POISON'S CAGE

POISON'S
CAGE

BREEANA SHIELDS

Random House 🏠 New York

To my three favorite musicians,
Ben, Jacob, and Isabella:
You are to my life as the score
is to a movie—the very best part.

Text copyright © 2018 by Breeana Shields
Jacket snake photographs copyright © Mark Laita
Jacket ornament copyright © Shutterstock

All rights reserved. Published in the United States
by Random House Children's Books, a division
of Penguin Random House LLC, New York.

Random House and the colophon are registered trademarks
of Penguin Random House LLC.

Visit us on the Web! GetUnderlined.com

Educators and librarians, for a variety of teaching tools, visit us at
RHTeachersLibrarians.com

Library of Congress Cataloging-in-Publication Data
Names: Shields, Breeana, author.
Title: Poison's cage / Breeana Shields.
Description: First edition. | New York : Random House, [2018] |
Summary: "Marinda and Iyla must work together to save themselves and the
ones they love from the wrath of the Snake King"—Provided by publisher.
Identifiers: LCCN 2017005970 | ISBN 978-1-101-93786-0 (hardcover) |
ISBN 978-0-525-57855-0 (international) | ISBN 978-1-101-93788-4 (ebook)
Subjects: | CYAC: Assassins—Fiction. | Poisons—Fiction. |
Brothers and sisters—Fiction. | Mythology, Indic—Fiction. | Fantasy.
Classification: LCC PZ7.1.S517 Pc 2018 | DDC [Fic]—dc23

Printed in the United States of America
10 9 8 7 6 5 4 3 2 1
First Edition

CHAPTER ONE

Marinda

It's too beautiful to die today.

Gita and I hike along a slender trail blanketed on either side by glossy green leaves shaped like teardrops. The path isn't steep, but I can hear Gita's breath—the rise and fall of it, the way it catches in her throat each time she speaks.

Her fear is like the moisture trapped in the humid air—hidden, but so heavy I can feel it pressing against my skin.

"Everything will be fine," she says. "Balavan just wants to meet you. I'm sure that's all it is."

"Or maybe he wants to execute me," I say, trailing my fingers across a plant with bright red blossoms. The flowers release a cloying scent and coat my fingers with a filmy residue that feels like drying blood. I snatch my hand away.

"No, Marinda," Gita says. "I won't let that happen." But I can hear the lie in her voice. She couldn't protect me from Gopal, and she won't be able to protect me from Balavan either.

The small palace that serves as Naga headquarters is nestled in a rain forest outside Sundari and far from the prying eyes of the Raja. Far enough that only the tigers and monkeys would hear a girl screaming.

I was a fool to think there was a chance the Naga would allow Gita to continue as my handler, to hope I'd be allowed to remain living on my own in Bala City, to believe that anything would be the same after my betrayal. Today I'll either get a new handler or I'll die for my disloyalty. Judging by the sweaty palm marks pressed on the middle of Gita's sari, she thinks it's the latter.

"Tell me about him," I say when I can't stand the silence any longer. We walk under a canopy of trees that provides shelter from the sun. Monkeys squeak and twitter above us like gossiping ladies.

"What do you want to know?"

"I want to know what to expect," I say. "Tell me something that might save my life."

Gita shakes her head. "I wish I could," she says. "But Balavan is unpredictable. Sometimes he is charming and personable. And sometimes . . ." She presses her eyes closed as if blocking out a memory. "He can be cruel."

She reaches for my hand and I resist the urge to flinch. Most days it takes all the restraint I have to look at her without grimacing, to touch her without wrapping my hands around her neck and shaking her like a rag doll. But if I want to bring the Naga down, I have to swallow all of my anger and play the part of the compliant follower.

Gita squeezes my fingers. "You must convince Balavan of your loyalty," she says. "You must tell him what you told me. How the Raja is holding your brother captive, how he beat you and imprisoned you. It's important that Balavan feels your hatred for the Raja. That he knows you will be loyal to the Snake King. Just tell him the truth."

Dread twists my stomach into a tight knot. Because it's not the truth that will save me today. It's how well I'm able to lie.

I curl my fingers into my palms. My hands always feel useless now, empty without Mani's tiny fingers threaded through mine. There's a hollow space in the center of my chest that aches with how much I miss him. But, for once, I'm grateful we're not together and that he's tucked away in the Raja's palace in Colapi City. He's safe. If I die today, at least I've given him that much.

Gita and I walk in silence for several minutes until two men emerge from the forest and step onto the path in front of us. Thick tattoos of snakes curl around their muscular forearms, and swords hang at their hips.

I take another step forward to explain why we're here, and in a single fluid motion one of the guards slides his sword from its scabbard and presses it against my neck. The cool metal bites into my skin. My breath gathers at the base of my throat, trapped.

"This is a broad and winding path," the guard says. The sword is heavy on my shoulder, and my spine starts to collapse under the pressure.

"The path that twists like a serpent always is," Gita says behind me, her voice calm and even. The guard lowers the sword and returns it to his side. I press a palm to my neck to check for blood as I try to make sense of the exchange. It must be some kind of password.

"Marinda is the *rajakumari*," Gita says, motioning toward me, and I try not to cringe at the title. I don't want to be anyone's princess, let alone the Nagaraja's. "Balavan has requested a meeting with her."

"Yes," the guard says, raking his gaze along the length of my body. "I bet he did."

"She's the *ra-ja-ku-ma-ri*," Gita repeats, emphasizing every syllable, her eyes blazing.

"For now," the guard says, looking everywhere except at my face. "But maybe not for long. Rumor is she's deadly with a blade."

He's heard, then—how I killed Gopal, how I stabbed the Nagaraja in the eye to save Mani. The memory makes bile rise in the back of my throat. That and the way this man is looking at me like I'm a piece of ripe fruit.

"See something you like?" I ask.

He grins wickedly. "I see a lot I like."

I step toward him and put a palm on his chest. "That's more like it," he says, throwing one arm around my waist and pulling me close.

I stand on my tiptoes so that my lips are just inches from his. "Didn't you hear?" I ask, running my fingers through his thick hair. "I don't need a blade to be deadly."

I see the flash of realization in his eyes as he remembers the rest of my story—how I can kill a man with only a kiss as a weapon. He wrenches away from me so fast that he nearly tumbles over. The other guard rushes forward with one hand on the hilt of his sword. "Leave that where it is," I say.

He clears his throat and drops his gaze to his boots. "Of course," he says, stepping off the path. "Forgive me."

We pass the guards and continue on the path. "I'm not sure that was necessary," Gita says once we're out of hearing range.

"Of course it was," I tell her. "If I'm going to die today, it won't be after letting some man look at me like I'm a rabbit roasting on a spit."

"It's better if he thinks you're about to kill him?"

I fix her with a hard gaze. "Yes," I tell her. "It's better."

I'm about to say more, but the Naga headquarters materializes in front of us and my words die on my lips. I understand why Gita has been calling it the palace.

It's a pyramid-shaped building made entirely of dark gray granite. Pillars carved with snakes, birds, tigers and crocodiles circle the perimeter like sentinels. It looks both majestic and like it's part of the landscape, as if it could have sprouted from the ground right alongside the bamboo and the soaring fig trees.

Gita reaches for my hand, and even though I hate when she touches me, I let her take it. Because I need to feel tethered to the earth. I need to feel the reassuring press of another human heartbeat against my wrist to remind me that I'm alive, that I'm not alone.

We climb the sheer staircase that leads from the bottom of the forest floor to the entrance of the palace. My heart slams against my rib cage, and I tell myself that it's from the exertion and not because I'm worried about what will happen once we reach the top.

The moment our feet touch the final step, a monkey off in the distance howls a single shrill note and the door swings wide. A chill races down my spine.

Gita gives my hand a squeeze that I think is meant to be reassuring, but it feels more like a warning. I let go of her as I step over the threshold.

It takes a few moments for my eyes to adjust to dimmer light, but when they do, my astonishment overtakes my fear.

I'm not sure what I was expecting—something more like the caves near Colapi City. A shelter made from the earth, thick with the musty scent of reptile and lit only by flickering candlelight. But this. This is something else entirely.

The palace is dripping with splendor.

My gaze sweeps over the walls, inlaid with gemstones in intricate mosaics that stretch from floor to ceiling. Millions upon millions of winking jewels—sapphires, rubies, emeralds, amethysts. The walls are literally made from treasure. The furniture is finely carved and gilded, and the floor is gleaming black marble, so shiny I can see my own reflection.

In the center of the room is a rug shaped like a huge white snake. But when I look more closely, I see that it's made not of fabric but of living flowers. Creamy magnolias—so many that the entire chamber is filled with the sweet, lemony scent of them.

"Do you approve?" I startle at the voice and spin around to face a woman dressed in a green-and-gold sari. Her hair is braided in half a dozen loops, and gold disks hang from her earlobes. She's several years older than I am. Maybe in her midtwenties. Her hand still rests on the doorknob, and she gives me an easy smile.

"It's breathtaking," I tell her.

"The Nagaraja would be pleased to hear it," she says, and my sense of wonder vanishes.

I think of the last time I saw the Nagaraja—his jaw clamped down on Mani's arm, his anger at my escape like a hot knife in my head—and I know that he wouldn't be pleased to hear anything from me right now.

The woman must see something shift in my face, because her smile fades and she clears her throat. "I'm Amoli," she says, pressing her palms together and dipping her head. "Balavan is waiting for you."

She motions for me to follow, but before I do, I glance once more around the room to commit it to memory, along with all the other scraps of information I've gathered today: the Naga headquarters is roughly 14,842 steps from the entrance to the rain forest; the path is manned by armed guards who require a password; the entrance to the head-quarters faces west. The lavish main foyer has only two visible exits—the one I just walked through and the one Amoli is headed toward.

Both Gita and I fall in step behind her, but a few moments later she turns and shakes her head. "I'm sorry," she says. "He only asked for the *rajakumari*." She gives Gita a forced smile. "You can wait here, and I'll let you know when it's finished."

When *what* is finished? My gaze flits to Gita, but the panic swimming in her eyes is no comfort.

I take a deep breath and square my shoulders. I can't afford to look weak or scared. This is the moment I've been preparing for. The moment I prove to the Naga that they can trust me again, that I'm one of them.

It's the moment I either live as a spy or die as a traitor.

CHAPTER TWO

Marinda

Balavan is the highest-ranking member of the Naga, save the Snake King himself, so as Amoli leads me down the long corridor, our sandaled footsteps echoing off the polished marble, I'm expecting her to escort me to a throne room.

Instead she opens the door to a bedchamber.

Against the far wall is a low mahogany bed covered in scarlet silk and piled with sumptuous, jewel-toned cushions in all shapes and sizes. A table sits off to one side, burdened with honey-drizzled wedges of pale cheese, a stack of flatbread, and a silver bowl filled with mangoes, apricots and pears.

A breeze blows in from the open window, carrying the delicate scent of earth. Climbing vines creep up the side of the building toward the sky.

I frown. "I thought you were taking me to meet Balavan," I say.

Amoli's gaze deliberately sweeps from my feet to my face. "You've been traveling," she says.

"I'm not tired," I tell her. "I'm ready to meet with him now."

She shakes her head. "You misunderstand," she says. "He won't want to see you in this state."

I open my mouth to argue, but then the voice of the Raja's spymaster, Hitesh, echoes in my memory. *You must be a vision of compliance, Marinda. Loyal followers of the Naga want to please their leaders.*

I swallow my frustration and give Amoli a tired smile. "Of course. Whatever Balavan wants."

"Good," she says. And then after a beat, "May I have your satchel, please?"

My heart stutters, but I keep my face passive, grateful that I listened to Hitesh and didn't load my bag with hollow coins and edible paper. *We'll get you the supplies you need later,* he said. *The Naga won't trust you at first. We can't take the risk.* Now the only things Balavan will find in my possession are a supply of clean saris and an ivory comb. Except for . . . I resist the urge to put my palm to my head and draw attention to the scarf in my hair. It's the one piece of contraband I did bring from the palace. Instead I slide the satchel from my shoulder and hand it to Amoli.

"I'll need your money too," she says.

I shake my head. "I didn't bring . . ."

Amoli reaches into the tiny pocket sewn at the hip of my sari and pulls out the few coins I tucked away. She frowns as she examines them. My palms start to sweat.

"Oh," I say. "I forgot those were there."

But it's not the money that seems to upset her. Her thumb traces the four members of the Raksaka etched on the surface: the Tiger Queen; the Great Bird, Garuda; the Nagaraja; and the Crocodile King. With a start I remember the coins I found in Japa's bookshop on the day he died. Coins that featured the Snake King alone.

Amoli clears her throat and drops the coins into the satchel. Her expression is unreadable. "Rest," she says. "Eat something. I'll be back in a bit to help you prepare."

I sink down onto the bed and rub my eyes. The silence wraps around me like an embrace. Despite my impatience to meet with Balavan and find out what he has planned for me, it feels like a luxury to be alone. Pretending to love Gita requires so much focus, so much tamping down of the hate that simmers in my chest, that it leaves my entire body aching.

I kick off my sandals, lie back against the pillows and close my eyes, but no matter how hard I try, I can't sleep. My gaze skips to the table of food, and my stomach grumbles. I sit up and pull one of the platters onto my lap, but I'm not sure I dare eat. The food could be laced with poison. It would be an elegant way to get rid of me—to serve me tainted food and let me die by my own hungry fingers. But the more I think about it, the more I doubt it's true. The Naga won't waste my death by killing me discreetly. If I'm to die, they'll want to make a spectacle of it.

I pinch a bit of cheese between my fingers and drop it onto my tongue. The flavors explode in my mouth—the sharp and the sweet both more pronounced when married. Just to be sure the food is safe, I wait a full twenty minutes before I take another bite. Then I eat most of the cheese, a loaf of flatbread and a pear before I finally feel less hollowed out.

The feast has made me sleepy, but before I lie down, I pull the scarf from my hair. The blue silk is printed on one side with deep golden stars, moons and suns. On the other side is what looks, at first glance, like a smattering of constellations. Only on close inspection could a person make out the subtle shape of Sundari and the brighter stars that indicate every dead drop in the kingdom—all the places I can leave whatever information I gather for the Raja. I fold the scarf into a small square and nestle it beneath one of the slats under the bed, examining it from every angle to make sure not even a hint of color is visible. When I'm satisfied the map is safe, I lie back and drift off to sleep.

* *

I'm dreaming of Deven when I feel a hand on my cheek. I nearly say his name—it's on the tip of my tongue as I sigh into the touch—but then awareness comes rushing back and my eyes fly wide. Amoli takes a startled step backward.

"I'm sorry," she says. "I didn't mean to frighten you. I called your name several times, but you didn't stir."

I sit up and pull my fingers through my hair. "It's okay," I say. "I must have been more tired than I realized." My head throbs lightly, and I take a deep breath and try to force the fog of disorientation to dissipate. I have to be more careful. What if I'd said Deven's name in my sleep? Am I certain I didn't? If anyone here suspects that I still care about him, both his life and mine will be in danger.

Amoli has a berry-colored sari draped over one arm and a basket full of supplies in the other. "Shall we do a bath first?" she asks, though her tone suggests it's not a question. And she doesn't wait for an answer before she unburdens her arms and makes her way through the open door of the bathing chamber at the far side of the room. She starts the water running and then pulls a vial of oil from her pocket. The room fills with the scent of jasmine.

While her back is turned, I close my eyes and steel myself for what's ahead. *Be compliant,* I remind myself. *Seem eager to please.* But the thought of letting Amoli touch me, when she serves the people who tried to sacrifice Mani, makes my skin crawl.

Amoli shuts off the water and I force my face to go slack, like curtains falling closed. By the time she turns toward me, my mind is empty, and I hope my expression is too.

"All set," she says, motioning toward the tub, where steam curls into the air like warm breath. She shifts away from me to allow at least the illusion of privacy while I disrobe and slip into the bath, but as soon as I'm submerged, she plunges her hands into the water and begins scrubbing at my skin with a rough cloth.

It takes all the self-control I have not to wrench away from her. The pressure on my bare skin is too familiar, too much contact when so few people have ever dared touch me. I bite my lip to keep from crying out.

Amoli freezes, the cloth in her hand hovering above my shoulder blade. "Am I hurting you?"

The question knocks something loose inside me, and tears threaten at the corners of my eyes. But I can't afford to let them fall. Instead I let out a light laugh. "No," I say. "You just seem to be under the impression that I walked here in a cloud of dust. Am I really so dirty?"

"I'm sorry," she says. "I just want you to make a favorable impression on Balavan." But her hands are gentler when she resumes scrubbing.

When every square inch of my body is red and raw, Amoli pours a handful of thick soap into her palm and lathers it into my hair, kneading my scalp with her fingertips. The motion is so relaxing that my eyes flutter closed and I slump deeper into the water. Cleaning my skin felt like an invasion, but this. This feels like the height of luxury.

I'm almost disappointed when Amoli disentangles her fingers from my hair and pours several pitchers of warm water over my head until all the suds are rinsed away.

She holds out a thick, creamy towel, and I wrap myself in its warmth as I step out of the tub. The scent of jasmine wafts from my skin, clings to my hair.

"Sit here," Amoli instructs, pulling up a low stool and placing it in front of a mirror. I want to argue with her, want to tell her to stop ordering me around like I'm a child, but I bite my tongue and follow her instructions.

Amoli uses a wooden comb to untangle my hair, leaving it hanging in a dark curtain around my shoulders. Then she wraps a strand tightly around her fingers and holds it there for a full minute before she unwinds it. She continues working one section at a time until my hair falls down my back in loose curls.

Next Amoli fishes a muslin cloth out of her basket, along with a shallow clay oil lamp and several small containers.

She fills the lamp with castor oil and holds a match to the wick. Flickering light dances across the mirror. She dips a corner of the cloth in one of the containers and then plunges it into the flame. The scent of sandalwood fills the air, and nostalgia overtakes me. *Kajal.* When Iyla and I were little girls, Gita would occasionally line her eyes and color her lips. We thought she looked glamorous and begged to try the cosmetics. "No, my loves," she said. "You are beautiful just as you are." A pang of sadness shoots through me at who I thought Gita was then. I wonder where she is right now. Probably pacing through the corridors, fretting over my fate, when she should be worrying about her own.

Amoli waits for the cloth to cool and then dips it in a pot of ghee and swipes the *kajal* over both my upper and my lower eyelids. Next she mixes powdered fruit rind with a splash of milk and applies it to my cheekbones with her fingertips, blending the paste into my skin in steady, sure circles. But when she dips a tiny brush in the mixture and moves toward my lips, I flinch away.

"Don't worry," she says softly, holding my chin firmly between two fingers. "I'll be careful." The brush is feather soft against my mouth, and the sensation isn't entirely unpleasant, but as Amoli applies layer after layer, my lips start to feel suffocated and I'm reminded of the poisoned lip balm Gopal used to make me wear when I was small and not yet deadly enough on my own. A shiver dances down my spine and finally Amoli pulls away.

Despite myself, I'm mesmerized by my reflection.

It was always Iyla who looked desirable, who smelled

like flowers and had color in her cheeks. Now that it's me, I'm surprised at how powerful it makes me feel.

But then I wonder why I need to look like this to meet Balavan, and my stomach sours. Is this the treatment of an honored guest or the ritualistic body cleansing before I'm put to death and my ashes are flung into the Kinjal River?

"Rajakumari?"

My gaze flits to Amoli, who is holding out fresh clothes and studying me with knitted brows. The look on her face suggests this isn't the first time she addressed me.

"Is something wrong?" she asks.

I give her a smile. "Of course not," I say as I wrap the plain end of the sari around my waist and pull the jewel-edged *pallu* over my shoulder. "I was just lost in thought for a moment."

"Do you need a break?" she asks. "I can come back later to finish."

I'm transformed from head to toe. What more could there possibly be left to do? "No," I tell her. "Really, I'm fine."

She searches my face without speaking for a few moments and then nods and motions toward the stool. "Let's start on your hands, then."

"My hands?"

She pulls a slender tube from her basket. "Yes," she says. "I'll be applying *mehndi*."

My breath catches. The intricate henna designs are only used for special occasions. Weddings. Funerals.

"Is he going to kill me?"

Amoli frowns, and it takes her a long time to answer. "I don't know," she says. "But I hope not."

She squeezes the henna paste from the tube with careful, practiced fingers, and soon the backs of my hands are covered in delicate, interlacing lines broken up by flowers and teardrops. It's as if I've slipped on a pair of black lace gloves, and the effect is breathtaking. Amoli applies the design all the way from my fingertips to my elbows and then starts on my feet, decorating them from toe to ankle. The designs conceal the dozens of scars left by years and years of snakebites. By the time she's finished, the sun has slipped beneath the horizon and I'm so captivated by her artistry that I've nearly forgotten why I'm here. But the truth comes crashing back when Amoli stands up and stretches. She pulls a final item from her basket, a ruby teardrop dangling from a golden wire. She fastens it around my forehead so that the jewel rests between my eyebrows.

"You're ready," she says.

CHAPTER THREE

Marinda

Amoli leads me down a dim corridor lit only by flickering candlelight. My heartbeat thunders in my ears, and I try to empty my thoughts of anything except service to the Nagaraja. At our last meeting the Snake King forcefully entered my mind, and it was only Mani's voice that kept me from losing myself. And while I don't think the Nagaraja's minions have the same power—Gopal certainly never did—the worry still gnaws at me. Finally we come to a set of golden doors at the end of the corridor, and Amoli gives a sharp knock before she enters. "Master Balavan," she says, her voice dripping with so much deference that it makes my stomach turn. "I present the *rajakumari*." She steps aside, and suddenly I'm face to face with the Nagaraja's most trusted servant.

And he doesn't look anything like I thought he would.

I was expecting another version of Gopal—a belly soft with indulgence, graying hair, a cruel face.

But Balavan is young and vital, with flawless copper skin and hard muscles. He has a square jawline, and his eyes are like bottomless pools of black ink, dark and unfathomable. And then he smiles, and for a moment I forget to breathe.

"Marinda," he says warmly, as if we've met a dozen times before. "I'm so happy you've chosen to join us." He takes both of my hands in his and plants a kiss on each of my cheeks.

My mind goes completely blank. I can't stop staring at the contours of his face, at the way a muscle jumps near his jaw, at the light flickering in his eyes. There's something so familiar about him that I'm suddenly sure I've seen him before. He must have visited Gopal when I was a child.

"Will there be anything else, master?" Amoli asks. Her question breaks the spell.

"You may go," Balavan says, his voice smooth and even. Amoli slips through the door without another word and closes it behind her with a soft click.

When Balavan turns his gaze on me again, all the warmth has evaporated from his expression.

"Why are you here, Marinda?" He asks the question softly, but it has all the power of an earthquake. I feel unsteady, like the ground might shift beneath me at any moment.

My tongue is glued to the roof of my mouth, but I need to find a way to speak, a way to erase the suspicion in his tone.

"To serve the Nagaraja," I say.

He clasps both hands in front of him and tilts back on his heels. "The same Nagaraja you tried to kill just a few months ago?"

I swallow the lump in my throat. "He had my brother," I say softly. "He would have killed him if I hadn't done something."

"Ah, your brother," Balavan says. "Mani, is it?" I nod, speechless. He is the first member of the Naga to refer to Mani by name instead of calling him "the boy" or referring to him as a pet.

Balavan blows a stream of air through pursed lips and then turns to examine his reflection in a large, diamond-shaped object on the wall. It's made not of glass but of luminescent pearl—the palace is so opulent that even the mirrors are made of gems. He smooths back his hair and plucks a piece of lint from his collar. "Gopal badly mishandled that situation," he says. He turns toward me. "Your brother, I mean." His eyes find mine, and again I'm struck by how endless they seem. "There was no need for male assassins. I already had a contingency plan for that."

I try to ignore the rage that explodes in my chest at the suggestion that Mani was nothing more than a failed experiment. Gopal was secretly poisoning him for years in an attempt to turn him into a weapon. In an attempt to turn him into me.

I can't let my emotion ruin this opportunity. It's the first chance for information that could actually help the Raja. "What was the contingency plan?"

He laughs. "All in good time, *rajakumari*. We have to find out if we can trust you first."

My pulse jumps. "Of course you can trust me," I say with as much force as I can muster. "Why would I risk my life and come here otherwise?"

"Oh, I can think of a few reasons," Balavan says. He presses his lips together and studies me. "Are you sure saving your brother was the only reason you turned on the Nagaraja?"

"Yes," I say. "Everything I did was for Mani."

"You didn't have another, more ideological reason for wanting our leader dead?"

"Of course not." Balavan doesn't say anything, but I hold his gaze. I won't be the first to look away. "What can I do to prove my loyalty?"

The lazy smile that spreads across his face raises the hair on the back of my neck. "My darling Marinda," he says. "I'm so glad you asked."

He circles me with the fluid movement of a lion stalking a gazelle. "The Nagaraja has a new target for you," he says. "We need you to kiss one of the Raja's advisers."

I look down at the gorgeous *mehndi* designs on my hands and feet, and all of a sudden the hours spent in preparation make perfect sense. I'm not dressed to die.

I'm dressed to kill.

* *

The dungeon smells like snake.

A wave of nausea sweeps over me, and I try to close off my mind, just in case the Nagaraja is near. But as I follow Balavan through the winding passageways lit by flickering torches, I'm forcefully reminded of the last time I was in a dungeon, and it gets harder and harder to keep the memories at bay.

Thoughts of Mani flood my mind—the desperate need to get to him, the worry that he'd be sacrificed to the Nagaraja before I found a way to escape. I take a deep breath and force myself to focus. Because this time is different. This time I'm in control, and any games we play will be my games.

I can hear the raspy breathing of the prisoners as we pass each cell, but unlike in the Raja's dungeon, they don't cry out or beat against the bars and beg for release. Perhaps they've learned there's no point. We're enveloped in the eerie silence of the hopeless.

Balavan stops so suddenly that I nearly run into him. He fumbles with a set of keys and slides the bars of the metal cell open.

In the corner, barefoot and chained to the floor by heavy leg-irons, is a man in a dirty Sundarian uniform. His jaw is covered in stubble, and a yellowing bruise discolors his left eye.

I long to kneel next to him and whisper that he will be okay, that Hitesh warned me the Naga might put me to the test but that the Raja would make sure anyone I might be asked to kill was immune. I can't risk saying anything to him with Balavan so close, though. Instead I give him a shaky smile and hope he will understand.

Balavan moves toward the man and towers over him. "I'll give you a final chance," he says. "Tell me where to find it."

The man shakes his head, sliding his heels across the floor until his back is pressed against the stone wall. Balavan kicks him in the stomach. I press a palm to my mouth and bite back a scream.

"I've brought a *visha kanya*," Balavan says. "If you tell me what I want to know, I will slit your throat. It will be a quick death. A merciful one. But if you don't . . ." He motions toward me. "A poisoned kiss. Which I assure you will be neither quick nor merciful."

The man's gaze darts to me. "Please," he says. "Don't do this."

Worry tugs at me. Is he not immune? Or is he simply playing a role, like I am?

"Don't speak to her," Balavan says. "Don't speak at all unless you're going to tell me where it is."

The man drops his head and turns his face toward the wall.

"Marinda," Balavan says softly, "kiss him."

My pulse flutters frantically like a moth in a jar. A few months ago, being a *visha kanya* was what got me thrown in the dungeon. Now it's the only thing that will get me out.

I kneel in front of the man and take his face in my palms. His eyes are wild, and with a start I realize that I've never killed someone who knows what I am. I've seen surprise in a target's eyes before. I've even seen desire. But until now I've never seen fear.

The expression sends something icy through my veins, and I hesitate, searching his face for an answer to a question I can't ask out loud.

"Kiss him," Balavan repeats more sharply than before. And I know there's no choice. If I refuse, both of us are dead.

"I'm sorry," I mouth. And then I brush my lips gently

across the prisoner's and hope that Hitesh has kept his end of the bargain.

I start to stand, but the man catches my fingers in his. "Wait," he says, his voice colored with urgency. "The Nagaraja—"

Balavan shoves me out of the way and steps between us. "I told you not to speak."

The man cranes his neck to see me. "The Nagaraja is hunting—"

But he doesn't get to finish his sentence before Balavan kicks him hard in the teeth. Blood sprays across the man's face, and he falls silent.

My heart constricts. Nausea threatens to overtake me.

Balavan takes my elbow and leads me out of the cell. I resist the urge to cast a final glance over my shoulder.

The man will live, I tell myself. Though he'll have a few broken teeth, he won't suffer the same fate as all the other men I've kissed.

But we haven't even reached the bottom of the stairs when I hear the labored sound of the prisoner's breath. I tell myself that it means nothing—the man is just in pain from Balavan's boot connecting with his face. Of course his breathing would be heavy and strained. But I've heard that sound a thousand times before—it's the way Mani used to breathe every day before I realized that Gopal was giving him poison and not medicine. If the prisoner isn't immune, in a few hours his labored breathing will turn to high-pitched wailing, and pain will rip through his body. My blood turns to ice.

And by the slow smile that spreads across Balavan's face, I can see that history is repeating itself.

The man will die tonight. But not until he's suffered for hours.

Balavan puts an arm around my shoulders. "Good work, Marinda."

Despite the cold wave of horror rolling through my chest, when his gaze finds mine, I give him my sincerest smile.

* *

Balavan doesn't say another word until we're out of the dungeon. At the top of the stairs, he clears his throat. "I planned to kill you tonight, you know." He says it evenly, as if he were ordering dinner. My pulse spikes, but I keep walking.

"Oh?" I say, equally serene. "And why is that?"

"I had this silly idea that the Raja had turned you. That you were only coming back to gather information for him."

I laugh, and it comes out harsh and brittle. "You don't know me very well if you think I would serve someone who is holding my brother hostage."

"Maybe," he says. "Maybe not. In time I hope to earn your loyalty. Perhaps even your love. But for now it doesn't really matter *why* you came back." His smile is calculating. Greedy. "Only that you're here. And that you're staying."

My step falters for just a moment. My mouth goes dry. I haven't earned his trust at all—this was only a test, a game to try to compel me to show my hand.

The realization pierces me—like the swipe of a paring

knife held too close. Or wielded too carelessly. For a moment I am paralyzed, just as I was the first time I cut myself slicing onions. I still remember the sharp gasp of surprise, the blood welling at the wound even before the pain set in, the throbbing for hours afterward. But most of all I remember Gita's gentle warning: *Use the tools, Marinda. Don't let them use you.*

I take a deep breath and forcefully press the panic down, make it so small that I can't even find it anymore. And then a wave of tranquility washes over me and I let it take all of my worry along with it. Because the people I love are safe, and playing games is exactly what I came to do. At least I'm not playing blind anymore. I've glimpsed my opponent. I understand the rules.

Now I just need to figure out how to force Balavan to reveal his strategy. Not only how to play, but how to win.

With someone so proud, flattery seems like a good starting point.

"Isn't it unwise to work with me if you really think I'll betray you?" I ask. "You seem far too cunning for that."

He stops walking and turns his liquid gaze on me. "I don't think I told you how lovely you look tonight, Marinda," he says. He reaches for me, twirls a lock of my hair around his finger and inhales deeply before letting it go. "You're a vision."

Prickles race up the back of my neck. I can almost see the machinations behind his eyes. A gentle deflection of my flattery and a shot across the bow in the form of a compliment of his own. If the proud like to feel powerful, surely the beautiful want to be praised for their appearance. But if that's what he thinks, he's got the wrong girl.

"Don't change the subject," I say. "Why let me live if you don't believe you can trust me? I'm no danger to you if I'm dead." I want him to say the words out loud. I want to know why I'm here if he doesn't trust me.

Balavan laughs and rubs his palms together. "Simple," he says. "A traitor willing to kill for me is still a traitor I can use."

My stomach is as tight as a clenched fist, but I force the muscles in my face to stay relaxed.

"So I'm nothing but a weapon to you, is that it?"

"Would you wish to be more?"

I leave the question unanswered, let it vibrate between us for several long seconds before I start walking again. Balavan hesitates for a beat, then falls in step beside me, and I smile to myself. I managed to fluster him, and the feeling of power that surges through me is intoxicating. But the victory lasts only a moment. We turn the corner and see Amoli standing stiffly at Balavan's door. And she's not alone.

Iyla is here.

CHAPTER FOUR

Iyla

Marinda is so focused on her conversation that she doesn't see me right away. Her face is a mask of studied compliance. She's more gifted at playing this role than I thought she would be. I might even believe it myself—that her loyalty to the Naga is sincere—if I didn't know her so well. If I couldn't see the way she pulls her stomach in tight like she's bracing for a punch, if her shoulders weren't creeping ever so slightly toward her ears.

Her whole body is a held breath.

Then she turns her head toward me, and her eyes go wide. The disappointment that darkens her expression hits me like a slap. But she quickly composes herself and gives me a smile that doesn't quite reach her eyes.

"Iyla," she says coolly. "I didn't realize you'd be here." She kisses the air around my cheek, her lips never landing.

"Where else would I be?" But we both know what she

expected. That I would stay tucked away in the Widows' Village, learning how to mend saris from Vara. That I would live a small life tending to my vegetable garden. That I would stay far away from the Naga.

I touch Marinda's arm, and her skin is on fire. A sheen of sweat has appeared on her upper lip. She's coming unraveled. I find her fingers and squeeze them, and when she meets my gaze, I give her a hard look.

I can see the question in her eyes, but I won't give her the satisfaction of an answer. She wouldn't have to wonder why I'm here if she'd thought about me before this moment, if she'd worried about securing my safety along with Mani's. But there's only room in her heart for him. I would willingly stand back to back with her, blade in hand, and help her fight her battles if she weren't always leaving me.

My stony stare must work, because Marinda takes a deep breath and stands up straighter.

Balavan gives me a wide smile. "Iyla," he says. "I'm glad you were able to get away."

"It took me a few days, but I managed." I resist the urge to look at Marinda. To study her expression.

"Were you able to get the information we needed?"

"Some of it," I tell him. "I'll need to go back again before I have a target ready."

"Excellent," Balavan says. He rests a palm between Marinda's shoulder blades and she stiffens. It's such a possessive gesture that it takes some work to keep a neutral expression on my own face.

"You should get some rest, my *rajakumari*," he says. "Iyla and I have business to discuss."

Marinda presses her lips together, and I'm not sure if she's reacting to Balavan calling her his princess or the suggestion that I'm still working for the Naga. But she covers her discomfort with an easy smile. "Of course," she says. And then, turning toward Balavan's handmaiden, "Amoli, could you show me back to my room? I'm afraid I've gotten turned around."

She's lying.

I have no doubt that she's counted every step since she arrived, memorized every turn. She gives me a final glance, and I'm expecting to find a raw expression of pain on her face, one I didn't realize I wanted to see until it was missing. Instead her eyes are weary and full of resignation. She can't even muster up enough affection for me to feel betrayed.

"Certainly," Amoli says. "I'd be happy to escort you back." Marinda threads her arm through Amoli's and lets herself be led away. And just like every other time she's left me, she doesn't look back.

* *

Balavan's rooms are sumptuous. The walls of the sitting room are covered in glazed-tile motifs of blue, yellow and green. Two identical sofas face each other, swathed in turquoise silk. Red velvet drapes hang from tall windows and fall in puddles on the glossy hardwood.

And he displays food like some people display flowers. It covers every surface—golden bowls of fruit, plates heaped with soft cheeses and flatbread, silver goblets overflowing with figs. It's as if Balavan has an appetite that can never be satisfied.

"Please," he says with a sweep of his arm. "Make yourself comfortable."

I kick off my sandals and sit on one of the sofas, curling my feet underneath me. Balavan remains standing. "Where would you like me to start?" I ask. I'm ready to fill him in on my mission. The last one Gopal gave me before Marinda put a knife through his heart. The one I ignored until two weeks ago, when it became clear that I had to come back if I hoped to survive. I'm ready with my excuses for why it took so long to make contact, but I doubt I'll need them. My assignments often require me to be gone for extended periods of time.

"We can talk about the boy later," Balavan says. "I want to discuss Marinda."

My pulse jumps, and a thread of worry curls in my stomach. She's the last thing I want to talk about.

"What would you like to know?" I ask.

Balavan smiles, but there's nothing warm in his expression. "Tell me what she cares about."

I narrow my eyes at him. "Why?"

He gives me an icy stare. "Your place is to answer questions," he says, "not ask them."

I swallow hard. He has me cornered. There's no way I can refuse to speak. "She cares about her brother," I say.

"And what else?"

I laugh sharply, surprised at how the question stings. "She *only* cares about her brother."

He doesn't speak for a full minute, and the weight of his stare makes it difficult for me to breathe. But I hold his gaze.

"Are you certain?" he asks.

"Yes."

"I want you to make sure."

This pulls me up short. I square my shoulders, put both feet on the floor, lean forward. "What do you mean?"

"Your next mission is to gather intelligence on Marinda. I want to know where she goes, who she speaks to." He pauses and searches my face. "I want to know *everything* she cares about."

"You want me to spy on her?"

His voice gets dangerously quiet. "Is that a problem?"

I pull my feet back onto the sofa and tuck them underneath me. "Not if you make it worth my while."

His face thaws and he laughs. "Gita was right about you."

"Oh? What did she say?"

"That you are heartless. That you would give away your own mother if you could be convinced that it would benefit you."

The swift flood of emotion is a shock. The sting behind my eyes, the choking sensation in my throat that makes it impossible to swallow. *Did she really say that? Does she think I'm so easily bought?* But I learned a long time ago that tears are the thieves of power. Instead I shrug. "True," I say. "But there's still the matter of the convincing."

Balavan's gaze skips to my hands, to the small age mark that I only noticed a few weeks ago. "I could give you back your youth."

I go very still. The past unspools in my mind like a

bundle of dropped thread—the visits to Kadru year after year, the pain as she extracted bits of my life in exchange for the poison that would make Marinda deadly. I lift my head and meet his eyes.

"How many years did Kadru take from you so that Marinda could become a *visha kanya*?" he asks. "Twenty? Thirty?"

My mouth is dry. "Fifty."

His triumphant expression tells me that he already knew this number. And I wonder who sat in this very spot and answered the question *What does Iyla care about?* Who told him that all I really wanted was my life back? Who betrayed me by giving him the one thing that would make it easy for me to betray Marinda?

"I could restore every one of those years," Balavan says. "You don't need to die young just to protect Marinda. You've sacrificed enough for her."

I curl my fingers around the edge of the cushion and squeeze. "What are you hoping to find?"

"I need to know if she's lying to me."

I shake my head. "Marinda isn't a gifted liar."

"No? And what about you?"

I ignore the ache in my throat. Disregard the sensation of being pressed against the soft silk of a spiderweb, of being slowly wrapped in delicate strands until it's too late to escape. I try to seem as cold as Gita said I am. "Only time will tell."

"But don't you see, *priya*? Time is the one thing you don't have."

CHAPTER FIVE

Marinda

From my bedchamber, I can hear the anguished screams of the prisoner. It's been three hours since I brushed my lips against his, since I saw the fear in his eyes that will forever haunt me. Maybe it's the reason Balavan chose this particular room—so that he would be sure I heard the fruits of my labor.

Hitesh promised me I wouldn't have to kill anyone to take the Naga down. Even when I protested that he couldn't possibly protect them all. "Believe me, Marinda," he said. "Anyone the Naga would target on our side is immune."

He was either lying or wrong, and neither possibility brings any comfort. I should have known to expect the worst when he warned me that the game of espionage is a game you always play alone.

I sit on the floor with my head in my hands and wait until the sounds of suffering finally fade and the only thing

I hear is my own racing heartbeat. I thought I could do this, thought I could carefully bury my humanity so deep that even I wouldn't be able to find it—at least until the Nagaraja was dead and his followers destroyed. But Iyla's sudden appearance is a stark reminder that I still have something to lose.

What is she doing here? Why would she choose to return when she worked so hard to escape? When she'd finally found safety?

The questions are an unrelenting drumbeat in my mind, a serpentine unease twisting through my gut. And the way she looked at me. Coldly. Like the last few weeks we spent in the Widows' Village stitching together the tattered remnants of our friendship never even happened.

How will I ever bring the Naga down with her so close, reminding me that there's more at stake than my own life? And why is she still working for them?

I have a sudden, aching desire to talk to Deven. It crashes over me like a wave—the need to have his arms wrapped around me, the longing to feel anchored to him. I think of the last time we spoke, his fingers tracing the line of my jaw, the familiar smell of him enveloping me like a warm blanket.

"Don't go," he said. But his voice was flat and hopeless. It was a request that had been made and denied a dozen times. So I gave him a kiss instead of a reply and hoped it would be enough.

When we finally pulled apart, breathless, his eyes were shiny. "Don't let them change you," he said.

The plea jangled inside me like a dropped sword.

The Naga had created me—fashioned me from flesh and poison—and I could see the worry etched across Deven's expression that my loyalty might shift back toward them, the people who'd made me what I was.

"Don't worry," I said. "I won't."

But then I thought of Kadru—about her promise that I would one day become her—and I shivered. Deven rubbed his palms up and down my arms. Then he pulled me to his chest, and my doubts flew away like startled birds. I would never be like Kadru.

But now I'm not so sure. I've been with the Naga for less than a full day, and already I've killed someone for them. What if I lied? What if they do change me?

I pull my fingers through my hair and release a groan. I can't just sit here marinating in guilt, obsessing about Iyla and missing Deven. I have to do something, anything, not to feel like I've just given up one prison for another.

I search through the drawers in my room until I find a stack of creamy parchment, a slender bamboo reed sharpened to a fine tip and a pot of ink. I write an impassioned letter to the Raja begging for Mani's release. It is precisely what Gita and Balavan would expect from me if everything I've told them were true. But embedded in the letter is my real message. A cipher where only every seventh word has meaning. *Arrived. Safely. Adviser. Dead. Nagaraja. Hunting. Something. Unknown.*

I read the letter over several times and make sure that it sounds authentic, that it is exactly what I would say if I were serving the Snake King and if Mani really were being held prisoner at the Raja's palace. When I'm satisfied it's perfect, I leave it on the corner of the desk, partially covered, but where I'm sure Amoli will find it and report back to Balavan that I'm doing everything I can to secure the release of my brother.

I change out of my sari and scrub my face until I recognize my reflection again. The *mehndi* designs will take weeks to fade, but at least I don't look like a stranger anymore. I climb under the silky covers and sink into the mattress, where it takes me hours to fall asleep. And even when I do, I'm startled awake by tortured screams. I lurch into a sitting position, gasping. I stuff a fist into my mouth and strain to hear, but several minutes pass before I realize that the sounds were only coming from my nightmares.

*   *

Gita is standing at the foot of my bed when I wake up the next morning. "Thank the ancestors he didn't kill you," she says the moment I open my eyes. Her hand is pressed to her chest like she's holding her heart in place.

"Iyla is here," I say before I can think better of it.

But Gita only shrugs. "Of course she is. We're all here. Now tell me everything. What did Balavan say? Did he punish you?"

I resist the urge to leap across the bed and wrap a hand around her throat. Did he punish me? Was making me kill an innocent man punishment? My very existence is a death sentence.

"No," I tell her. "But he doesn't trust me."

Gita pats my knee. "He will," she says. "In time he will."

She smooths the hair away from my face. "Are you hungry?" she asks. "Do you want me to bring you something to eat?" An image of Mani tied up on the altar in the Snake Temple rises in my mind. Gita has no right to act like she cares about me. No right to touch me.

I put a hand over my mouth and pretend to stifle a yawn to keep myself from screaming.

"I'm tired," I tell her finally. "I think I just want to be left alone to rest."

"Of course, *rajakumari*," she says. "Of course."

Gita leaves and I pull the covers over my head, bury my face in my pillow and, for the first time since I got here, let myself cry.

* *

The next few days pass with no sign of Balavan, Iyla or even Gita. Amoli brings me meals in my room—thick curries and tender loaves of flatbread.

And when I complain that I can't stand the sight of the same four walls for another second, she walks arm in arm with me around the palace. We stroll past a cluster of Naga members, who fall silent at our approach, nodding to Amoli and regarding me with a mixture of curiosity and suspicion. I surreptitiously study their faces—two men I've seen before and a woman I haven't—and add them to the growing tally in my head. So far I've counted at least sixty-five members of the Naga.

"What's through there?" I ask as we pass a corridor that Amoli has never turned down. It's one of the missing pieces of the mental map of the palace that I've been trying to construct.

She hesitates a moment before answering, as if weighing whether to tell me the truth. "The hatchery," she says finally.

"Can I see it?"

In truth, there's almost nothing that I'd rather do less. But I need as much information as possible to pass along to the Raja's men.

Amoli shrugs. "I don't see why not."

She leads me into a room lined with dirt-filled wooden boxes. Thousands of pale snake eggs lie half-buried in dark soil.

"Where are their mothers?" I ask. I was expecting to see full-grown snakes coiled atop the eggs, keeping them warm, protecting them.

Amoli laughs. "Snakes aren't like chickens," she says. "Snakes abandon their young."

"Oh," I say, a pang of sympathy tugging at my heart for the orphaned babies. Until I remember what is inside all those eggs—and then my stomach turns over. "Why are there so many?"

"The Nagaraja needs more than just human followers," Amoli says.

I think of Kadru and all her snakes, and my throat starts to close. "Can we go now?" I ask. "I think I've seen enough."

Amoli returns every day to keep me company. She's willing to walk through the corridors with me, but she never leaves me to wander the palace alone.

So it's a relief when Balavan finally summons me to his rooms for a meeting. I'm almost grateful to see his obsidian eyes and his dazzling smile. But seeing Iyla stretched across his sofa like a lazy cat is a swift kick to the gut. I force my mind to become a blank page, tell myself that I am an empty shell. That I care about no one. That Iyla's lack of loyalty means nothing to me.

But my heart knows I'm lying. It flings itself against the bars of my rib cage, as if staging an escape.

"We have a new target for you," Balavan says. *We.* As if he and Iyla are a team.

Suddenly the full weight of my choices crashes into me and snatches the breath from my lungs. I've never felt as alone as I do in this moment.

An empty shell. A servant of the Nagaraja. Nothing. No one. My stomach clenches. No. A tool. A weapon.

"Finally," I say lightly. "I'd begun to think you didn't need me anymore."

Iyla's gaze finds mine and something passes between us. Maybe she understood that I was talking to her even though I was looking at Balavan. But then her expression goes slack and she looks away. Maybe I was only seeing what I wanted to see.

"We will always need you, *rajakumari,*" Balavan says. "As long as you're loyal, that is."

I ignore the warning and sink into one of the chairs. "Who is the target?"

"Iyla will introduce you," he says.

This time I can't keep the surprise from showing on my

face. "But what about tradecraft?" Gopal never allowed me and Iyla to be seen together in front of a potential target.

"Let me worry about tradecraft," Balavan says. "You worry about following orders."

So Iyla is to be my warden.

CHAPTER SIX

Iyla

I can't stop staring at my hand—at the way the age spot has vanished, at the way my skin seems just a little smoother than it did before. Balavan didn't give back everything Kadru took from me—only five years. A down payment, he called it. A good-faith deposit for services yet to be rendered. Still, I have 10 percent more of my life than I had when I got here, and my skin looks like it did months ago, before the tiny signs of age started showing up all over my body—a single silver hair, an age spot, a knee that perpetually aches. Maybe now I can fall asleep at night without worrying I won't wake up again.

Marinda and I are due to leave the palace this morning at dawn. I arrive outside her bedroom just as the sun creeps over the horizon and tiles the corridor in pale pink light. Her door swings open before I have a chance to knock, and she doesn't meet my gaze as she closes it softly behind her.

She's dressed in a simple navy-blue sari and wears a gold-and-blue scarf in her hair.

We leave the palace in silence. The only sounds are our footsteps echoing across the polished ebony floors and Marinda's too-steady breathing, as if she's schooled her lungs into calm submission. She walks stiffly beside me.

A blanket of early-morning mist hovers over the canopy of trees, so that we can't see more than a few feet in front of us. We hike down the path, past the guards, who only nod as we go by them. Once we're far enough from the Naga palace that we can't be overheard, Marinda clears her throat. "What are you doing here, Iyla?"

I shrug. "Where else would I be?"

She spins to face me. Finally I see pain in her expression, and it's not nearly as satisfying as I hoped it would be. "In the Widows' Village," she says, her eyes wild. "Where you were safe."

"You can't be serious. You thought I would be safe after you came back here? You don't think the Naga would wonder where I went?"

"Who cares if they wonder, as long as they don't know?"

I groan. "We were living on borrowed time, Marinda. The Widows' Village wasn't nearly secure enough—eventually the Naga would have found us. Our only hope was to have the protection of the throne, but that was a privilege you only bothered to secure for Mani when you decided on this little adventure. You left me for dead."

Slow horror creeps over her face. "Is that what you think?" she asks. "That I don't care what happens to you?"

I curl my fingers into my palms and dig crescent-shaped

marks into the tender skin there. "What other reason could you have for not making sure that the Raja kept me safe too?"

Her voice is soft. "I thought you wanted to be done with all this," she says. "I wanted you to be happy."

I turn and start walking again. I don't tell her that it was Deven who sent me here, that when he found out I was planning to leave Sundari, he begged me to make sure Marinda was safe first. "The Naga won't trust her after what she did," he told me. "But they don't know that you've been with her all this time. They'll trust you."

I didn't tell him that he shouldn't trust me. That no one should.

"What did he give you?" Marinda asks, falling in step beside me. A bright green bird trills above us, and a breeze shivers through the trees. At first I think she means Deven, so I don't say anything. But then she sighs. "Balavan must have some reason to trust you. I'm not stupid, Iyla."

"It doesn't matter," I tell her. "No one owns me." But a trickle of unease touches the back of my mind. Because now I'm craving life. Longing for it.

Marinda's gaze flicks to me and she frowns, but she doesn't press me for more information. She's quiet for a moment before she says, "Where are we going?"

"Ultimately? To interrogate a man named Pranesh who Balavan suspects has ties to the Pakshi." Those who worship the great bird Garuda want nothing more than to see the Naga destroyed. Balavan wants the members of the Pakshi identified and eliminated.

"Ultimately?" Marinda repeats. "Are we going somewhere else first?"

"Yes," I tell her. "We're going to see Deven."

The spasm of joy that crosses her expression is a splinter in my heart. "Wait," she says. "Really?"

I nod. "Really."

She reaches for my hand and squeezes it. Her gratitude presses against my guilt and rubs it raw.

* *

I was eight the first time Gopal threatened to take Marinda from me.

We were in a training session—he was teaching me how to lie without being discovered and how to spot a liar. "Tell me you love me," he said, and I winced. There was no bigger lie. No greater challenge.

"I don't want to," I told him.

His face hardened. "I didn't ask you if you wanted to. Tell me you love me."

I wrinkled my nose. "I love you," I said.

Gopal slammed his hand down on the table. "This is not a game, Iyla. The *rajakumari*'s life may depend on your ability to deceive anyone at any time. You are worthless if you can't protect her."

It was an oft-repeated sentiment spoken from the time I was small enough to sit on Gopal's knee. *You are not as important as the* rajakumari, *little one. But your life will have purpose if it is dedicated to protecting hers.*

I folded my arms across my chest. "Marinda doesn't think I'm worthless."

It was a deliberate provocation. Referring to Marinda

by her name instead of her title. Suggesting that her opinion mattered more than Gopal's, that her opinion was different from his. And worst of all, implying that there might be loyalty in our friendship that he hadn't created. I hadn't yet learned that with Gopal, power needed to be wielded subtly if it was to be wielded at all.

"The *rajakumari* thinks what I tell her to think." He spoke the words through a clenched jaw, as if he were hanging on to the side of a cliff by only his fingertips. And still I couldn't resist stepping on his hands.

"No," I tell him. "She loves me and there's nothing you can do about it."

Gopal grabbed my chin and pinched it between his thumb and forefinger. "I own Marinda's affections," he said. "And I can make her stop loving you anytime I choose."

I glared at him. "Prove it."

His fingers slipped from the cliff of self-control he'd been clutching. He reared back and slapped me across the face so hard that stars exploded in my vision. I sat on my hands to avoid pressing a palm to my cheek. Tears stung my eyes, but I blinked them away.

His nostrils flared. His breath was shallow and sharply punctuated. Seeing him lose control made me feel power when I should have felt fear.

"I love you," I said. My voice was genuine. My smile crinkled the skin at the corners of my eyes. I couldn't have appeared more sincere if he had given me a bouquet of flowers instead of a slap.

His lip curled. "Yes," he said. "That's more like it."

Gopal's efforts at taking Marinda from me weren't successful right away. Though it wasn't for lack of trying.

One night at dinner he turned to Marinda and said, "Perhaps Iyla could give you some advice on how to care for your skin. She's so much more naturally beautiful than you are."

Any other girl would have bristled at the comparison. It should have driven a wedge between us, but Gopal didn't know Marinda like I did. Not yet.

"It's good that Iyla's more beautiful, though, right? My looks don't really matter for a quick kiss." She swept her bread through the red sauce on her plate and popped it into her mouth without another word.

Appealing to her vanity would never work. A few days later he tried the opposite approach. I had just left the room, but I lingered in the hallway, my back pressed against the wall to listen to their conversation.

"Your work is more important than Iyla's, *rajakumari*," Gopal said. "You must remember to keep her in her place."

"But if not for Iyla, I wouldn't have any work. Isn't she the reason the Raja knows which men he should target? Because she collects the information?"

Gopal sighed heavily. "Well, yes, but you must keep her at a distance. She's not worthy of your time."

"We don't violate tradecraft, if that's what you're worried about."

"You aren't allowed to love her," he said, and his voice had a desperate edge that made me smile to myself.

"Oh," Marinda said. "Okay." Her voice was both

compliant and dismissive. He'd given her an order that he had no way to enforce, and they both knew it.

He spent the next two years trying to drive us apart. Comparing us, pitting us against one another, punishing one for the other's disobedience. But at every insult or insinuation, Marinda would find my hand under the table and lace her fingers through mine. The message was clear. We were a matched pair, and whatever happened, we were in it together.

It was only a matter of time before Gopal would realize that our shared suffering had forged a bond that he'd never be able to break, that Marinda would always love me more than she feared him. And then he'd never let us be together. When Marinda turned ten, I begged her to run away with me. She wasn't hard to convince. For years we'd dreamed about escaping, whispered our plans in the middle of the night after I'd snuck into her room and climbed into her bed. We'd lie forehead to forehead, our warm breath mingling, and dream of a life far away from there.

A few weeks later I knelt in the grass outside her bedroom window, my heart lodged in my throat. What if she didn't come? What if Gopal caught us? Finally a creak, a bump, a sandaled foot dangling in the night. We were seconds from freedom. I reached out to steady her but froze when I heard her sharp intake of breath.

"Are you going somewhere?" Gopal asked. His voice made my stomach plummet. Not because it was angry, but because it was careful. Controlled. Almost cheerful. It was the voice of someone who knew he'd already won.

"Who is she?" Marinda's voice was full of wonder, and I

longed to stretch on my toes and see what Gopal was up to. See what had calmed his insecurities.

Gopal laughed. "Not she, *he*. He is your brother, Marinda."

I inched toward the edge of the window and risked a glance inside. Gopal held an orange-swathed bundle. A baby. My hope sputtered out like a candle in a stiff breeze. If Gopal couldn't turn Marinda against me, he would give her the kind of love that would eclipse anything she'd ever felt for me. A sibling born of blood instead of circumstance.

Marinda pulled her leg back inside. The window slid closed. And she forgot I was ever there at all.

CHAPTER SEVEN

Marinda

I don't realize how much I've missed the city until Iyla and I are swallowed up in the swiftly moving river of people—men pushing rumbling carts filled to the brim with coconuts, children playing stickball in the street, women carrying baskets of ripe fruit, their bangled bracelets ringing with every step. The cacophony of color and noise engulfs us in a sea of anonymity.

I haven't felt this secure in weeks.

Deven is supposed to meet us at a safe house in the heart of Bala City, but we get there before he does. It's not the same location where Deven took me after the Naga killed Japa and kidnapped Mani, but it's close enough that my heart still clenches at the sight of the nondescript alley. Iyla digs a key from her bag and slides it into a small opening in the wall, and a door-shaped portion of the stone swings inward.

The safe house is a small flat with two beds shoved against

one wall and a small table wedged into the corner. Shelves stacked with nonperishable food—bundles of dried fruits and meats, canteens of water, baskets of nuts and seeds—line the walls. In the back are a small shower and a chest of drawers with changes of clothes in various sizes.

Iyla kicks off her sandals, stretches out on one of the beds and closes her eyes. But I'm too excited to sleep. I search through the drawers for paper and write down all of the information I've memorized about the Naga so far—the location and layout of the palace, what I've been able to decipher about their hierarchal structure, a description of Balavan. Soon the table is covered with notes, maps, lists of names. But still the minutes tick by without any sign of Deven, and a knot forms in my stomach. If he doesn't show up soon, we'll have to hide the information at one of the dead drops and leave without seeing him.

"Stop pacing," Iyla says. "You're giving me a headache."

"Maybe he's not coming," I say. "How much longer do we have?"

"Relax." She turns onto her side and tucks an arm beneath her head. "Balavan isn't going to question your absence as long as I'm babysitting you."

I give her a halfhearted glare. I hope that she doesn't take her duties as my warden too seriously, because I need to find a moment alone with Deven to tell him my concerns about her. I want to believe that she won't betray me, that she's only pretending to work for Balavan, but I can't bring myself to fully trust her. Not yet.

The minutes stretch into hours, and my nerves are pulled so taut I feel like I could snap at any moment.

Finally we hear the sound of a key turning in the lock, and the door swings open. I've been seeing Deven in my dreams since I left him, so I thought I remembered the planes of his face, the shape of his eyes. But my imagination didn't capture him perfectly. It's as if his features have rearranged themselves in my absence—he looks at once familiar and foreign.

I launch myself into his arms, bury my face against the warm skin of his neck and breathe him in. His arms wrap tightly around me and I feel small next to him.

"Mani?" I ask when he releases me, though I should know better than to hope.

A shadow passes over Deven's face, and my joy deflates. "Is he okay?" I ask.

"Yes, of course," he says gently. "It just wasn't safe to bring him." He plants a kiss on my forehead. "Next time. I promise."

Iyla has unfurled herself from the bed. "I have something I need to take care of," she says. "I'll be back in a few minutes."

"Thank you," I say, grateful for the privacy.

She gives me a tight smile. "I won't be long."

Iyla slips out the door and Deven pulls me closer. His fingers trace the shape of my face, the long line of my neck, the contours of my mouth. By the time his lips find mine, I'm trembling. I close my eyes and let his touch fill my mind with light, let it crowd out all the darkness. The kiss deepens and I forget where I am, forget that I'm an assassin, a spy, a *visha kanya*. In his arms I can just be a girl.

But not forever.

I pull away, dizzy and disoriented. "We need to work," I say.

He kisses my neck just beneath my ear. "Are you sure?"

I don't answer. Instead I lead him to the table and I fill him in on everything that has happened since I left the Raja's palace. His eyes widen when I tell him about the man I kissed, but he doesn't look at me differently, doesn't recoil like I thought he might. "Did you actually see him die?" Deven asks.

"No," I say. "But I don't think someone could have faked those screams." The memory washes me in a fresh wave of guilt.

Deven tucks a strand of hair behind my ear. "I'm sorry," he says. "I'll talk to Hitesh and make sure it doesn't happen again."

I curl my fingers into my palms. "It won't matter," I say. "He won't be able to protect everyone."

Deven rakes his fingers through his hair. "You're right. He won't. But he can try."

It won't be enough. I chew on my lower lip and Deven catches my hand in his. He slips his fingers under the wide bracelets around my wrists and traces the scars there. "You don't have to do this," he says. "You can come back to the palace with me right now and forget any of this ever happened."

I hold the temptation of his offer close to my heart, just for a moment. "I can't," I say finally. "If I leave now, every death caused by the Naga will be my fault. I have to try to stop them."

"Marinda, please. At least—"

I hold up a hand to prevent him from saying anything. If he keeps talking, I might agree to go with him. I could be holding Mani in my arms within days. "No," I say. "I'm staying."

His shoulders sag. The light goes out of his eyes. But he doesn't argue.

I clear my throat. "I don't know what Iyla told you when she asked you to meet us here," I tell him. "But she's working for the Naga again. I don't know if we can trust her." The look on his face pulls me up short. "You knew," I say.

"The Naga were never going to trust you at first," he says. "Iyla had a better way in."

I grip the edge of the table. My heartbeat thunders in my ears. "You asked her to come back? How could you do that? She'd finally gotten away from them, and now you've traded her safety for mine."

His eyes flash. "That's a trade I would make again and again."

"You had no right—" My argument is robbed of breath by the sound of the door opening. Iyla stands at the threshold, her gaze skipping between us.

"Sorry to interrupt," she says.

I wave a hand in front of my face. "No," I say. "You weren't . . . you didn't . . ."

Deven lays a palm on my shoulder and squeezes. "Hello, Iyla," he says. "Come tell us about your next target."

✳ ✳

The man Balavan wants us to question works on Gali Street. I haven't been anywhere near Japa's bookshop since he died, and the thought of going there now makes dread slick through my veins. But we have no choice.

Deven walks silently between me and Iyla. His grief is tangible—Japa was like a second father to him—and it echoes off my own sadness, amplifying it, making it unbearable. I try not to look at the bookshop as we pass, but my gaze is pulled over and over like a shell caught in the tide. I wonder who nailed the thick boards across the entrance. Who packed up each book? Who moved Japa's body?

Despite our earlier disagreement, Deven and I reach for each other at the same moment. I lace my fingers through his, and it gives me the strength to keep walking.

Iyla leads us to the far end of Gali Street—past the bookshop, past the butcher and the flower peddler, past the windows exhibiting brightly colored pottery and barrels of dried peppers. She stops in front of a display of blades.

I turn to her, wide eyed. "We're interrogating someone who works *here*?"

She flashes me a grin and pushes the door open.

Deven and I follow her inside and my breath catches. A dizzying array of weapons covers every surface. Gleaming swords, *katars*, and axes hang from the walls. An enormous collection of *chakrams* lie on a table in the center of the room. Daggers in every imaginable size are piled in baskets. And in one corner is a collection of items I've never seen before: a silver weapon with slots for fingers and three long tines, turning the wearer's hand into a giant, deadly claw;

a forked-tongue knife that flicks open, splitting into twin serrated blades; and a *haladie,* two curved swords attached to a single center hilt.

Each weapon is a work of art, and I wonder what drives the impulse to make the instruments of death beautiful. A jewel-encrusted dagger. A golden-pommeled sword.

A kiss.

Like we can make murder less ugly by performing it with something splendid.

"Pick something," Iyla says under her breath.

As if I need a weapon to be deadly.

But the expression on her face leaves no room for argument. I select an enameled dagger set with rubies and turquoise. Iyla picks a knife with a snake on the handle. The man behind the counter watches us with detached interest. He can't be more than twenty-five, and everything about him is sharp, from his lanky body, made of only angles, to his beak-shaped nose and long face.

Iyla saunters to the front of the shop and sets her knife on the counter, though she leaves her hand wrapped tightly around the handle. "I'm looking for Pranesh."

"You found him," the man says. "How can I help you?"

Iyla gives him a chilly smile. "Actually, I'm wondering if there's someone else here I can talk to?"

The man's forehead wrinkles in confusion. "But you said you were looking for me."

Iyla shrugs. "I changed my mind. Could you get me someone else, please?"

"Sorry," the man says. "I'm the only one here today, so if there's something you need, you're stuck with me."

"I'm so happy to hear that," Iyla says. "Deven, the door, please."

Deven draws the shades and slides a sword through the handles on the door to jam it closed. Pranesh sucks in a sharp breath and reaches under the counter for a weapon, but Iyla's too fast for him. She unsheathes her knife with lightning speed and has it pressed against his neck before his fingers have fully closed around his blade.

"Drop it," she says. Pranesh unclenches his fist, and his weapon clatters to the floor.

Iyla is on her tiptoes, so I grab a stool from the corner and put it in the center of the room.

"I don't know who you think I am," Pranesh says. As he speaks, Iyla's blade vibrates against his throat, distorting his voice. "I'm nobody."

"Sit," she says, and the man shuffles to the middle of the room and sinks onto the stool. She nods toward Deven. "Tie him up," she says.

Deven folds his arms across his chest. "Is that really necessary?"

Her eyes blaze. "Is he speaking yet?"

"You haven't asked me anything," Pranesh says through clenched teeth.

Iyla presses the knife more firmly against his neck, and a bright red drop of blood beads on his skin. "When I do, are you going to cooperate?"

Her cheeks are flushed with pleasure. She's enjoying this.

Deven secures Pranesh's hands behind his back with a rope. "Don't overdo it," he tells Iyla in a voice just above a whisper. "He could be on our side."

But I'm not sure that Iyla's side and our side are the same. She tugs at the ropes with her free hand to make sure they're secure before she lowers her knife.

She circles the stool until she's facing Pranesh. He has a faint smear of blood on his forehead and a sheen of sweat on his upper lip. "Who do you work for?" Iyla asks.

"I work here," Pranesh says. "For the man who owns the shop."

Iyla growls and takes a step forward, but I put a hand out to stop her. "Our orders are to kill you after we interrogate you," I say softly. The color drains from Pranesh's face. "But we're willing to let you live if you cooperate."

Pranesh shifts in his seat. He bites his lower lip. "What do you want to know?"

"How long have you been working for the Pakshi?" Deven asks. "I thought I knew everyone who follows Garuda, but I don't recognize you."

Pranesh shakes his head. The confusion on his face seems genuine. "The Pakshi? I don't—"

So it's a trap. No wonder Iyla treated him so harshly. Balavan sent us to one of his own men to see how we would perform. I throw a worried glance at Deven. We can't let the Naga find out we were together. We might have to kill Pranesh after all.

"How long have you been working for the Nagaraja?" I ask.

He sucks in a sharp breath. "Never," he says. "I would never."

The look of horror on his face is genuine. He's either a

gifted liar or we have the wrong man. Deven strides forward and lifts Pranesh's sleeve.

"What are you doing?" I ask.

"Looking for a tattoo," Deven says. "If he's Naga, we can't let him live."

Many of the Naga have tattoos of black snakes circling their forearms. Deven wears a tattoo of Garuda on his biceps. It's not foolproof, but it's a good idea.

"Not my arms," Pranesh says softly. "You'll find what you're looking for on the back of my neck."

Iyla circles behind him and yanks the collar of his shirt down. Her face goes still and Deven and I rush to her side to look for ourselves. Pranesh has a tattoo, but it's neither the Nagaraja nor the great bird Garuda.

It's a large, oblong head with giant eyes and a gaping mouth full of sharp teeth.

Pranesh has a tattoo of the Crocodile King.

CHAPTER EIGHT

Iyla

I thought I had considered every possibility.

I knew there was a chance that the assignment to interrogate Pranesh was only a test. That perhaps he was a member of the Naga who had stepped out of line, and my task was to provide a helping of fear as a side dish to his death. I also thought it was just as likely the man might really be Pakshi. That Balavan wanted to analyze my skill as a spy with a low-level target.

I didn't expect to return with actual intelligence. With a secret so big that, for a moment, I wonder if Balavan even knows it.

But of course he does.

He sent me on the hunt, and he will expect me to return with treasure.

"I thought the crocodile and the tiger were dead," Marinda is saying. She paces in front of Pranesh, the enameled dagger still dangling from her fingers as if she's forgotten it's in her hand.

"Who told you they were dead?" Pranesh asks. Marinda's eyes flick to Deven.

He shrugs. "Most people think they are. They haven't been seen for centuries."

Pranesh snorts. "And I suppose seeing is believing? No one has seen Garuda either, and yet so many people cling to the hope that she exists."

Deven pins him with a steely gaze. "Careful," he says. "We could still decide to kill you."

We're wasting the day away letting Pranesh talk in circles and half answer questions. It's time to get some real information.

"Where is the Crocodile King?" I ask.

Pranesh swallows hard. "I don't know."

I walk forward and kneel in front of him. I unsheathe my knife and polish it on my sari, first on one side, then on the other. I take my time before I start to speak. "There are two kinds of spies, Pranesh. The first are the ones who are in it for the thrill. They relish the feel of their hearts pounding in their chests, the rush of danger when they're in the field. They're spies because they love it, because it makes them feel alive. Those are the ones who are easy to turn." I stand up and run the tip of the knife along his hairline, down his face, along the V-shaped lines of his throat. Not deep enough to draw blood, but with enough pressure that he stops breathing. "And then there is the other kind of spy—the spies who really believe in their cause. The ones who would give up anything for their convictions. They're the kind who can't be bought. They're also the ones who die when captured."

I drop the knife back to my side and lean down so that I'm only inches away from his face. "The question is, which kind of spy are you?" I drop my voice to a whisper. "And which kind of spy are you willing to bet your life that I am?"

I stare at him until he starts to tremble. "Give me some paper," he says finally. "And I'll draw you a map."

* *

"We can't really give Balavan that map," Marinda says several hours later. Deven is headed back to the Raja's palace with Pranesh. The only way to keep the man alive is for him to disappear. He may still be breathing, but his former life is over; his identity, his friends, his home—all must be abandoned without a parting glance. Deven will help him start fresh. It's the only way.

"We have to give it to him," I say. "He must know that Pranesh was working for the Crocodile King. If we return with nothing, our cover will be blown."

Marinda gives me a searching look that makes my jaw go tight. "Is there a cover to blow?"

"Don't be ridiculous," I say. But it isn't an answer and we both know it.

The sun dips below the horizon, bathing the city in salmon-colored light. One by one the shops close, and the crowds begin to thin. Sundari is beautiful like this. Drowsy. Half-empty. The day—good or bad—nearly finished.

Marinda's movements are stiff. I can tell she's holding

back, that she's teeming with questions she's too proud to ask. But even if she did, I don't have answers for her.

"Balavan will want information on you," I warn her. "He'll want to know who you saw. What you did."

She pulls a golden, pear-shaped pin from the back of her head and her dark hair tumbles around her shoulders, cascades down her back. "Tell him I sent a letter," she says.

"A letter to whom?"

"To the Raja."

I release a stream of air through pursed lips. "And the letter said what?"

She shakes her head. "You wouldn't know unless you'd stolen it."

"And I didn't?"

She gives me a rueful smile. "You didn't." And then after a beat, "Do you think it will be enough of a report? The letter?"

I shrug. "It's hard to know with Balavan." I know what she's really asking. Will I tell him that she saw Deven? Will I put her life in danger? Or more importantly, will I put Mani's life in danger?

We walk in silence for several minutes, each lost in our own thoughts. Then Marinda stops abruptly. "Let's go to the marketplace," she says.

A ripple of unease goes through me. "No," I tell her. "We don't have time."

"Of course we do," she says. "You said Balavan wouldn't miss me as long as we were together."

She's already started walking in the opposite direction

and I have to hurry to catch up. "This is a bad idea," I tell her. "What do you need at the marketplace, anyway?"

"I need to see Kadru."

I stop walking. "No."

Marinda looks over her shoulder. She blinks. "Oh. Then I guess I'll see you back at the Naga palace? I won't be long."

She knows I can't leave her. Knows if I show up at the Naga palace alone, Balavan will lose what little trust he has in me. Without a second thought, he would snatch away the five years he returned. My thumb finds the smooth skin at the back of my hand and traces a circle. I hurry to catch up with Marinda, fall in step beside her and try to ignore the smug smile that tugs at her mouth.

"Why would you choose to go back there?" I ask. "Ever?"

"I need to ask her something," Marinda says. "It's important."

"I'm not going inside."

"You don't have to." Marinda squeezes my arm, and I resist the urge to swat her away. She has no right to offer comfort. Not about this.

I haven't seen Kadru in years. Not since the last time she pricked the base of my neck with her sharp claws and sent pain exploding through me. Not since she pulled the life from my body with skilled, greedy fingers.

"Think of how wonderful your next life will be, darling," she said once when I was six and had learned to arch my back, to kick, to scream.

That was always the promised trade-off—a miserable life now for the hope of a golden and glittering one later. A life lived for Marinda with the guarantee that someday someone would live a life for me. But I liked my rewards more immediate. What if I was already on my tenth life? What if this was my last chance?

By the time we make it to the marketplace, most of the vendors have long since boxed up their wares—folded their silk scarves, scooped up their baskets full of gems, put away their remedies—and carried them home. An eerie silence hangs over the street like a fog. Goose bumps race along my arms.

"Do you think they're really all alive?" Marinda asks, her voice cutting like a knife through the stillness. "Garuda, Bagharani, the Crocodile King?"

I sigh. "It's starting to look that way."

Her gaze gets misty and far away. "If it's true, it changes everything."

But I think she's wrong. I don't see how it changes anything at all.

CHAPTER NINE

Marinda

It wasn't until I saw Iyla's hair gleaming in the twilight that I studied her more closely. The small age spot on the back of her hand—the one her thumb hasn't stopped tracing since she found it several weeks ago—is gone. Her skin is dewy. Her cheeks have more color, and her hair is just a little thicker, the color just a little richer.

The realization unfurled in my stomach with a snap. Balavan has offered her the one thing beyond my reach, beyond Deven's. Life.

It's not that I haven't thought about how to restore Iyla. How to give her back the years Kadru stole to turn me into a killer. I asked Deven if the maraka fruit would work, but he didn't know. It's an antidote to the poison, but it probably can't give her years she doesn't have.

But if I'm going to win in a game against Balavan, I

need to be on equal footing. Iyla is too big an advantage for me to concede.

Kadru is the only person who might have the answers. Iyla waits at least a hundred steps from the entrance to the tent. She has one fist tightly clenched around the opposite hand, as if she knows she can rely only on herself for comfort.

It tweaks something inside me to see her like this—her shoulders slumped forward as if she's carrying an invisible weight, her eyes wide and rigid. It's an expression I've never seen on her before, but one that can only be described as fear.

I take a deep breath before I part the flap of Kadru's tent and step into her small, sumptuous kingdom. White snakes are everywhere—curled around the legs of a mahogany table, suspended from a bamboo pole, lounging on a velvet chaise.

Kadru sits cross-legged in an overstuffed chair, her gaze pinned to the entrance as if she's been expecting me. She is dressed in a plum-colored sari. Amethyst stones rest in the hollow of her throat and dangle from her ears.

"I heard you were back," she says. Her fingers idly brush the head of the snake curled on her lap.

I keep my face impassive, my muscles loose, but there's nothing I can do to stop the hammering of my heart or the prickle of fear that races over my skin. The reptilian stench of the tent curls around me, making it impossible to breathe deeply. If only the snakes would move, would give me some space, I might be able to gather my thoughts.

Suddenly every snake in the tent moves at once, slithering away from me, gathering around Kadru.

I release a sigh. "Thank you," I tell her.

She throws her head back and laughs. The sound makes the hairs rise on the back of my neck.

"Oh, my darling, I didn't command them." She smiles, catlike. "You did."

I take a step back. Shake my head. "No," I say. "That's not possible."

"Did you wish for them to move away from you?"

My blood runs cold. The last time I saw Kadru, she told me I would become her, that her path was my path. I fight back tears.

"How?" I say. "Why?"

Something like sympathy flashes in Kadru's eyes. "It happened for me the first time I saw the Nagaraja in person," she says. "I felt his mind touch mine, and from then on I had a connection to all snakes. Though it took me years before I could do what you just did."

Horror wells in my chest as I remember my encounter with the Nagaraja. How I finally made him release Mani by opening up the connection in my mind even more completely to him. How I pushed all of the pain and sorrow from my memory into his. I cover my mouth with my hand. What have I done?

Kadru stands up and places a palm on my arm. Her skin is warm. "Don't fight it, darling. There's power in being the Nagaraja's chosen one." She takes my face in her hands and pins me with a searching look. And suddenly her voice is in my mind, far more forceful than the one she usually uses. *The game you're playing is a dangerous one.*

I gasp, but Kadru gives me a warning glare, a subtle shake of her head. "Be a good girl," she says aloud.

I feel naked, but without any sense of which way to twist my body to avoid scrutiny.

I can't stop shaking. My gaze darts around the tent, as if I might find answers on the intricately embroidered pillows or the gold-rimmed teacups.

Kadru strides back to her chair. She curls her feet underneath her. She waits.

Several long seconds pass before this question occurs to me: If she can see inside my mind, can I see inside hers?

Not unless I let you in.

I stuff a fist into my mouth, pull air slowly through my nose. I shouldn't have come here.

"Why *did* you come here, darling?" Kadru asks.

"Why are you asking when you already know?" My voice comes out hoarse and just above a whisper.

Kadru raises one delicate eyebrow. "Come now, *rajakumari*. Don't play games."

I want to rip her hair out. Claw at her face. Shake her like a bag of rice—viciously, until the exterior rips and her pearly-white secrets come spilling out.

If she sees my violent thoughts, she doesn't show it. Her face is calm, expectant. Maybe I imagined her voice in my head. Maybe I'm losing touch with reality.

I glance at the entrance to the tent. It's dangerous to approach Kadru when I know she serves the Nagaraja, when I know she's loyal to them. But she's helped me before. When I asked for venom to make Deven immune, she gave it to me instead of turning me over to Gopal. She made me pay a steep price, but she didn't tell me no. And right now she's the only one who can give me what I want. I thought it was worth the risk.

But that was before I knew she could see my thoughts.

I turn to leave, but then I think of Iyla standing outside, of the fear in her eyes. I spin back toward Kadru. "I want you to give Iyla her life back."

She sighs and her expression gets dreamy and distant. "I had a counterpoint once," she says. "That's what Balavan called her—my counterpoint. The girl whose life was slowly drained to make me deadly. Her name was Tamira." She swallows. Her gaze drops to her lap, to the thick white snake coiled there. She strokes his head, her jewels flashing, her purple fingernails looking like blooming bruises against his pale scales. With a start I realize that I know the snake is male. That I know he enjoys being caressed.

The air in the tent suddenly feels too thick to breathe. "What happened to her?" I ask, as much to distract myself from the snake as to get an answer.

"She died young, while I grew more deadly, more powerful." Kadru lifts her head and meets my eyes. "She got the better deal."

"I doubt she would agree," I say.

"No," Kadru says. "You're probably right."

The silence stretches between us. Questions tumble around my mind, but they are so disjointed I can't put them into words.

"I cared a great deal about Tamira," Kadru says. "You might even say I loved her. But in the end it didn't matter. It didn't matter for me, and it won't matter for you. What you're asking, Marinda, it isn't possible."

"I don't believe you," I say. "I think Balavan has already given some of her life back."

"And you're hoping if you can help her, you'll wield some control? That she'll be loyal to you?"

"No, it's not like that." But even as I say the words, hot shame licks up my neck. Because the truth is that I do want to control Iyla. I want her loyalty. I want her friendship. I want her to feel about me the way she did when we were children.

Kadru shakes her head. "Not possible." I don't know if she's responding to my statement or my thoughts. But then her gaze sharpens and she frowns. "Iyla will never be loyal to you."

I curl my fist around a bamboo pole and squeeze until my knuckles turn white. "She will," I say. "She has before." I think of all the times we spent as children whispering secrets in the dark of night, hiding in the belly of the huge teak wardrobe in Iyla's room and giggling as Gita huffed around the girls' home shouting our names. Iyla wasn't just loyal to me. She loved me.

"You are the reason she's dying," Kadru says. "How could she possibly ever love you?"

My throat burns. I've had the very same thought before, but somehow hearing her say it out loud makes it seem irrevocable.

"But I didn't take her life—*you* did."

"You must know by now that it's more complicated than that. If I could help you, I would. But Iyla has lost more years than I could ever return."

"You could if you wanted to," I say softly. "What's fifty years to you when you have so many?"

"Fifty? Oh, if only it were so few. Iyla has lost five hundred, my darling. And even I don't have that many to spare."

I take a step backward. "That's not possible," I say. "How could you have taken five hundred years from her when she'll only live . . ." But even as I speak, the knowledge settles over me like a blanket made of steel. It presses all the air from my lungs. "You took years from lives she hasn't lived yet, lives she hasn't even been born to?"

The question hangs in the air between us.

"Not for myself," Kadru says finally. "The lives went to the Nagaraja. But they're gone all the same."

My voice feels trapped at the base of my throat, and I have to force my next words out. "How much longer does she have?"

"She's on her last life," Kadru says. "And if she's started to show signs of age . . ." She pauses, as if reading my thoughts for confirmation. "A few years at most. Possibly not even that long."

I think of Iyla's face when she learns the truth—that she's lost so much more than she even knows. I think of the hate that will twist her features, that will forever change the way she sees me.

The snake on Kadru's lap slithers to the floor as she stands. She runs the back of her fingers along my cheek. "It was meant to be this way," she says. "You were never supposed to have human connections."

For just a moment Mani's face springs into my memory. His impish smile, the way his hair looks first thing in the morning—sticking up in every direction. My heart curls protectively around the image and I force it from my mind. I can't ever let myself think of Mani in Kadru's presence. I let my thoughts drift back to Iyla, but that's hardly any better. I don't want to lose her either. But I will. She's going to blame me even though it's not fair.

Kadru tilts her head to one side and studies me with a knowing expression, as if she's following every thought, and I swallow hard. Her eyes soften. "The heart doesn't concern itself with what's fair. You had already lost Iyla before you even knew her name. It's time to let go."

But I refuse to believe her. There has to be another way to keep Iyla alive, to keep Mani safe. To take down the Nagaraja. And whatever it is, I'm going to find it.

"I have to go," I say. I ignore the way the snakes perk up at my words. The way I can feel their restless energy pulsing through my own mind. I smooth my palms along my sari to dry them. "Are you going to tell Balavan I was here?"

Kadru laughs. "Oh, darling, I won't need to. Iyla will tell him."

CHAPTER TEN

Iyla

Marinda looks like she's seen a ghost. Her lips have drained of color. Her hands flutter at her sides like injured bird wings. I forget all about keeping my distance from Kadru's tent as I rush to her side.

"What happened?" I ask.

"Nothing," she says, but the word is too quick, too strained. She doesn't slow down, doesn't meet my gaze.

"Marinda, wait." I lay a palm on her forearm. "Don't lie to me."

She stops then. She turns to me, slowly. Her smile is tremulous and her eyes are so full of pain that my heart pinches in my chest. I know that expression—it's one I've given her many times—bleak and bled of hope. It's the sting of being betrayed. What did Kadru say to her?

"I'm fine," she says. "Can we just go back to the Naga palace?"

I drop my hand back to my side. "Of course we can."

Marinda walks likes someone is chasing us, and my thighs burn as I struggle to keep up. Her sandals slap against the street in an unrelenting, angry rhythm.

"Nothing good ever comes from visiting Kadru," I tell her. She doesn't answer. I'm not certain she even heard me.

We walk in silence while I wait for her to calm down. To turn to me, as usual, and tell me what's bothering her.

But she never does.

Something inside me starts to fray. I've never seen Marinda like this. She's never been so far away that I couldn't reach her. It makes me feel like I'm standing on quicksand.

And yet all the way back to the Naga palace, I'm rehearsing what I'll tell Balavan. What if the letter isn't enough? How I can betray Marinda in pieces without betraying her completely?

Knifelike worry twists in my gut. What if I can't satisfy Balavan without giving him Marinda, whole and unprotected? What if it's like giving a snake a mouse and expecting him not to eat it?

But it won't come to that.

A little voice in my head whispers that this is a lie, that if I have to choose between my life and Marinda's, I won't be able to trust myself not to go too far. But if tradecraft has taught me anything, it's that sometimes lies are necessary. Sometimes they're a matter of survival.

Marinda still seems lost in thought when we approach the guards on the path to the Naga palace. They step in front of us, hands on the hilts of their swords, and block us from moving forward.

"A tiger can hide in the bushes, and a bird can take cover in the trees," the younger of the two men says.

Marinda's head snaps up. Her gaze sharpens. I make a mental note to tell her she needs to be subtler when she's collecting intelligence.

I roll my eyes at the guard. "We just left this morning. You watched us go."

"And perhaps you've fallen from Balavan's grace in the meantime and he's decided to change the password," he says. "I still need to hear it."

I smile sweetly, even though I'd like to snatch the sword from his hands and liberate his head from his neck. "But the most dangerous enemy is the one that can hide underfoot," I say.

The guard grins as he steps off the path. "Now, was that so hard?"

Out of the corner of my eye, I see Marinda's fingers curl into fists at her sides. I put a hand on her elbow and pull her forward before she does anything stupid.

Once the Naga palace comes into view, she twists away from me. My hand falls to my side and my throat burns.

"I'm exhausted," she says. "I'm going to rest." She doesn't wait for an answer before she trudges off and climbs the palace steps. Her movements are leaden, and I wonder what Kadru said to finally make her understand how costly it is to have two different identities. How dangerous.

The guilt is a smoldering ember in my chest. Balavan

is giving my life back, so why do I still feel like I'm steeped in poison?

* *

Balavan wastes no time in summoning me to his rooms. I don't even have a chance to scrub the dust from my feet before he sends Amoli to fetch me.

He's bouncing a plum in his hand when I arrive, the dark fruit flying wildly through the air before smacking his palm with such force that I expect the tender flesh to tear at any moment and send the juices dribbling to the ground like spilled blood.

When he sees me, he catches the fruit and holds it out to me. Impressions of his fingers dent the surface. "Would you like a snack?"

My stomach turns over. I shake my head. "No," I say. "I'm not hungry."

He shrugs and tosses the plum into a bowl on the table. "You're late," he says.

"Pranesh wasn't cooperative at first," I tell him. "It took longer than I expected."

His chin dips and he levels me with a cold gaze. My heart trips forward, but it's important that I remain calm. Nonchalant. Balavan doesn't say anything for a long time. He just stares at me, as if waiting for a confession. It's an old trick—to let the silence stretch to the point of discomfort. An inexperienced person will try to fill it with something, anything. Usually prattle that reveals more than she intended.

But I'm not inexperienced. I match his silence breath for breath and wait for a question to materialize. Finally it does.

"How is our *rajakumari*?"

"Marinda is fine," I say, answering the question precisely.

He smiles as if I've pleased him. "Did you go anywhere besides the weapons shop?"

"Marinda mailed a letter," I say.

He paces in front of me. Entwines his hands together and steeples his fingers under his chin. "A letter to whom?" he asks.

"It was addressed to the Raja in Colapi City."

"And what did it say?"

Marinda's own words pool at the tip of my tongue. "I wouldn't know that unless I'd stolen it. Did you want me to pry it from her fingers and rip it open? I thought you intended for me to be subtle."

"A gifted spy might have been able to read the contents and then reseal the letter before the *rajakumari* was any the wiser."

I narrow my eyes. "Then perhaps you should give this assignment to a gifted spy."

He laughs and rubs his hands together. "I like you more and more," he says.

"Funny," I say. "I like you less and less."

Balavan doesn't even break his stride. "What did you find out about Pranesh?"

"He's not working for the Pakshi," I say. "But I suspect you already knew that."

"Were you able to find out who he is working for?"

"Of course," I tell him. "I would still be questioning him if I hadn't." Balavan keeps pacing and makes a circular motion with his hand to indicate I should continue. "He works for the Crocodile King."

At this Balavan stops and turns toward me. "And did you get a location?"

I pull a folded piece of parchment from my bag. "Even better," I say. "I got a map."

His eyes glitter. He snatches the page from my fingers and shakes it open. His gaze darts hungrily along the crookedly drawn lines. "This," he says, "is perfect."

A shudder goes through me as I wonder what kind of weapon I've given him. He hands the map back to me, and I raise my eyebrows in question.

"You'll need to infiltrate them, of course."

I don't cover my surprise quickly enough, and his expression fills with dark amusement. I open my mouth to speak. Snap it shut again. "I thought you wanted me to spy on Marinda," I say finally.

He splays his fingers against the back of a chair, his hands crushing the azure velvet. "Oh, I think you can do both," he says. His lips curve up in a smile, but his eyes are hard as flint. "You're practiced at doing two things at once, aren't you? Just like how you're trying to protect the *rajakumari* even as you betray her."

Blood roars in my ears. "I don't know what you're talking about."

Balavan circles the chair and stalks toward me. It takes

all of my self-control not to back away. He puts one finger under my chin and lifts my face until I'm gazing into his bottomless black eyes. "Yes, you do."

He never takes his eyes off me as he reaches for a drawer in a low table, slides it open and pulls out a folded sheet of parchment. He hands it to me. "Is this the letter you wish me to believe that the *rajakumari* mailed today?"

I skim the page—a plea for Mani's release in Marinda's small, even script. My chest tightens. She obviously meant for Balavan to read the letter, but how sloppy of her to tell me to use it before it was destroyed. My pulse thunders in my ears, but I force a laugh. "Are you suggesting she's only written one letter?" I shake the paper gently. "She sounds desperate. I wouldn't be surprised if she's written to the Raja a dozen times."

Balavan pushes off the chair and clucks his tongue as if I'm a child caught with her fingers in the cookie jar. "Iyla, my love, let's not play games. Today was the first time the *rajakumari* has been out of the palace since she arrived. Why would she write another letter when she had yet to send the first?"

My mouth goes dry. Fear skitters against the back of my neck. Balavan rests a hand on my bare shoulder. His fingers are dry and cold against my skin. "Now," he says softly. "Let's try this again. Where else did you go besides the weapons shop?"

Suddenly I'm grateful that Marinda insisted on going to the marketplace. She's handed me a less deadly weapon to wound her with.

I swallow. "She went to visit Kadru."

"I see," he says. "And what did they discuss?"

"I don't know," I say. "I stayed outside the tent."

A muscle twitches in his jaw. "How did she look afterward?"

This time I tell him the whole truth. "Like she'd just glimpsed her own death."

Balavan's smile is victorious. "Good," he says. "Very good."

CHAPTER ELEVEN

Marinda

"Are you sure you're all right, *rajakumari*?" Amoli says. "You look ill."

I try to gather my thoughts, but they are dashing through my mind like panicked children. A dull ache pulses at the base of my skull. "I'm fine," I say. "Just very tired."

It's as if Kadru has tugged on a loose thread in my soul and I'm slowly unraveling. The room looks different than it did before. Before I knew that Iyla appeared suddenly younger, that the Crocodile King not only lived but was amassing followers. Before I knew that I could see into the minds of snakes. The world has shifted under my feet, and there's no safe place to stand.

Amoli studies me, a crease appearing between her eyebrows. "Can I get you anything? Something to eat, perhaps?"

I have a sudden sharp urge to pick up the vase on the

table and launch it at her head. Why does everyone keep offering to fill the hole in my heart with food? *Bring me my brother,* I want to shout. *I don't need anything else.* Instead I paste on the false smile that has become as much a part of me as the ache in my chest. "No," I say. "But thank you."

She doesn't move. "It's brave, what you do," she says. "Though I imagine it must take a toll."

I stare at her, speechless, until it dawns on me what she means. I have to suppress the unhinged bubble of laughter that rises in my throat. She thinks I look ill because I killed Pranesh. She's impressed with my ruthlessness because she assumes it's directed at her enemies.

A small weight lifts from my heart. Maybe the day is not a total loss. "It does," I say. "But the Nagaraja knows what must be done."

The corners of her mouth turn up. It's the first genuine smile she's offered me since I got here. *I am not one of you,* I want to tell her. *I never will be.*

But Gopal's voice echoes in my memory, cries out from the dust. *You already are,* rajakumari. *You already are.*

* *

The table in the dining hall is laden with food. Balavan sits at the far end, his elbows propped on the glossy surface. He doesn't rise as I enter.

With a sweep of his arm, he directs me to sit on his right. "Thank you for coming," he says.

As if I had a choice.

Amoli woke me early this morning and informed me

that her master had invited me to dine with him. But we both knew it was an order, not a request.

I sit in the chair at Balavan's elbow. My plate is already filled—two fluffy pieces of warm *idli,* a bowl of *sambar* and a small dish of coconut chutney. I keep my hands on my lap, hidden under the table, so they won't betray me by trembling.

"How are you finding our palace thus far?"

So he's not going to explain why he summoned me here. And I won't give him the advantage by asking.

I reach for my water glass. Condensed droplets bead on the surface. It was obviously ice cold at one point and has been sitting here for some time. I take a sip.

"It's beautiful," I tell him.

He smiles. "I'm delighted you think so." And then, after a pause, "Well, don't just sit there. Eat."

I swallow. The plate in front of Balavan is empty, and his dark eyes hold a challenge. I can't refuse his request without arousing suspicion. He doesn't take his gaze from me as I tear off a section of *idli* and dunk it in the *sambar.* He's still staring when I place the savory cake, dripping, on my tongue.

He watches me like a man starving. The room feels overly warm. A bead of sweat trickles down my back.

Finally Balavan clears his throat. "It's time to officially present you to the rest of the Naga, *rajakumari.* They're all dying to meet you."

The jubilation in his voice makes me nervous. I wipe my fingers on a napkin. "I've already met many of them," I say.

"I was thinking something a little more formal," he says. "We're having a celebration."

My pulse spikes. "A celebration for what?"

Balavan reaches across the table and touches the back of my hand. "For your return to us, of course."

I pull my hand away and take another sip of water. I don't say what I'm thinking—that one can't return to a place she's never visited, a place she's just discovered exists.

The corners of his mouth turn down. His eyelids are half-closed and heavy. "You're not excited." He leans forward, elbows on the table. "Are you unhappy to be with us, *rajakumari*? Is there somewhere else you'd rather be?"

The hair on the back of my neck prickles to life. "Of course not," I say. I don't look him in the eye.

"Iyla tells me you visited Kadru," Balavan says. "How is she?"

The goblet in my hand trembles. Water sloshes onto the surface of the table as I set it down. Kadru was right. I shouldn't be surprised—Iyla has betrayed me before—but still, the knowledge is like a dagger sliding between my ribs.

"Kadru is well," I say. "She sends her regards."

Balavan laughs like I've just told him an amusing story. "Does she?"

I ignore his question and ask one of my own. "When are we celebrating?"

He touches my hand again and this time he curls his fingers around mine so that I can't pull away. "Tonight, my love. We celebrate tonight."

* *

Amoli takes great care in dressing me. I wear a deep green sari, edged in gold. Emeralds dangle from my ears, and thick golden bracelets circle my wrists and ankles so that the Naga will be spared from seeing my scars, shielded from remembering how they made me one of them.

A single long braid falls past my hips, and Amoli has woven a column of small golden disks imprinted with snakes down the entire length of my hair. My head already aches with the weight. I can only imagine how heavy it will feel by evening's end.

By the time I enter the main room of the palace, the celebration is already in full swing. Colorful paper lanterns hang from the ceiling, and hundreds of candles flicker from every surface, sending dancing firelight across the black marble floor. The members of the Naga mill around the room, drinks in hand, each of them dressed in the most gorgeous clothes I've ever seen—the women wrapped in elegant saris and dripping in jewels, the men swathed in silk dhotis.

There are more of them than I ever imagined. Hundreds. And I can't help but wonder which of them were in the cave the night that Mani almost died. Which of them would have sat idly by and let a little boy be sacrificed to the snake they worship?

The fluttering in my stomach slows. Stops. Morphs into diamond-hard rage. I will make them pay. Every one of them.

Across the room a woman lifts her head. Catches my gaze and holds it. She makes her way to me and takes my elbow in her palm. "You must be Marinda," she says. There's an edge to her voice that I don't understand.

"Yes," I say. "And you are?"

She gives me a cold smile. "Chara," she says.

"Nice to meet you."

Her lips twist into a wry smile. "Is it?"

"Of course it is," I say. "I'm always pleased to meet another of the Naga."

She laughs. "*Another* of the Naga. Oh, aren't you adorable."

Before I can stop myself, I take a step back. Chara closes the distance between us and touches my elbow again. "I find it fascinating, your sudden change of heart," she says. "Tell me, what convinced you to come back?"

I wrench away and fix her with a stony stare. "Loyalty," I say. "Now if you'll excuse me . . ." But before I can leave, she grabs me again, forcefully this time. Her fingertips dig into the flesh of my upper arm.

"You aren't fooling anyone," she says, her lips near my ear. "And you won't get away with it."

I sweep my gaze across the room, searching for the one person I can communicate with at a glance. The one person who might rescue me from Chara's clutches before I do something stupid, like kiss her. But Iyla is nowhere to be found. I crane my neck; I'd even settle for Gita at this point. I catch a movement from the corner of my eye and turn to see Kadru watching me. She's dressed in a black silk top with matching pants. Her midriff is bare and glistening. A white snake curls around her neck like a scarf.

Do you need me? Her voice in my head makes my heart leap from my chest to my throat. But the answer floats to the surface of my mind before I can stop it.

Yes.

"Balavan may have accepted you back into the fold," Chara hisses in my ear. "But that doesn't mean he trusts—"

"Chara," Kadru says behind us, her voice as rich as melted chocolate. "How wonderful to see you again." The woman's next words die in her throat with a strangled gasp. She lets go of my arm and takes a step back, her eyes suddenly filled with abject, naked fear. Kadru could kill her with only a touch, and Chara knows it.

"Balavan will be so interested to hear that you were schooling the *rajakumari* on his true motivations," Kadru says. "It's good he has you to speak for him."

Chara's face drains of color. "No," she says. "It wasn't like that."

"Wasn't it?" Kadru circles the woman, coming so close her breath ruffles Chara's hair. The snake flicks his tongue. "Because it seemed like you were suggesting that Balavan was lying."

Chara shakes her head. She opens and closes her mouth, fishlike, but no sound comes out. Her expression plucks at a cord of sympathy inside me, and I lay a palm on Kadru's arm. She's made her point. Chara's gaze follows my hand, and her mouth falls open at the realization that I can touch Kadru without dying.

For the first time all evening I feel powerful. Kadru takes a step back. "Marinda is more forgiving than I am," she says. "But remember that Balavan is more ruthless." She strokes the snake's head, and he closes his eyes with pleasure. "I wouldn't risk his wrath."

"No," Chara says, sidling away from us. "No, of course not."

Once she's out of hearing range, Kadru turns to me. "Gopal was her mate."

The floor drops from under me. The self-satisfied warmth that filled my chest a moment ago cools to an icy, rolling horror. It's no wonder Chara hates me. I killed the man she loved. I put a knife through his heart. She probably watched me do it.

I press a hand to my mouth—I think I might be sick.

"You can't afford mercy," Kadru says. "Chara never felt it for you." She surveys the room coldly. "None of them did."

No, I think, *they didn't.* We stand together for a full minute, the silence wrapping around us like a shawl. Finally she turns to me. "Go," she says. "Mingle. Be their *rajakumari.* You can't afford to risk Balavan's wrath any more than Chara can."

Again she's right. I step forward and let myself be swallowed by the throng.

Later I see Kadru moving through the crowd, regal, beautiful. The Naga stare at her in awe, but they give her a wide berth. And for the first time it strikes me how lonely it must be to be that deadly. To be that feared. At this thought Kadru's gaze finds mine. And she smiles.

* *

The party wears on.

Balavan finds me and threads his arm through mine. We dart from one cluster of people to the next like bees in a flower garden. He whispers so many names against my ear that I have no hope of remembering them all. The members of the Naga regard me with suspicious, cool expressions. Still, Balavan holds me out like a jewel on his hand.

"Trilok," he says to a man with a close-cropped beard and a row of straight white teeth. "Meet our *visha kanya*."

The man takes my fingers in his and kisses the backs of my knuckles. His lips feel like dry paper.

"It's an honor," he says. "Perhaps with your assistance we can make some headway with the re—" Balavan silences him with a sharp look. The man's face goes slack. He licks his lips.

"Let's not discuss business tonight," Balavan says smoothly, his cool hand resting on my back. "It's a celebration." My fingernails bite into my palms.

Trilok scratches the back of his neck. "Of course," he says. "My apologies."

If I didn't understand before, the exchange makes it crystal clear. I'm nothing more than an exotic bird in a gilded cage. The kind its master takes out at parties so that his guests can watch it spread its wings and admire its jewel-toned feathers before it's locked away again. I'm a symbol to be admired, but never trusted. And never free.

* *

Sleep refuses to find me. My worries gather until they are a tangled throng in my mind, twisting around one another, squeezing, choking, until I'm not sure which problem is the worst. The deadliest.

I need to bring down the Naga and get back to Mani and Deven before this place changes me. Before I forget what's real and what's performance. But no one trusts me here. No one will ever say anything useful in my presence. It's not an ideal situation for espionage.

Except . . . a germ of an idea wriggles into my mind. I try to dismiss it. It's reckless. It would likely never work. And worst of all, it would be another step down the dark path that leads to becoming Kadru. And yet I can't stop turning it over in my mind. Poking it. Examining it from every angle. And then I let the idea drift down into the fertile soil of necessity, where it takes root and starts to grow. I slip out of bed, tiptoe to the door and ease it open. I make sure no one follows me as I make my way down the corridor in my sleep clothes.

Remnants of the celebration are everywhere. Half-empty glasses smudged with fingerprints, bits of glitter dusted across the black marble floor, pools of wax at the bases of cold candles. But the room is empty and unguarded.

I've spent so much time committing every detail of the Naga palace to memory that I could navigate it in my sleep. I walk with hurried, silent steps all the way to the hatchery. Hundreds of dirt-filled wooden boxes line the walls, but I pick up only one. Five pale eggs are nestled inside. I clutch the box to my chest and hurry back to my room.

I close the door softly behind me, climb onto the bed and pull the box into my lap. It takes several long minutes, sitting with my eyes pressed shut, pulling air in slowly through my nose, before I find the courage to lift one of the oblong eggs and cradle it carefully in my palm. The wrongness of it scoops the breath from my throat, and I resist the urge to fling it back into the box. It's not hard like a bird's egg, but leathery and rough. And it has a little give to it, like I could curl my fingers, squeeze, and collapse it like soft clay.

I hold the egg up to the light and see the tiny snake coiled within the translucent shell. *Hello,* I think, and the snake curves toward me as if it can hear the timbre of my thoughts. As if it wants to. I pick up each of the eggs in turn, examining them from every angle. Learning to touch them without fear creeping down my spine.

I think of Kadru and how, even before she could see into my mind, she always seemed to know more than I told her. I think about the snakes wrapped around her neck and coiled at her feet.

If Balavan won't trust me with his secrets, I'll create an army of spies that can take them from him.

And they'll only report to me.

CHAPTER TWELVE

Iyla

The mosquitoes make it nearly impossible to hold still. They nibble at my cheeks, my neck, my fingers. I long to kill them with a slap of my palm, but I can't risk the noise.

Or losing my balance.

I've been perched in a tree for nearly three hours. My muscles ache, and a branch digs viciously at my lower back.

The lair of the Crocodile King wasn't hard to find. Pranesh's map was accurate, even if the knife at his throat made the lines shaky and poorly drawn. But finding the location and actually getting here were two different things.

Pranesh labeled the lair Crocodile Island, but it's actually a tiny peninsula off the coast, surrounded on three sides by sparkling blue water and connected to land by a network of craggy cliffs. Traveling by boat would have been more straightforward, but it also would have made me easy to spot. Instead I was stuck going the hard way—scaling rocks and tripping over stones. In a pair of sandals.

I'm grateful I didn't wear a sari. The hems of my pants are soaked with water and mud. I shift in the tree and long for a warm bath.

The peninsula is so densely populated with trees that the only way to get a decent vantage point is from the air. More climbing. More scratches up and down my arms. But now, from my perch in the tree, I can see a clearing with a fire pit and a stone altar. The area was empty when I first arrived, but eventually I spotted small rowboats launching from the mainland. Now dozens of people—all of them male—work together gathering kindling, collecting water, peeling vegetables. They're too far away for me to hear conversation, but that can wait for later. My only mission today is to decide on a target.

I shift in the tree, trying to find a more comfortable resting place for my back, but no amount of adjusting turns the branch into a sofa. My gaze roams over the crowd. I quickly dismiss the men who sit alone and focus on their task without interacting. If they are inhibited even among friends, the chances of my getting close are remote. I also ignore the handful of men who are giving orders with gruff voices and pointed fingers. Leaders are too invested to part with information easily. I want someone in the middle of the pack—someone with enough connections to be useful but not so devoted that a little flattery can't win him over.

And I want someone who seems restless.

A group of young men around my age stand off to one side discussing something intently. Even though I know

I'll never be able to hear them, I lean forward. They stand in a circle. The boy who is speaking gestures wildly with his hands, and the others listen, their arms folded across their chests. The speaker looks like the perfect target. He's obviously charismatic—he has the undivided attention of the group—and he looks angry too. It's the perfect combination.

But then one of the other boys in the circle throws back his head and laughs so loudly that the wind carries the sound all the way to my perch in the treetop. It's a noise so unrestrained, so full of joy, that I can't help but shift my attention to him.

No. He's all wrong.

He's tall and lanky, with hair cropped so short that it covers his scalp like a fur cap. His face is too open, too friendly. He's completely devoid of the kind of rage Deven first saw in me—the fidgety dissatisfaction with life. The impatient desire for escape. All the qualities that will make a person turn on the people he works for. This boy has none of that. And yet . . .

The other young men in the circle have unfolded their arms, unclenched their fists. They lean toward him as he speaks. He's not powerless. His power just isn't marinated in anger.

I wish it were.

I try to turn my attention back to the first boy, but I can't remember which one he was. Their faces are all softer now. Their jaws unclenched.

I watch them until the sun dips below the horizon. And then I climb down from the tree and make my way across the cliffs so that I will be there to meet the boats when they come ashore.

* *

His name is Fazel.

It takes me six days before I hear it for the first time. I follow him all over Sundari—to the flat at the far edge of Bala City where he lives alone, to the small farm where he works tending chickens, to the town square where he plays game after game of chess for coin. But it's the old woman at the marketplace selling spiced nuts who finally reveals his name.

"Fazel," she says when he steps up to her stall. "I saved a bag of the sweet cinnamon almonds just for you." She pulls a small burlap sack from a basket on the ground and shakes it gently.

"Aw, Lina, you spoil me," he says. He kisses both of her cheeks before he takes the bag and drops several coins into her palm. She deposits the money into a green glass jar and then puts both of her hands on Fazel's cheeks.

"You're a good boy," she says. "Shall I set aside a bag from the next batch?"

"Of course," he says. "But let's live dangerously and go spicy next time."

She grins. "I can make a batch of almonds laced with capsicum that will strip the bumps from your tongue."

He laughs with the same uninhibited delight that I've heard from him a dozen times now. I roll my eyes. It's as if he's incapable of seeing the evil in the world. "I'll look forward to it," he says. "Thanks, Lina."

He starts walking, and I scoot from beneath the umbrella where I've been hiding to follow him. I take a deep breath. It's time to arrange a meeting.

Fazel hums softly as he wanders through the marketplace. The sound grates on my nerves, and I find myself wishing I'd picked a different target. He's too content to make a good double agent.

I could have followed any one of the boys from Crocodile Island. They were all there for the picking when the boats came ashore—boys who looked angrier, boys who looked on the verge of drifting away, boys who looked at their leaders with a hint of disdain. And yet I followed Fazel. His whole countenance annoys me, but I still find myself drawn to him. Maybe it's a gut instinct. Maybe my intuition knows something I don't.

Fazel pours a handful of almonds into his palm and lifts his face to the sky as he tips them into his mouth. I use the moment of distraction to step directly in his path. He crashes into me with a surprising amount of force for someone strolling along with a tune in his head. I cry out as my ankle turns and I fall harder than I intended.

Sugared almonds rain down on my head.

Fazel's quick intake of breath is as sharp as the pain in my foot. I curl on my side and cup my ankle in my palm.

"I'm so sorry," Fazel says, kneeling beside me. "You came out of nowhere." In any other circumstance I might laugh at the irony, but I'm in too much pain to find it funny. I silently curse myself. I only meant to *fake* an injury.

"Let me see," he says, gently taking my leg in his hands. He slips off my sandal, and his fingers explore the bones that make up my ankle with tender precision. He turns my foot in a circle and I bite back a yelp.

"I don't think it's broken," he says. "But it's going to swell. We need to get some ice on it."

I'm too stunned to speak, and Fazel's dark brows pull together in concern. "Did you hit your head?"

"I don't think so," I say, but my mind feels foggy. Did I?

He puts a finger under my chin and lifts my face so that he can look into my eyes. My cheeks flame as he studies me. He's so close that I can see the gold flecks in his eyes.

"Are you dizzy?" he asks.

My gaze wanders to his lips—they're full and slightly parted. "No," I say.

He offers his hand and helps me to my feet. "Can you walk?"

Gingerly I set my injured foot on the ground and try to put weight on it, but a sharp pain shoots through my ankle. I wince and grab Fazel's forearm.

"It's okay," he says, wrapping an arm around my waist. "I can carry you." With that, he scoops me into his arms.

"Put me down," I say. My voice is tight.

"It's really no trouble," Fazel says. "I don't live far. We just need some ice and then—"

"Put. Me. Down."

He stops walking and lowers me to my feet. I gasp as soon as my injured foot touches the ground.

Fazel cocks his head to one side. His mouth quirks in amusement.

"I'm not helpless," I snap.

"I'm sure that's generally true," he says. "But at the moment it seems like a blatant lie."

He's right, of course. I can't hop all the way back to the Naga palace on one foot. I bite my lip and try to nudge my pride aside, but it won't move.

Fazel smiles as if he can see my struggle. "It was rude of me to sweep you off your feet before I'd even introduced myself," he says, sticking out his hand. "I'm Fazel." His name sounds different as it falls from his own lips, and I let the sound of it settle in my mind. Fazel. He leans close to me and whispers in my ear. "This is the part where you tell me your name."

The rebuke was teasing, but my cheeks still flame with humiliation. "Iyla," I say. "My name is Iyla." My voice comes out sharper than I intended, but Fazel's smile doesn't falter. His hand swallows mine. His skin is cool against my palm.

"It's a pleasure to meet you, Iyla. Now, may I help you?" He dips his head toward the ground where I'm balanced on one leg. "You must be getting tired of standing like that."

I give him a small nod as permission, and he gathers me into his arms like I'm weightless.

My heartbeat takes off at full speed. It wasn't supposed to happen like this. I was supposed to control our first touch, the first time our eyes met. It was supposed to be Fazel's pulse that raced under my fingers, not the other way around. I've completely lost control of the situation.

"I'm really sorry," Fazel says as he walks. "I'm not usually clumsy." The muscles in his arm strain beneath my cheek, tight with the effort of lifting me.

"It's nothing," I say. "I'll be fine."

Fazel laughs and the sound vibrates through my chest, cracks my heart open. I close my eyes and try to pretend I'm somewhere else, anywhere else. I remind myself why I followed Fazel in the first place. I need him to fall for me—at least enough to loosen his lips and dislodge his secrets. And I can't do that if I let myself be charmed by his easy laugh. By the way his skin feels like velvet against mine.

I need Balavan to agree to give me my life back. I don't want to die before I've really lived.

I slip on the role of seductress like a silky robe. I let my head fall against Fazel's chest, smile as I feel his breath catch. "Thank you for rescuing me," I say. I slide my fingers along the skin exposed by his open shirt. "I'm not sure what I would have done without you."

He stops in front of a small brown building and sets me down. "If not for me, you wouldn't be injured at all," he says, pulling a key from his pocket and sliding it into the lock. "So I'm guessing what you would have done without me is to go about your day uninterrupted."

I lay a palm on his arm. "Some men would have just left me there," I say. "I'm so glad you didn't."

His gaze travels from my hand to my face. He blinks. "Does that usually work?"

I swallow hard. "I don't know what you mean."

Fazel opens the door and guides me to a chair in the

corner. "Sit here," he says, "and I'll find you a stool to rest your foot on."

He disappears around the corner, and I have a chance to study the flat. It's nicer than I would have expected for a man who lives alone. The fabrics are dark and masculine, but the furniture is artfully placed—clustered into several different conversation areas, as if he often has guests. Sunlight floods in through a large window and makes the space open and cheerful.

Fazel returns with a small cushioned stool and a bag of ice. He props up my leg and presses the ice to my throbbing ankle. Reflexively, I pull away from the sudden chill, but he holds my foot in place.

"What I mean," Fazel says, picking up the thread of the previous conversation, "is that you suddenly poured on the charm. It's fairly transparent, and I'm wondering if it usually works or if I can pat myself on the back for being particularly intelligent." He flashes me a grin, and my mouth goes dry.

"I'm not . . . It wasn't like that."

"Wasn't it?"

I glare at him. "No," I say. "It wasn't."

"So you went from the prickliest person I've ever met to a silver-tongued vixen in the space of a breath?"

My carefully laid plans slip and unwind like a dropped spool of ribbon. I've never failed to win a boy over before. It's always been effortless.

"What do you want, Iyla?"

My mind is suddenly crowded with all the things I

want. They nudge up against each other with sharp elbows. *I want to own all the years I was born with. I don't want to have to betray Marinda. I want a life that doesn't require me to be two different people.*

"I don't want anything," I tell him.

His expression closes like a slammed door. He stands abruptly and pulls at the back of his neck. "I'll make some tea to help with the pain."

Fazel storms into the kitchen, leaving me alone with my mistakes. They sit in my stomach like sour milk. I have no choice but to go back to Crocodile Island and pick a new target. I pull my fingers through my hair. So much time wasted. Balavan will be expecting a report soon, and I'll have nothing to give him.

My thoughts drift to Marinda. I wonder if she's surviving Balavan's games. I wonder if she's missing Mani and Deven.

I wonder if she's missing me.

CHAPTER THIRTEEN

Marinda

The snake eggs become my new obsession. Several times a day I pull the box from where I hid it at the back of the mahogany wardrobe in my room, concealed by dozens of hanging saris so Amoli won't find it. I hold the eggs one by one. I cradle them in the hollow of my palm so that before they are even born, they will know the color of my thoughts.

It's the only thing at the palace that keeps me grounded.

Balavan can't seem to get enough of me. He requests my presence beside him at every meal, summons me to his rooms to coax promises of loyalty from my lips, walks through the rain forest with me on his arm. And all the while I cling to thoughts of the snake eggs. To the freedom hidden inside them like a gift.

But today when I pull the box onto my lap, one of the eggs has a large tear in the leathery surface.

My stomach turns at the sight—bubbling fluid oozes from the opening, and the tiny pink nub of a snake head presses through the sludge. I didn't expect the hatching to be so gruesome. But then I find the thread of the snake's thoughts. The single-minded focus on escape, the relentless determination despite the monumental task ahead. It's how I feel every day.

I'm transfixed. Hours pass, and slowly the other eggs split apart as well. Now five snakes reach for my mind as they fight their way to the surface.

It's a female snake who wriggles from her egg first. She has a moment of jubilation before she turns her attention to me.

I reach toward her, but my hand freezes in midair. I can't do it. I can't willingly pick up a snake. I squeeze my eyes closed and force myself to breathe. Memories crowd in my mind—sharp fangs sinking into my flesh, the sting of venom coursing through my veins, fear so intense that it was like heat, leaving my soul feeling blistered and raw.

I can't do it.

The snake's mind pokes at mine like a child grasping for a toy, and I open my eyes. This is not one of Kadru's giant snakes. She doesn't want to hurt me. And I won't let her.

I hold my breath and pick her up.

The snake's mind flushes with pleasure, and she wraps herself around my wrist as if she needs the comfort of my touch along her entire body. Oddly, the gesture makes me think of Deven—of the way his whole arm presses against mine when he holds my hand, like having our fingers twined together isn't enough. An ache blooms in my chest.

But the more I think of Deven, the more I notice the worry that crouches at the back of my mind. What would he make of the snake wrapped around my wrist? "Don't let them change you," he said. But I'm not changing *for* the Naga. I'm doing this to destroy them. I'm doing this so that Deven and I can be together. So that Mani can be safe. So that Iyla can have revenge for her lost lives.

The snake rests her head against my palm, and Kadru's voice echoes in my mind. "I used to be you," she told me once. "And when the Nagaraja grows tired of you or when you become too deadly to be useful, you will become me." What if I'm making a mistake? But then I push the thought away. This is not the same as Kadru. It's not as if I'm collecting snakes like pets. It's not as if I love them.

The snake flicks out her tongue and tastes the skin on my hand. And I don't pull away.

* *

It takes some practice to train the snakes to understand me.

I sit on the bed, my legs crossed, my mind emptied of anything but communicating with my new subjects.

Come to me.

All five snakes slither from their hiding place under the wardrobe and start across the room. But then a breeze rustles through the window. The snakes falter. The light outside shifts, and a shadow falls across the glossy hardwood. It makes the snakes think of food, and they race to the patch of darkness. Their minds are young and easily distracted.

No. I refocus their attention. *Come to me.*

They slither to the foot of the bed, and I drop a handful of lizards on the floor in front of them and turn away while they feast. Soon they'll be able to hunt for their own food, but for today I gather their prey from the forest outside—tree frogs, small reptiles, various bugs—to give as training rewards. Mani and I used the same method to teach our cat new tricks. We would feed Smudge bits of chicken when she'd do something we wanted—return a toy we'd thrown, roll over for a belly scratch. But that didn't make my skin crawl like this does. I tamp down my revulsion and close off my mind so I don't have to feel the snakes' pleasure in swallowing the lizards whole.

Once they finish their meal, we keep working. We practice until the sun goes down and the room is swathed in darkness. Until I'm sure that my thoughts are more forceful in the snakes' minds than their own.

But the real test comes the next morning when Amoli breezes into the room with a tray laden with *dosas* and fruit.

"Good morning," she says, sliding the tray onto the table beside my bed. "Balavan is busy today, and so he asked that you have breakfast in your room."

The snakes flick their tongues. Taste the air. Smell Amoli with the tissue on the roofs of their mouths. They start to peek from beneath the wardrobe.

Stay, I tell them. *Search her mind.*

"Is Balavan away from the palace?" I ask.

Amoli's eyes tighten at the question, and it takes her a beat to answer. "Yes," she says, unfurling a cloth napkin and draping it across my lap. "He is."

But the snakes' minds fill with an image of dozens of Naga gathered in one of the rooms of the palace. They sit facing each other on brightly colored cushions, and candle-light flickers over their features. Their eyes are trained on Balavan, who is positioned at the top of the circle.

Amoli is lying to me.

"When will he return?" I ask.

Her glance skips away from me. She busies herself straightening the food on my tray. "I'm afraid I don't know," she says. "He's asked that you stay in your rooms until he calls for you. But I'm happy to get you anything you need to be comfortable."

The snakes sense her anxiety, like a mouse in the grass. But she's not concerned about me. She's worried about missing whatever Balavan is telling his followers. She wants to leave so she can join him.

"No," I say. "I'll be fine here."

Amoli gives me a weak smile. "I'll check on you later," she says.

Once Amoli leaves, I call one of the three female snakes to me. The oldest. I've started calling her Jasu. She was the first to hatch, and she seems the least prone to distraction. It's a huge risk to let the snake out of my presence while she's still so young, while I'm unsure how far our connection reaches or if I can be certain she'll return. But if I'm going to get any useful information to pass to the Raja, it's a risk I have to take.

I lift the snake onto my lap and stroke her small head with my index finger. *Follow Amoli,* I tell her. *But you can't be seen.* Jasu's mind touches mine, and I know she understands. I set her on the floor and watch as she slithers beneath the door and out of sight.

* *

Jasu's progress is slow, and for a long time all I see in her mind is the memory of Amoli's smell. It's the only way the snake knows how to find her. As Jasu searches, I keep testing our bond—tugging on the threads that bind our minds together, fearful of feeling them snap.

The connection holds. But as the minutes pass, a knot forms in my stomach. It's been too long. Jasu's thoughts are gathered into a single sharp point—*Find Amoli.* She can't focus beyond that, can't think about where she is or where she's going. She won't know if she's lost.

I reach for Jasu's mind to call her back to me, when the snake's vision suddenly expands. Amoli's scent bursts into my mind, along with her scattered, frenetic thoughts. The itch on the back of her neck. The ache in her knee as she sits, legs crossed, on an oversized cushion. The rumbling in her stomach because she had to skip her breakfast to bring me mine. Balavan's voice drones in the background, but I can't reach his words. Jasu is too firmly attached to Amoli, too focused on the deeper areas of her mind, where her stray thoughts live.

I try to nudge the snake to tune out the distractions. *What is she hearing? Focus.*

Jasu's mind is pierced with the sting of reprimand. I startle at her strong reaction, remind myself that she's still a baby. And she wants so hard to please me. A wave of tenderness washes over me, and I try to fill my thoughts with calm reassurance. *You're doing well, Jasu. Keep going.*

Jasu tries to obey. A fly buzzes near Amoli's face, and the woman waves it away with a flick of her hand. Jasu's mind latches on to the distraction and follows the fly.

I take a deep breath and nudge her back to Amoli. *I need to hear what she hears.*

Finally Balavan's voice enters my mind. *Yes. Good.*

". . . didn't get any useful information from his death," he says. "We can't make that mistake again."

"I would have been happy to question the prisoner," one of the women says. "If you'd let him live."

"We'd tried questioning him," Balavan says. "Many times. He gave us nothing. But when I brought the *visha kanya* to the dungeon, he suddenly found his voice. He tried to tell her we were hunting relics. *After* she'd already kissed him. I had to silence him before he could say more."

"But that's not Marinda's fault." Gita's familiar voice scrapes inside my mind. "Do you still not trust her?"

Balavan sighs. "The question is why a member of the Pakshi thought he could trust her. Especially when she was there to kill him."

"But she *did* kill him," Gita says. "Surely that proves her loyalty?" Her desire to protect me brushes up against something raw inside my soul, like soft cloth dragged across a fresh burn.

"You're too close to the girl," Balavan says. "You can't be objective."

"If you'd just let me talk to her, I'm sure—"

"Enough." Balavan doesn't raise his voice, but his words slice through the room as if he shouted. "I've told you to stay away from her. Amoli is in a better position to determine her loyalty."

I can't see Gita's face in Jasu's mind—Amoli isn't looking at her—but her expression must be contrite, because Balavan's tone softens. "Perhaps the man was playing games with me. Maybe he mistook the *rajakumari* for someone else. It doesn't matter." I can picture Balavan waving a hand in front of his face. "We don't need her to find the other relics. Iyla is in place to bring down the Crocodile King. I need the rest of you to focus on finding Garuda. And more importantly, finding the feather."

My sharp intake of breath nearly makes Jasu lose her focus. Her mind turns to mine, questioning, but I gently redirect her attention. *Keep listening.*

"Kamlesh," Balavan says, "how many of Bagharani's followers are dead?"

"All of them," the man answers. "After we destroyed the Tiger Queen, they lost their appetite for fighting. Some joined our cause. The rest we slaughtered."

Balavan's dark laugh fills Amoli's mind, darkens Jasu's, overtakes mine. "One down," he says. "And two to go."

* *

I lie on my bed with my knees tucked to my chest. Jasu is back with the other snakes beneath the wardrobe, but her mind still reaches for mine. She mirrors the horror I feel, amplifying it until it grows so large it closes off my throat.

The Naga are hunting relics. And somehow the relics—whatever they are—provide the key to taking down the other members of the Raksaka. Bagharani—the Tiger Queen—is dead. There's so much to take in, so much I still don't understand. But one thought especially haunts me, a thought I know will stalk my nightmares.

I helped them do this.

I helped the Nagaraja grow so powerful that his followers are on their way to building a world where only one of the guardians of Sundari exists. And I have no idea how to stop them.

I feel like a naive child who has spent her whole life peering through a keyhole, thinking the sliver I could see was all that existed. Foolishly believing I had the power to change that slice of reality, to shape it into something just and lovely. Now the door has swung wide. And I realize I didn't know anything at all.

I think of the many depictions of the Raksaka I've seen—the ones created from gems, where the great tiger is fashioned of amber, her head in profile, her eyes alert as she stalks through a thicket made of jade. I used to believe they were legends, the four guardians of Sundari—nothing more than symbols of a kingdom in perfect balance. That was before the Nagaraja tried to kill Mani. Before he entered my mind and I tasted the evil that lurked there.

I don't know much about Bagharani, but she must have been better than the Nagaraja. And now she's dead. The people who followed her, slaughtered. I think of Deven and his friends who follow Garuda. Of what could happen to them when the Nagaraja finds the relic he's looking for. I think of Iyla, somewhere in Sundari, plotting to take down the Crocodile King. Does she know what Balavan is planning? Does she know he plans to remake the world?

Fear scrapes at my throat. There's so much more at stake than just my own life, so much more than Mani's. Thousands of lives press against my conscience; their weight squeezes the air from my lungs. For once I feel like the poison pulsing through my blood isn't nearly as deadly as it needs to be.

At this moment I would gladly take up the burden of Kadru's loneliness if it meant I could kill the enemy with a brush of my fingertips.

A movement on the floor catches my eye, and I lean over the side of the bed to see five small white snakes, their minds reaching to comfort mine. I scoop them into my palm and place them on the pillow next to me. They slither closer and wrap themselves around my wrists and ankles. They cover the scars that their ancestors made. They infuse my thoughts with their compassion. And finally I find enough peace to fall asleep.

CHAPTER FOURTEEN

Iyla

Fazel put something in the tea.

The room has gone fuzzy around the edges. The furniture blurs into the walls. Fazel sits across from me, nothing more than a smudge.

I stare reproachfully into the bottom of my cup, where only dregs remain.

"What did you give me?"

"Does your leg feel better?"

I reach down, but it takes me three tries before I'm able to find my ankle. The throbbing is gone, but it still feels tender to the touch. I sit upright and my head swims. It takes me a moment to realize that Fazel didn't answer the question.

"What's in this?" My words melt together. My tongue feels thick.

"My grandmother was a healer," he says, as if this

explains everything. "She made me this tea when I broke my arm." He laughs. "All three times."

"But why . . ." I forget what I was going to ask. Something about . . . something.

"Do you want to lie down?" Fazel asks.

"I have to go," I say. "Balavan will want . . ." I stop. I don't think I was supposed to mention Balavan's name.

"He'll want what?" Fazel asks.

I shake my head. "I can't stay here." I stand up, and the room starts spinning. Fazel hops to his feet and grabs my elbow.

"At this point you don't have much of a choice." Pain pulses in my ankle and I slump against him. He smells like citrus.

"Did you give me a truth serum?" I ask. I think about moving away from him, but I don't.

He laughs softly, his breath rippling through my hair. "No," he says. "But I'm starting to think I overdid it on the valerian root. I don't think Naniji's tea ever made me quite so silly."

I lift my chin and find his gaze. "I'm not silly," I say. "I'm just tired."

"Which is why you should lie down."

It's a good idea. I lay my head on his chest. Some part of me thinks this isn't what he meant, but I'm so sleepy and my limbs feel so heavy. For the third time today Fazel scoops me into his arms, and then he lays me down on the sofa. I reach up and drag my palm over his scalp. His short hair is just as soft as I imagined.

"I've been wanting to do that all day," I tell him.

He smiles. His face is only inches from mine. "Well then, I'm glad you got your chance." He covers me with a thin blanket. I pull it up to my chin and let my eyes slide closed.

"I'll check on you later," he says. His voice already sounds far away, like I'm slipping underwater while he waits onshore. I intend to answer him, but I never do.

* *

Pale sunlight falls across my face and I turn toward it, eyes still closed, and let it warm my cheeks. I stretch my arms above my head, arch my back, flex my toes. A sharp pain shoots through my ankle, and I freeze as a memory of the injury rustles at the back of my mind.

I crack an eye open. "Morning," Fazel says. He reclines in the chair across from me, his foot resting on the opposite knee, his hands behind his head. He's smirking.

Heat creeps up the back of my neck. I scoot into a sitting position and wrap the thin blanket more tightly around myself. I'm trying to piece the previous day together, but there are gaping holes in my memory. *Did I touch his hair?*

"Stop looking at me like that," I snap.

He laughs. "Oh, so it's the prickly one."

I give him a hard stare. "What's that supposed to mean?"

He leans forward and rests his elbows on his knees. "I just wasn't sure which version of you I was going to get this morning. The irritable one, the seductress or . . ."

"Or what?"

"Or the girl from yesterday. The one who accused me of feeding her truth serum."

A wave of nausea rolls over me. "I said that?"

His face is solemn, but his mouth twitches like he's repressing a smile. "You did. Right before you ran your fingers through my hair."

My mouth goes dry. I hoped that part, at least, was a dream. "Your hair is too short to run my fingers through."

"Yes," he says. "So you discovered."

I groan and let my face fall into my hands. There's no way to salvage my dignity. I should have chosen my target more carefully—I knew there was a reason to pick the angry guy instead of the one with a sense of humor. I stand up, toss the blanket aside and try to smooth the wrinkles from my sari with my palms, but it's no use.

"Have you seen my sandals?" I ask without meeting Fazel's gaze. "I need to go."

"Anxious to get back to Balavan?"

A sharp knife of horror pierces my heart. Mentioning Balavan by name is a serious violation of tradecraft. If I said anything else, if I compromised the Naga in any way . . . I swallow hard. I can already feel the metal blade of Balavan's anger pressing at the hollow of my throat.

"What did I say about him?" I put as much air into my voice as possible. Casual. Easy.

"Only that you seemed to think you needed to hurry back because he'd want something." Fazel gives me a mischievous grin. "I can't imagine what your boyfriend might be waiting for."

"He's not my boyfriend." I say the words before I can stop myself and then immediately wish I could take them back. Balavan would be better explained that way. It would be effortless, believable. But attaching myself to him, even in the midst of a lie, makes my skin crawl.

"Then who is he?" Fazel asks. "And what does he want?" His voice has lost its playfulness, and I know I need to choose my next words carefully. I disguise my trembling hands by picking up the blanket I tossed aside. I keep my face turned away as I fold it into a neat square.

"Balavan wants food," I say, setting the blanket down on the end of the sofa before I finally meet Fazel's gaze. "And he's my dog."

His eyes widen, and then he bursts out laughing. The sound is like drinking hot tea on a cold day. I can't resist smiling, and the expression feels foreign. I can't remember the last time I smiled without forethought or calculation. Fazel's eyes soften.

"How is your ankle feeling?" he asks.

"Better," I say. "Thank you."

"I'm sorry I bumped into you."

"I'm sorry I touched your hair."

"I'm not."

This time it's my eyes that widen.

The tips of Fazel's ears turn pink and he shrugs. "It will give me something to hold over your head if I ever need to blackmail you."

He's teasing, but the joke hits too close to home. I look away, but not quickly enough to miss how his smile falters and then disappears. I spot my sandals tucked neatly under a side table, and I try to imagine Fazel slipping them off my feet last night and setting them there, the heels and toes precisely lined up, like they were placed with care. I snatch them and slide them onto my feet.

"Thank you again," I say. "I need to be on my way."

"Wait," Fazel says. "Let me grab my shoes and I'll walk you."

I wave him off. "No," I say. "I can manage alone."

"Are you sure?"

"I'm sure," I say, but my heart clenches at the lie. I try to smile, but my mouth won't cooperate. "Balavan doesn't like strangers."

Fazel stares at me for a beat longer than is comfortable. "Okay, then," he says. "Have a safe trip home."

My throat feels thick. Because I've never had either one of those things. Never safety. And certainly never a home.

＊　＊

It gives me some comfort to think of Balavan as an animal—as the dog I told Fazel he was. Every time Balavan questions me about the Crocodile King, I picture him sniffing at my pockets for bits of meat. I imagine his wet nose pressing against my palm. I envision him licking himself in the corner after I leave.

It makes me less terrified.

I don't tell Balavan that I need to select a new target. I don't confess that I mentioned his name to one of the followers of the Crocodile King. I report that everything is going according to plan.

"It will take some time before he trusts me," I say one

afternoon a few days after my meeting with Fazel. Balavan and I are sitting outside on a large stone terrace at the back of the palace. A pair of peacocks strut in front of us, and every so often Balavan throws the birds a bit of bread. "If I question him too soon, he'll withdraw and I'll have to start all over again."

"Don't wait too long," he says. "I need to know where the relic is. If you can't find it, I'll need to send someone who can." I wonder if he has someone else who can. If he has dozens of girls like me dotted all over Sundari, being managed by handlers like Gopal and Gita. Or am I the only one? It might shift the power balance if I knew he had only me. But it's not something I can count on.

"What does the relic do?" I've been waiting to ask the question since he first told me to infiltrate Crocodile Island, but with Balavan, questions always need to be timed carefully. This one wasn't.

He freezes. A muscle jumps in his jaw. "Does it matter?"

I shrug. "I always find things faster when I know what I'm looking for."

The statement dangles between us for a moment. Finally Balavan looks away and tosses another handful of bread to the peacocks. They viciously stab at it with their beaks, as if they think they need to kill it before they can eat.

"You're looking for a tooth," he says.

At first I don't think I heard him correctly. I envisioned the relic as something splendid. Something gilded and lined in velvet. "A tooth?"

"Yes." He smiles as if my shock pleases him. "A giant crocodile tooth. I imagine you'll know it when you see it."

"But what does it do?"

He regards me coolly, like I'm an insect he's considering flattening. Just when I think he won't answer, he does.

"It's infused with the blood of the ancients," he says. "It makes it so the Crocodile King can live forever."

"And you want me to find it so . . ."

He throws another piece of bread onto the stone terrace and then watches with relish as the birds attack it. "So I can destroy the Crocodile King?" He turns toward me and gives me a smile that freezes the blood in my veins. "Yes, *priya*. That's exactly what I want."

CHAPTER FIFTEEN

Marinda

The snakes finally give me something I haven't had in all the weeks I've been at the Naga palace—freedom. Or at least the promise of freedom.

I train Jasu and the others to search the minds of anyone who passes my door. To let me know when Amoli is coming, when Balavan is nearby, when meetings are scheduled that will provide information I can bring to the Raja. Finally I feel like I'm getting somewhere.

Now I just need to find a time to slip away from the palace. I hold the possibility of escape—even a short-lived one—close to me. It's like a flower in a garden I stroll through daily. I touch the delicate petals, I lean forward and inhale the heady fragrance. But I don't pluck it. Not yet.

My opportunity comes one evening after I've eaten in the dining room with Balavan. All through the meal he seemed distracted. His fingers thrummed the table. He stared into space for long stretches. At one point he slipped and called me Marinda. Not "*rajakumari.*" Not "the *visha kanya.*" Not "my love" or "my pet." It's as if he forgot to put me in my place. Forgot to remind me that he owns me.

When I get back to my rooms, I send the snakes to investigate. They return with their minds full of chaos. Images assault me from five directions—a long journey, copper-colored cloaks made to look like snake scales, an underground cavern lit with flickering candlelight. Bags packed. The air vibrating with anticipation. I run to the window and find the moon—a bright coin against a velvet sky. Just a few days from being a perfect circle.

The Naga are going to the Snake Temple. A shiver runs through me, and Gita's words echo in my mind. *The Nagaraja must be fed.*

Another sacrifice. Another man, woman or child who will be devoured by the Snake King. I could try to stop it from happening, but I have no chance of overcoming the dozens of Naga who will be there. And trying to prevent the sacrifice would most certainly end any hope I have of staying in a position to collect information that might actually be useful in figuring out how to destroy the Nagaraja.

The choice is a weight on my heart.

But the Raja's men know that the Nagaraja eats at the full moon. Maybe they'll find a way to stop him this time. To stop all of them.

For the first time I wonder if I weakened the Snake King when I rescued Mani. When I deprived him of his monthly meal. The thought gives me a sharp stab of satisfaction.

I call Jasu. Her mind perks up and bends toward me. *Tell me when they've gone.* Her thoughts swivel to the bustle in the rest of the palace, to the frenzied thoughts of those who are packing and preparing. And then suddenly my own face enters my mind. Someone in the palace is thinking about me, but it's not Balavan or Amoli. The thoughts are laced with too much tenderness, too much guilt.

Iyla.

A lump forms in my throat. I didn't know she was back. I haven't seen her since the day we questioned Pranesh. Since the day Kadru told me Iyla would report my activities to Balavan. And she did. I nudge Jasu's attention toward Iyla, and the thoughts of the rest of the Naga fade away. Iyla paces back and forth in her room.

Her mind is a chaotic jumble of images that don't seem to have any connection to one another—a tree, a sprained ankle, an out-of-focus room, a palm touching close-cropped hair, a peacock, a giant tooth. *Stay with her,* I tell Jasu. But no matter how I try, none of it makes sense. Iyla's thoughts are colored with a choking sensation of panic. And my face seems to dance around the edges of her fear.

Is it that she's worried I'll find out she betrayed me? Or is she actually worried for my safety? It's impossible to tell.

A sharp warning pierces my mind. An image of Amoli from one of the other snakes. *Go,* I tell them. *Hide.*

The snakes barely have time to slither under the wardrobe before the door swings open.

Amoli comes into the room with several freshly washed saris thrown over one arm and a stack of clean towels in the opposite hand. One of the male snakes reaches for her mind without my even having to ask. All of my training is paying off. Amoli's thoughts are tinged with disappointment. Resentment. My stomach pitches forward as I realize what it means.

She's not going to the Snake Temple with the rest of the Naga. Balavan is making her stay here and serve as my warden. Which will make it considerably harder to slip away from the palace.

"Is everything okay?" I ask.

Amoli's gaze sharpens. "Of course," she says. "Why do you ask?"

"You look . . . I don't know . . ." I glance up at the ceiling and pretend to search for the right word. "Disappointed."

A spark of panic flares in her mind. Then shame. Then resolve. Her face goes forcibly relaxed. "Not at all," she says. "I'm just tired."

"You don't have to wait on me," I tell her. "I'll happily take care of my own clothes." I try to take the saris from her, but she steps away and heads toward the wardrobe.

"Don't be silly," she says. "Balavan wouldn't have it any other way."

Stay, I tell the snakes. All five of them are focused on her now, and the last thing I need is one of them emerging to curl around her ankles. "Because he wants you to keep an eye on me?" I ask.

"Because you're the *rajakumari*." She steps away from the wardrobe, and the pressure on my chest lifts.

"I'm not sure I believe that," I say. I'm trying to stall to give the snakes enough time to rifle through her mind.

With all five of them searching, I'm hoping to find something I can use to help me win my freedom tonight.

Amoli gives me a patient smile. "I'm not sure it matters what you believe."

She didn't mean to say it. The regret that leaches from her mind to the snakes' minds to mine is instantaneous and sharp. But her anger over being left behind has gotten the better of her. She spoke without thinking, and now her gaze roams over my face to assess the damage. I don't intend to make it easier on her.

"See, that's what I suspected, but Balavan keeps telling me differently."

"I only meant that you are important whether you believe it or not," she says. Her face doesn't betray her thoughts. Her expression stays as smooth as glass.

I make a noncommittal noise at the back of my throat, and the anxiety in her mind blooms.

"Is there something I can bring you? Something that would make you more comfortable?"

I almost feel sorry for her. She's forced to walk the tightrope of Balavan's approval—he has declared me untrustworthy, tasked her with making sure I don't step out of line. At the same time, he's affirmed my status as the beloved *rajakumari*. And Amoli is supposed to hold those two things in tension, skepticism and reverence. But I don't feel bad enough not to take advantage of it.

"You know what I'd really like?" I ask.

"What is that?"

"I'd like to go to bed early and sleep uninterrupted as late as I want. I'm so tired."

The relief that floods her mind almost makes me laugh. She worried I would ask for something she couldn't give me. "Of course, *rajakumari,*" she says. "Rest as long as you like. I won't disturb you until morning."

"Late morning," I say. "If it's not too much trouble."

Her smile is genuine. "No trouble at all," she says.

As she leaves, each of the five snakes searches her mind. But the only thing they find is a warm glow of anticipation. With every other member of the Naga away from the palace and me sleeping late, Amoli has the rare gift of time all to herself. And she plans to spend it alone in her room.

* *

I leave a few hours later with a scarf in my hair and Jasu tucked into the bag slung over my shoulder. I should be back before sunrise, but I hope that my conversation with Amoli will give me the luxury of more time if it comes to that.

The guards don't question me as I leave, and their silence unsettles me. I have the excuses on the tip of my tongue, steel coated and ready to offer up like weapons. But they barely look in my direction as I pass. Maybe they think I'm headed for the Snake Temple, like the rest of the Naga. Maybe they haven't been informed that I'm a prisoner. Or maybe they know all of that and they're just biding their time. Jasu searches their minds and finds that, just as I feared, their uninterested, faraway gazes are only a ruse. Their thoughts record every aspect of the moment—the color of my clothing, the scarf in my hair, the bag on my shoulder, the precise time I pass by.

Every detail will be reported to Balavan. I'm allowed to leave, but I don't leave unnoticed.

My stomach twists into a hard knot. But it's too late to turn back now. The damage is done. And the sooner the Raja has the information he needs to destroy the Snake King, the sooner I can be with Mani and Deven again. The thought quickens my steps.

Moonlight bathes the forest in soft light, and the sound of crickets trills in the air like a lullaby. My fingers instinctively go to my pocket, to find the wooden carving Deven made for me, but then I remember it's not there. It was one of many things I left behind when I returned to the Naga. When I lost Mani, the cricket became a kind of talisman—a reminder that no matter what happened, I had loved and been loved. I could use that reminder now. But until I escape the Naga's clutches for good, the chirping of real crickets and the darkness that wraps around me like a blanket will have to be enough.

Once I emerge from the rain forest, I pull the scarf from my hair and study the constellations printed on the silky fabric. The brightest stars indicate dead drop locations— places where I can leave information for the Raja's men to find. The closest one is just a short distance from here.

I walk along a dirt path dotted with small houses nestled on sprawling land populated by chickens and goats. Most of the windows are dark. But a few glow with flickering candle-light, and I wonder what keeps their occupants awake. A sick child? A lovers' quarrel? A late-night meal of bread and cheese?

My heart bends toward the idea of home, and I wonder

what it would be like to have a place of safety. A place where I could take a breath without worrying about who was watching and whether my pattern of breathing had given anything away.

A noise behind me pulls me up short. I freeze. A snapping twig? A gust of wind whistling through the trees? My mind reaches for Jasu, but she's fast asleep, lulled by coziness at the bottom of my bag and the motion of my gait. I'm probably only being paranoid, but I can't afford a mistake. Not when so much is at stake. I reach into the bag and stroke the top of Jasu's head with my index finger. She is slow to wake, and when she does, her mind is sluggish and groggy. It takes a few tries for her to understand my command, to reach out toward the thoughts of anyone who might be following me.

Jasu sends me fragmented images of dreams, the half-awake sounds of snoring, the thoughts of goats sniffing for food. Anyone who might have been following me before is gone now. I shake off my worry and keep pressing forward.

Finally I spot the location marked on my scarf, but the only thing here is a gnarled tree in the middle of an abandoned field. I turn in a circle, looking for somewhere to leave a message. Nothing. I search the base of the tree, run my hands along the trunk, and my palm skims over a loose knot in the wood. I tug at it, and it comes away in my hand like a lid off a pot. I lean closer and see that there's a small opening dusted with tiny scraps of parchment and bits of fabric, as if many messages have been left here before.

I pull a piece of parchment from my bag and scrawl a quick message. *Meet me after dark tomorrow. At the place where the maiden sings. Bring the monkey.* I fold the note into a small square, stuff it into the opening and replace the knot. I hope the Raja's men will find it in time. I hope they will know it's for Deven.

CHAPTER SIXTEEN

Iyla

I'm headed to the kitchen for a glass of water when I see Marinda slip out the front door of the Naga palace like she has a death wish.

Her hair is pulled up and tied in a scarf. She's wearing pants and leather boots, as if she plans on hiking for an extended period of time. She can't possibly be stupid enough to walk out of here the moment that Balavan leaves for the Snake Temple. The moment he has everyone on high alert that she might try to go. And yet she does.

I'm paralyzed by incredulity for a few seconds before I grab a pair of sandals and follow her into the night. Marinda strolls past the guards and then slows down and cocks her head to one side as if she's listening for something. Her shoulders tighten. At least she has the sense to be nervous.

One of the guards gives me a smirk as I pass. I can tell he's about to make a sarcastic comment, so I press a finger to my lips. "I'm following her on Balavan's orders," I say. "If you mess this up, he'll have your head on a stake."

A flicker of anger flashes over his face, but then his expression goes stony. He shrugs one shoulder and motions for me to pass. Marinda trudges all the way through the rain forest, and I follow behind her at a safe distance, careful to stay in the shadows.

A few minutes after she emerges from the foliage, she pulls the scarf from her hair and studies it. I try to edge closer to see what's printed on the fabric, what's creasing her forehead and making her bite her lip, but the night is too dark. She shoves the scarf into her bag, takes a sharp left and keeps walking.

I thought Marinda would go to the bookshop, or to the girls' home, or maybe straight to the Raja's palace to see Mani and Deven again. I didn't expect to follow her to a humble settlement of tiny homes. She stops and gazes toward one of the houses. The light in the window changes her face—turns it wistful and sad. It's an expression filled with such aching that it tugs on something low in my belly. My throat is thick with emotion. I'm torn by the desire to go to her and the need to keep Balavan satisfied. I shift my weight, and a twig snaps in half.

Marinda freezes. Her expression of longing vanishes, and stark fear takes its place. I'm too exposed here. I turn and sprint into the darkness, careful to make my steps as light and silent as possible, but I don't find a place to hide right away. I run until my lungs burn, until I find a house with an open gate. I slip through and press myself against the side of the house, deep in the shadows.

I wait until I'm sure Marinda is too far away to hear my footsteps before I step back onto the path. I catch up with her just in time to see her slipping something into an opening in a tree trunk. She replaces the knot of wood that conceals the hole, looks both ways and then hurries back up the path in the direction of the Naga palace.

How many years would Balavan give me for clear evidence that Marinda is spying for the Raja? Could I convince him to give me all of it?

I wait several minutes, the sound of my heartbeat rushing in my ears, before I remove the knot of wood and unfold the message. *Meet me after dark tomorrow. At the place where the maiden sings. Bring the monkey.* My chest constricts as I remember Marinda taking me to the waterfall and telling me the story of the maiden and the prince. It was a peace offering during our time in the Widows' Village. Even after she realized I'd betrayed her, she so often tried to mend my heart, to offer up a gift in her open palm. And I so often smacked her hand away. If it wasn't life she was holding, I wasn't interested.

Bring the monkey. It's what Marinda calls Mani in moments of great tenderness—monkey. As if that's the most lovable creature she could possibly imagine. She never had a nickname for me.

The letters start to swim in my vision. A single teardrop falls onto the parchment and blurs the signature— just a simple letter *M*. I fold the message along the creases Marinda made so that it looks just as she left it. The note feels heavy in my palm. It's worth more coin than I could possibly carry. It's worth more years than I've lived so far.

I picture Balavan's face when I hand him the parchment. I imagine him opening it, his gaze sweeping over the words, realizing that the handwriting matches the letter he took from Marinda's room. I envision telling him about the waterfall, about Mani, about Marinda meeting with Deven. I see his face turn to stone.

This message is the most valuable thing I've ever held.

I return it to its hiding spot and follow Marinda back to the palace.

* *

I expected the guards to stop Marinda. I thought I'd have to intercede on her behalf to keep her alive. But when one of the men utters the first half of the new password, his hand already reaching for the weapon at his hip, Marinda stares into the distance for just a beat and then gives him the second half with a steady voice. It's as if she plucked it out of the air like a ripe piece of fruit.

I spend hours tossing and turning before I finally give up on sleep. I pace back and forth across the length of my room until bright light seeps around the edges of the drapery. In the short time I've been here, the rug has already grown threadbare in the center.

Balavan would never have given Marinda the password, never have trusted her not to leave in his absence. That means she has someone else helping her on the inside. The realization cinches up my heart like a silk purse.

She doesn't trust me—not that she should, not that I've given her any reason to—but the thought of her whispering her secrets to someone else, trusting another person to hold her life in their palm—it fills me with so much darkness that I can hardly breathe.

Before I can stop myself, I'm striding down the hall to her room. I slap the door with my palm. A long pause. And then a groggy "Come in."

I swing the door wide. Marinda is lying in bed, her sleep clothes rumpled, her hair a mess. As if she's been here all night.

"Iyla," she says pleasantly. "How are you?" She scoots into a sitting position. She doesn't look surprised that I'm here, even though it's been weeks since she's laid eyes on me.

"Do you realize how reckless it was to leave here last night? What will happen to you if Balavan finds out?" I didn't intend to show her my hand so early, but there's something dangerous and raw pulsing through my veins.

She frowns. "You followed me?"

"How did you get the password to tell the guards?"

Her chin juts forward. "You followed me." A statement this time, her voice filled with certainty.

"Answer the question."

"Why, Iyla? So that you can be thorough in your report to Balavan? So that you can get the maximum payment from him? My entire life for a few years of yours?"

"You don't know what you're talking about," I say. "That's not how it is." But I feel like I'm standing at the edge of a lake, studying my own reflection. And Marinda's words are a stone dropped in the water. A weight that fractures my image. And no matter how I try, I can't make it look the same again.

Marinda gets the same faraway expression she wore earlier. Her face softens. "Then tell me," she says. "Tell me how it is."

"I don't want to die," I tell her. I'm startled at my own honesty, at the way the words leapt from me without forethought. At how they make my throat burn.

Marinda's eyes go wide, and then they fill with tears. "I don't want you to die either." A single drop escapes, trickles down her cheek, drips from her chin. She's always been willing to give me this gift—to cry for me when I am too hollow, or too scared or too broken, to express emotion. And somehow, seeing her weeping always makes me feel like I don't have to.

"I don't know what else to do," I tell her.

She starts to say something, and then her expression abruptly changes. She swipes the tears from her eyes and straightens her spine. "What's wrong?" I ask, but she just gives me a quick shake of her head.

The door swings open and Amoli comes in with a breakfast tray. She sees me and narrows her eyes. "Oh," she says. "Hello, Iyla."

I smile and snatch a grape from the tray. "I hope you brought enough for two." I pop the fruit into my mouth and talk around it. "Marinda wanted some company."

Amoli slides the tray onto the nightstand. "I thought you had work to do," she says, giving me a pointed stare.

"Oh, I'm sorry," Marinda says. "I bumped into her in

the kitchen last night when we were both getting a glass of water, and I begged her to join me this morning. I've been lonely, but I didn't mean to keep Iyla from her assignment. Is it something I can help with?"

Amoli flinches. Balavan expressly cautioned us not to discuss Naga business in front of Marinda. He doesn't want her curiosity piqued, doesn't want her asking questions. But somehow Marinda knew that this was exactly the tool to use to make Amoli back away. And it worked. I can see it all over the attendant's face.

"Nothing important," she says. "Enjoy your breakfast, girls."

The exchange catches on something in my mind. Tugs at it. How did Marinda know that I went to the kitchen last night? Her quick lie matches reality too closely to be a coincidence. Someone must have been watching me. A prickle races up the back of my neck.

Who is she getting her information from, if not Amoli? Who else is even in the palace right now?

Marinda stands up and pulls her fingers through her hair. "That was close," she says.

I bite my lip as I study her. "How did you know she was coming?"

Marinda glances away. "I heard her footsteps," she says. "I've gotten a lot of practice. The woman never knocks."

"How did you know I went to the kitchen for water last night?"

"I've known you since we were small," she says. "You go to the kitchen for water every night. At least twice."

Maybe I'm being paranoid. Marinda has been trained

to think quickly under stress just like I have. Of course she knows my habits. Of course she knows that Balavan is keeping her at arm's length. And it's not surprising that she would leverage that information to get what she needs. It's what we've been taught to do.

I sigh. Amoli walked in right when we were on the precipice of something big, right as we were about to cut through all of the suspicion and mistrust and split open our friendship to remake it into something new. And now it feels like the opportunity has vanished.

Marinda clears her throat. "That day at the market? The day we questioned Pranesh?" Understanding vibrates between us. Marinda is trying to reclaim the moment. To capture what we lost when Amoli walked in. I move closer to her, and we sit on the edge of the bed, facing each other.

"I remember," I say.

"The reason I wanted to visit Kadru . . ." She pauses and wraps her finger around a loose thread on her sleeve. When she looks up, her expression is raw, vulnerable. "I asked Kadru if she could help me get your life back."

"You did?" A seed of hope sprouts in my heart. My chest is tight with it.

Marinda squeezes her eyes closed and shakes her head. "Kadru wouldn't do it," she says. "Or she couldn't. I don't know which."

The seed withers and dies. And it's so much worse than if it had never been planted. "I'm sorry," Marinda says. "I didn't mean to . . . I just want you to know that I do care what happens to you. I know you don't think so, but I do."

"I'm going to die." As I say the words, I can feel their truth settle deep in my bones, their inevitability.

"You're not," Marinda says.

But she can't stop it from happening. If I don't serve Balavan, I can't reclaim the years I've lost. And I'm tired of choosing people I hate over people I love.

"So you keep serving him," she says, as if she's seen my thoughts. "You give him just enough that he keeps giving you your life back, and when you have what you need, you get out."

I stand up and pace back and forth. "It won't work," I tell her. "He wants information on you."

Her gaze is sharp. "So give it to him."

I can't figure out if she's a genius or if she's lost her mind. "But . . ."

She stands up and takes both of my hands in hers. Her scars are scattered like pearls against the smooth insides of her wrists. I rarely see her without her bracelets. Rarely see the reminder that I'm not the only one the Naga stole from. "We have to stop letting Balavan divide us," she says. "We're stronger if we stand together."

I don't know if I trust myself to make that promise. I'm not sure it's one I can keep. Marinda doesn't look away. Her expression is expectant, hopeful. "You followed me last night," she says.

I thought we'd already established that. "Yes," I say. "I did."

She holds out her hand. "Can I have the note I left for Deven?"

I shake my head. "I didn't take it," I tell her.

But she knows I don't have it. I can see from her expression that she already knows. Still, she keeps her gaze glued on me. "Why?"

And then I understand. I've already made my choice. When I left the note in the tree, I declared my allegiance, even if I couldn't admit it to myself. I blink several times to clear my eyes, and then I express the same sentiment I did years ago, when we were little girls riding on the top of an elephant and gazing at the entire kingdom sprawled before us like a spilled jewel box.

"Because," I tell her, "I choose you."

The words shimmer between us like a bridge of glass.

Marinda crosses it. She wraps her arms around me and holds me close. She smells like the jasmine Balavan favors. I think of sitting across from him and agreeing to spy on her. I think of all the days he has access to. All the sunsets he could give me. I try to put a boot on the neck of my worry, to deprive it of air until it stops moving, but my thoughts spin away from me.

Marinda lets go of me. "I need to meet Deven tonight," she says. "But we'll need a way to slip past Amoli. I don't think telling her I'd like to go to bed early is going to work twice in a row."

"I have an idea," I say. A mischievous smile tugs at Marinda's mouth. Her expression wraps me in nostalgia and makes me itch for adventure. It makes me believe I can do this, be just one person.

"What is it?" she asks.

"We're going to offer her a cup of tea."

CHAPTER SEVENTEEN

Marinda

The city is burning.

Iyla and I are at the edge of the rain forest when we notice the black smoke curling above the treetops, the sight reaching us a moment before the acrid smell does. We quicken our steps. As we get closer, we hear the clamor of angry voices, the roar of things smashing. The screams. We break into a run.

It feels like it takes forever to get to the heart of the city, and when we do, the scene stretches before us, glorious and horrible. Flames lick up the sides of buildings, glass glitters on the street, a mob of people presses toward the Raja's soldiers, held back only by the swords pointed at their throats.

The crowd shouts for justice. They promise retribution. When I get closer, I see that their faces are painted to look like tigers. My mouth goes dry. My heart thrums in time with the chorus of voices. Clearly, the Naga were wrong.

Not all of Bagharani's followers have been destroyed. Not even close.

"Silence," one of the Raja's men calls. The throng quiets. Somewhere not far off a baby cries. I wait for the soldier to promise to find whoever killed the Tiger Queen, to assure these people that justice will be done. I curl my toes inside my boots. I'm itching to run to Deven, to bring him news that will help make retribution possible.

The soldier clears his throat. "Return to your homes immediately or we will cut you down."

My stomach plummets. For just a moment there is a pregnant silence, as if the entire crowd is taking a breath at once. Rage trembles in the air like the final notes of a melody. And then all at once the mob surges forward.

The Raja's men don't hesitate. Their swords slice through necks and torsos. They show no mercy.

I start toward the commotion, but Iyla puts a hand on my shoulder. "No," she says. "We can't do anything."

Anger roils in my gut. "We can't just stand here. We can't do nothing."

I wrench away from her, but she catches my arm and yanks me back. "Marinda." Her voice is near my ear, urgent. "Think. You can only help them if you're alive."

My breath comes in ragged gasps. I wrap my arms around my middle. She's right. I have the best chance of taking the Nagaraja down. Of making him pay for what his people did to Bagharani. But the Raja is supposed to have the same goal. So why are his men killing her followers just like the Naga did?

Iyla brushes a stray hair from my forehead and tucks it

behind my ear. "If we're going to make our meeting with Deven, we need to leave now."

I can only nod in response. We duck through a side alley. I try not to look behind me. I tell myself no good can come of it. But, in the end, I can't help throwing one fleeting glance over my shoulder. I wish I hadn't. The streets are slick with blood.

* *

Iyla doesn't say anything until we're far from the chaos. And then, softly, as if she's approaching an injured animal, "Something must have happened to the Tiger Queen."

I pull my wrap more tightly around my shoulders. The night is frigid. The mountainside is crusted with frost.

"The Naga killed her." My voice is wooden. My entire body feels numb.

Iyla stops walking. "They killed her? Are you sure?"

"Yes," I say. "I'm sure."

"But how do you know?"

I swallow. I can't tell her about the snakes. Our relationship is too fragile, our alliance too tenuous. And she hates Kadru—I don't know if I can bear to give her the truth and watch her face as I become someone different in her eyes. My heart is already too heavy. "I overheard Balavan talking about it," I say.

Her eyes tighten. "I find it hard to believe that he would be so reckless." She doesn't say the rest of what she's thinking, though I can guess. *Especially around you.*

"He wasn't," I say. "I was careful."

"But—"

"What kind of spy would I be if I didn't figure out a way to actually spy?"

Iyla lets it drop, but I can tell she's still turning my words over in her mind.

We keep hiking, and I try to focus on my surroundings—the moonlight hovering above the tree line, the barren branches stretching spindly fingers toward the sky. It keeps me from replaying the horror of the evening over and over. I already know what I'll see behind my eyelids when I sleep tonight. The blood of angry men. The screams of their loved ones as they were cut to ribbons.

The roar of rushing water pulls me back from my dark thoughts and urges me forward. Mani sits at the edge of the waterfall, a bright blue blanket wrapped around his shoulders. Deven sits beside him. Their heads are bent together, lost in conversation.

My heart expands until my chest can barely contain it. "Mani," I call. He turns at the sound of his name. His eyes light up. He scrambles to his feet, tossing his blanket aside, and launches himself into my arms. I pull him close to me and sob into his hair.

The sight of his left arm missing below the elbow is still unfamiliar—a fresh shock each time I see him. My fingers stroke his cheeks, smooth his forehead.

"I missed you, monkey," I say.

His good arm wraps tightly around me. "I missed you too."

Deven puts his hand on the small of my back. His lips find mine and he kisses me slowly, tenderly. Mani groans.

Deven laughs and ruffles his hair. "I warned you, pal."

Mani wrinkles his nose. "Still."

Iyla stands stiffly off to the side. I reach for her hand and pull her into our circle. Deven puts his arms around her shoulders and gives her a quick squeeze. Mani stands on his tiptoes and kisses her cheek.

Her expression changes. Her smile trembles. She's trying to control some emotion, but I can't tell what it is.

"Come," Deven says. "Let's sit."

He brought extra blankets and hot drinks, which we sip from canteens. We fill him in on everything that has happened since we were last together: Bagharani's death, the riots, Balavan's search for the relics.

Deven rakes his fingers through his hair. "There have been skirmishes all over Sundari," he says. "Not just in Bala City. My father's men are trying to control them, but the crowds keep growing."

I shake my head. "They weren't trying to control it. They were making it worse. The people were begging for justice, and instead the soldiers killed them."

"How do they expect to get justice when they're burning buildings? When they're destroying things? The Raja's job is to protect the kingdom, not to bend to the will of the mob."

I thought Deven would be horrified when I told him what had happened tonight. I thought he'd be enraged. I didn't expect him to defend his father.

"Their leader is dead," I say softly. "Their comrades have been slaughtered. And their kingdom refuses to defend them. I think a little anger is justified."

Deven's face is rigid. A muscle jumps in his jaw. "Their leader," he says, "is my father."

The words snuff out the conversation like a pinched candlewick. Suddenly I'm painfully aware that we have an audience.

My gaze cuts to Mani, and for the first time I notice the shadows under his eyes. "Are you tired, monkey?"

He shrugs. "A little. I'm not sleeping very well."

I run the back of my hand along his cheek. "Why not?"

He lifts his chin, and his eyes meet mine. "Nightmares," he says. His voice is just above a whisper, as if he's ashamed. As if he's too old for bad dreams.

"Nightmares about what?"

His face tightens. His gaze is haunted. "The Nagaraja."

I pull him onto my lap and hold him close. "I'm so sorry, monkey. What happened to you was terrible. Any boy would have bad dreams."

The hopeful look he gives me rips my heart in two. "Really?"

I bend down so that my lips are near his ear. "I have nightmares sometimes too."

He wraps his arms around my neck. "Will you come back to the palace with me, Marinda? Please?"

I bury my nose in his hair. I breathe him in—the little-boy scent of him. It would be so easy to leave now. To never go back to the Naga palace. To never see Balavan again. To leave Sundari to its own fate. But I can't shake from my mind the vision of Mani tied to the stone altar in the Snake Temple. Of Bagharani's followers crying out for justice.

Could I live with myself if I turned away? Would Mani still respect me when he grew older and realized what I'd done?

Both Iyla and Deven are watching us with solemn expressions. I take Mani's face in my hands. "Soon," I tell him. "I promise. But I have to stop the Nagaraja so that no other little boys will have to live with nightmares. Can you understand?"

His eyes swim with tears. "Yes," he says. But his expression says no. His trembling lip begs me to reconsider. I hold him closer and rock him back and forth.

Deven's face has softened, and it gives me the courage to speak.

"The Raja governs them," I say. "But Bagharani made them feel like they belonged. Your father would do well to remember that."

He sighs. "I'm sorry. I've just grown weary of the Raksaka."

"How can you say that? You have a tattoo of Garuda on your arm. Is that just for show?"

"Of course not. But I don't think she's alive, Marinda. She would have shown herself by now."

"She's alive," I say. "She has to be. And if you don't find her before the Nagaraja does, he's going to kill her."

* *

Mani falls asleep in my arms. His breathing grows deep and even. His face goes slack. But it's not until he begins snoring gently that I dare ask Deven the question that's been thrumming at the back of my mind since I got here. "Could it be *vish bimari*?" I ask. "Does he have poison disease again?"

Deven shakes his head. "No. He's not sick, I promise. But he's restless all night, every night. And sometimes I find him acting out his nightmares—sleepwalking, destroying things without being aware. He often wakes up screaming."

Something lurches in my chest. "Maybe I should go back to the palace. Maybe taking down the Nagaraja is better suited to someone else."

Iyla scoots closer and puts a hand on my back. "He'll get through this," she says. "We'll make a safer world for him so that he never needs to have bad dreams again."

I hear a sound in my mind like a heavy step on thin ice—a groan, a crackle. And a fissure opens in my heart. I lay my head on her shoulder, and Deven lays his head on mine. I sit like that for a long time, surrounded by everyone I love.

And even so, the darkness gathers around me. I can feel it closing in.

CHAPTER EIGHTEEN

Iyla

Crocodile Island isn't any easier to manage than it was a few weeks ago. Although, at least this time I wore boots.

I scrabble up the tree, hand over foot, until I find a spot that affords me a decent view of the empty clearing below. Now there's nothing to do but wait.

And worry.

The bleak expression on Marinda's face as I left her this afternoon is a sliver in my heart. Seeing Mani unraveled her. She held on to him for an impossibly long time before she let Deven lead him away. She watched the two of them go with her hand pressed to her mouth. And then she didn't speak all the way back to the Naga palace. We wove through the streets of Bala City in the predawn mist in complete silence. If not for Marinda's breath curling in front of her like a ribbon of sorrow, I might have forgotten she was there at all.

When we got back to her room, she sank onto her bed, pulled her knees to her chest and closed her eyes. But I don't think she slept.

"We can leave," I told her a few hours later, when we both had given up on the idea of rest. "We can walk out of here right now and never come back. But we need to decide today. Balavan will be back tomorrow. He'll expect me to be on Crocodile Island trying to gather information about the Crocodile King. If we're going, we need to go now."

She met my gaze then. Her eyes were vacant. "No," she said. "We have to stop the Nagaraja. We have no choice."

"Marinda." My voice caught on the word. "Please."

"There's no one else," she said. "It has to be us."

But I'd never seen her more empty. It had cost her to walk away from Mani when he begged her to stay. It had cost her more than she could afford to lose.

And now I'm in a tree and she's all alone at the Naga palace. But I can't think about that. I need to focus on the mission at hand. The sooner we get the information Balavan is looking for, the sooner I can get out of here. The peninsula is bathed in apricot light. The sun is setting. If the Crocodile King's followers don't come soon, I'll have to climb down, find a place to sleep and then return again tomorrow. I crane my neck to try to get a view of the shore and breathe a sigh of relief when I see boats in the distance.

It takes another two hours for the men to come ashore and gather around the stone altar in the center of the clearing. There are at least triple the number of men and boys as last time. I search the crowd for Fazel. When I see him, his broad shoulders hunched over a crackling fire, his hands splayed toward the flame, my stomach swoops out from under me and I have to grab a nearby branch to steady myself, to convince my body I'm not falling.

Even after our last humiliating encounter, my traitorous fingers still itch to stroke his hair. I pull my gaze away and try to focus on finding another, more suitable target. One with greasy locks that don't beg to be touched.

But the men aren't talking in small groups like last time. They gather quietly. They move without speaking. It's impossible to find only one who is restless, because that describes all of them—restless, fidgety, expectant. Something about the charged feeling in the air is familiar. I glance up at the sky. A full moon. If the Crocodile King feeds on the same schedule as the Nagaraja, that would explain the mood shift. The thought sends a zing of anticipation through me. I would finally be able to see him. To know for sure that another member of the Raksaka exists.

The leader of the group—a tall, muscular man with jet-black hair—steps to the top of the circle, and a hush falls over the crowd. "Welcome, my brothers," he says. "Who will feed me tonight?"

The question rattles around my mind, reverberating with a wrongness I can hear but don't quite understand.

No one in the circle moves for a full minute. The silence stretches and bends, growing into something frightening. Finally a man steps forward. His hair is the color of ash, his shoulders curved with age.

"I will," he says.

A gasp behind him freezes him in place.

"Father, no." A palm on his arm. A voice full of pleading.

The older man turns and fixes his son with a gaze that I'm too far away to see in the dark. Is it sharp? Tender? Wistful? Whatever the expression, it makes the younger man drop his hand and fall silent.

The older man turns back toward the leader. "I am ready," he says. He steps up to the altar, and several other men rush forward to lift him until he rests, kneeling, on top of the stone. He clasps his hands in front of him and tips his face to the sky.

The leader touches his shoulder. "Go in peace, my friend," he says.

As he pulls his hand away, it shimmers. I scrub at my eyes, sure that my lack of sleep is making me see things.

But it doesn't help.

The leader's whole body seems to take on an ethereal, distorted quality, like the air above a hot pan. I watch awe-struck as his neck elongates, as his skin ripples, as his body transforms. Terror steals the air from my throat.

In the leader's place is an enormous reptile the size of a felled kapok tree. The man who called the meeting to order, who stood here a moment ago, is not the highest-ranking member among the Crocodile King's followers. He is the Crocodile King himself.

My vision swims. The earth seems to tilt beneath me.

My heart knows what this means a moment before my mind does. A single slow beat. And then a quickening as I realize that Marinda is in terrible danger. The giant croc can take human form. Which means that it's likely *all* of the Raksaka can take human form.

And who could the Nagaraja be except Balavan? My

pulse spikes. Marinda has been sharing a home with the creature who tried to eat her brother, who possessed her mind so completely that he nearly convinced her to kill Mani herself. And I left her there. Alone. Panic claws at me, but I'm trapped here. Thoughts of Mani on the altar at the Snake Temple draw my eyes downward. The man on the stone slab trembles as the giant croc snaps his jaws, but the man doesn't run. Why doesn't he run?

Who will feed me tonight? That's what the leader said before he transformed into the Crocodile King. The old man on the altar is a willing sacrifice. But why?

My fingers whiten as I grip the branch above me. The giant croc swishes his tail, slamming it against a tree trunk. A crack splits the stillness of the night, and the tree groans before falling slowly downward and hitting the ground with such force that it nearly shakes me from my perch. Suddenly the clearing around the altar makes more sense.

The men all take a knee. They bend their heads low, and I can't tell whether it's out of respect or out of a desire to avoid seeing what comes next. But I can't tear my gaze away. The Crocodile King snaps his giant teeth together once more and then opens his jaws. The man on the altar squeaks—a raw and vulnerable noise that betrays his earlier bravery. The noise splits my heart in two.

One man in the crowd looks up—it has to be the son— just in time to see the croc scoop up his meal and toss it back like it's nothing more than a sunflower seed. I squeeze my eyes closed.

The chanting begins then—a low keening noise that scrapes my soul raw. It's the sound of worship and grief blended together into a melody that only knows pain. I have to get out of here.

It might be a mistake to leave. Once the ritual is over, the men will be more relaxed. It will be easier to find a new target, to see which of the followers are more celebratory and which look like they want to bolt. My smartest move would be to find the son of the man who was sacrificed tonight. He will be vulnerable. He'll probably be angry. And nothing makes the secrets flow more freely than a desire for vengeance.

But I can't stomach it. Not tonight.

The two desires war inside me—the need to get to Marinda, to warn her, and the hope that by staying I'll find some piece of information that will save us both.

I look right and then left, in front of me and behind, but there isn't a clear path down that won't put me in reach of the giant croc or deposit me in the midst of his followers. I bite the inside of my cheek and lean my head against the rough bark. The moonlight filters through the trees and falls on my face with a chill glow. The night deepens, and eventually—what seems like hours later—the chanting subsides. I risk a glance down. The Crocodile King is gone, transformed back into a man, though it's too dark to find him in the crowd.

The men start to disperse. One smothers the fire. Another wipes at the blood on the stone altar with the sleeve of his cloak, as if it can be made clean again. Nausea roils in my stomach.

I can't stand to stay here for one more second. I start climbing down. If I'm quiet, I can slip away in the opposite direction and the men will be none the wiser. Halfway down, the heel of my boot catches on an unsteady branch. My still-tender ankle turns painfully. I smother a gasp as the smooth inner edge of my boot's sole slides along the branch. I try to regain my footing, but it's too late. The wood snaps, and suddenly I'm plummeting downward, weightless and screaming.

I'm going to die. My mind catches the thought from the air like a handful of dandelion seeds. The realization is soft and painless. A relief. I stop screaming. And then my back slams into the ground, knocking the air from my lungs, and the world goes black.

CHAPTER NINETEEN

Marinda

Balavan returns to the palace like a conquering hero.

Amoli and I are sitting at the dining table eating bowls of thick, hearty *rajma* when the front door flies open and dozens of voices spill over the threshold. The sudden noise is too loud, too jovial.

It rankles in the mournful silence, chafes against the raw pain of leaving Mani. My appetite abruptly vanishes and I push my bowl away.

Amoli's face sparks to life like a lit candle. She rushes to greet Balavan, but I stay where I am. I have no desire to see him. No wish to hear about the sacrifice he just witnessed.

But that doesn't stop him from finding me. A few minutes later he strides into the dining hall with the energy of ten men.

"*Rajakumari,*" he says. His voice is strong and he wields his gaze like a weapon. This is hardly the same man who left here a few days ago unfocused and distracted. He must find the ritual at the Snake Temple refreshing. The thought sickens me. "Have you enjoyed your break?"

There's something dangerous dancing in his eyes. It feels like a trick question. I wish that I had thought to bring the snakes with me so that I could see inside his mind, but they're back in my room, tucked beneath the wardrobe. I don't dare risk trying to call them to me.

"Not particularly," I tell him.

"No? Your excursions weren't all you hoped they would be?"

I swallow. I expected nothing less. I knew the guards would tell him that I'd left, and I'm prepared to answer his questions. But something about his triumphant tone chills me.

"I wasn't aware I was a prisoner," I say lightly. "You should have been more specific if you didn't want me to leave."

He smiles and covers my hand with his. "Of course you're not a prisoner," he says. "Why would you think such a thing?"

I stare at him, speechless.

"Did my guards try to stop you from leaving?"

"No."

"Did they punish you when you returned?"

I press a hand to my throat. The idea of the guards being ordered to punish me hadn't even crossed my mind. But it has obviously occurred to him.

"No."

He cups my chin in his fingers. "I don't blame you," he says. "The pull must have been irresistible." Looking into his eyes is like sinking into the depths of an ocean made of tar. Unpleasant. Inescapable. I resist the urge to wrench away from him.

"I'm afraid you've lost me," I say. "What pull?"

"Your brother," he says. "I assume that's why you left here? To see him?"

Fear curls in my stomach. I try to shake my head, but Balavan is still holding on to my chin. He lets go and strokes my cheek with the backs of his fingers. "I must say, *rajakumari,* you look beautiful today. Far better rested than Mani."

A spark of shock flies through me. I heard him wrong. I must have. "What do you mean?"

He laughs, but there's no humor in it. "Relax, my darling. It was a compliment. Your skin is dewy and your eyes are radiant." He pauses for a beat. "There aren't any hollows under them."

All the heat drains from my face. He's seen Mani. Or knows someone who has. I'm certain of it. Panic blooms in my chest.

"What have you done?" My voice comes out high and thin.

"Nothing," he says. "But I would hate for something to happen to the boy. Something worse than nightmares." He touches my nose with the tip of his index finger. "It would sour your expression, and it would be a pity to ruin such beauty."

My heartbeat is a roar in my ears. Balavan smiles as if

he can hear it, as if he already knows he's won. "I'm going to ask you a question, *rajakumari*," he says. His voice is low and silky. "And I want you to think carefully before answering, do you understand?"

I swallow the lump in my throat and nod.

"How have so many of the Raja's men survived your kiss?"

He already knows. He must. This is only a test to prove my loyalty, and it's one I can't afford to fail. It's the kind of choice I've been trained to make. The kind of choice I promised Hitesh I would.

I clear my throat. "The Raja has an antidote to the poison," I say.

His expression is blank. "What kind of antidote?"

"A fruit that the Raja grows in his orchards," I say. "But I suspect you already knew that."

"Is that why you didn't tell me?" he asks. There's a bite in his voice that makes my skin prickle.

"Of course," I say. "I assumed you have spies stationed all over Sundari—ones who know far more than I do. You haven't exactly sought out my opinion since I arrived here. I've been more decoration than anything else." It's a risk to speak with such insolence, but it has the desired effect. Balavan lets out his breath in one long exhale. His expression relaxes. "If I'd known you wanted information . . ."

He waves away the rest of my thought. "I'm sorry that I haven't made you feel important to our cause," he says. "You are far more than decoration, my darling."

I school my features into submission. Force my expression to stay relaxed so that my face doesn't give away my rage. My left eyelid twitches.

"That's nice to know," I say from under my lashes. "I was beginning to wonder."

"Yes," Balavan says. "So was I."

* *

Balavan's mind is impenetrable. I send Jasu to try to discover his secrets, but she returns in despair. I send all five snakes at once, with the same result. At first I think that they've lost their abilities, but they have no trouble accessing the minds of everyone else. They still warn me before Amoli enters my room. They continue to report on the thoughts of the rest of the Naga as they come and go.

It's as if Balavan's mind is encrusted in ice.

I think of my meeting with Kadru a few weeks ago and the chill realization that she knew my thoughts but could close the door on her own. Balavan must have the same ability. And if he can keep me from his thoughts, does that mean he can see mine? I'd be dead by now if that were true.

I sit on my bed and stare blankly into the distance. The snakes curl around my wrists and ankles—it's an apology and a comfort all at once. I sort through my options, lay them before me like playing cards and try to select the best one.

The choices seem endless, but the more I turn them over in my mind, the more I see that they boil down to only two: stay or go. If I stay, I have a better chance of getting enough information to destroy the Nagaraja. But if I go, I can protect Mani.

And Mani's safety is the one thing that I've never been willing to risk.

But I can't just leave without Iyla. I sigh and drop my head into my hands. I wish that I'd listened to her, but I insisted we stay focused on the mission. I told her to go to Crocodile Island. Told her to keep gathering intelligence on the Crocodile King's followers. I knew we couldn't win a game against Balavan without having the same information that he did. Now who knows when she'll be back? When we were younger, sometimes she'd find the information she needed quickly, and sometimes it would take her months of slowly getting to know her target before she discovered his secrets.

If I go before she comes back, it could put her in danger. But if I don't leave soon . . . A shiver runs through me. Balavan has someone watching Mani. Someone who could hurt him at any moment. I rake my fingers through my hair. There are no good solutions.

Jasu's body suddenly goes still. Her mind perks. I focus my attention on her and feel the slow convergence of various thoughts flowing in the same direction like a river that winds toward Balavan. The Naga are meeting again.

I stroke Jasu along the length of her body. *Can you reach them from here?* She tries, but it's too far. *Go,* I tell her. She slips under the door into the hallway, her thoughts focused on moving along the crevice where the wall meets the floor so she stays out of sight. The other snakes clamor for my attention. *Do you want us to go too?* But I don't dare send all five—the risk that they will be spotted is too high. *Stay with me,* I tell them. *I need you here.*

Jasu doesn't reach the Naga until the meeting is well under way. She immediately goes for Amoli's thoughts again as an easy access point, and I wonder if familiar minds are easier for her to enter than strangers' are. But this time Jasu doesn't fumble around the edge of Amoli's thoughts. She dives right in, and Balavan's voice slips into my head as effortlessly as sinking into a warm bath.

"The sacrifice was adequate, but we'll need much more if we hope to accomplish our goals. It's the willingness we're lacking."

A thick cloak of fear drops over Amoli's mind that I can't make sense of. She shifts on her cushion.

"Volunteers won't be a problem," a male voice says. "I'm sure we all agree. Isn't that right?"

A low murmur of assent moves through the room. Amoli's voice joins the others, but her hands twine together in her lap.

"Good," Balavan says. "I need more than lip service."

Amoli feels his gaze land on her. The thoughts gather in her mind like storm clouds punctuated with the thunderous sound of her heartbeat in her ears. But when she speaks, her voice comes out steady. "You'll have it," she says. "I give you my word."

I try to make sense of what Balavan is asking and why Amoli is so frightened by it, but I can't quite put the pieces together. And it doesn't help that she's trying not to think explicitly about it. She's shoving the request out of her mind before she even looks at it fully.

And I don't have time to linger on it either, because Balavan abruptly changes the subject. "Speaking of volunteers," he says, "I need someone willing to go to Crocodile Island and infiltrate the clan there."

"What about Iyla?" someone asks. "I thought she already picked a target."

Balavan doesn't answer for a moment, and Amoli's mind is full of dark anticipation. When he finally speaks, I wish he hadn't.

"Yes," he says. "She did. But that doesn't matter anymore. Iyla is probably dead."

My thoughts spin away from me in slow motion. It can't be true. The rest of Balavan's words filter through Amoli's mind and then mine in a haze of disbelief. I barely hear the rest of the details. "Iyla missed her scheduled check-in. She wouldn't have gone dark without a reason. Could be captured. More likely she was killed."

Balavan's words are like a bucket of stones thrown in my direction. I see them coming toward me and I want to flinch away, but there are too many and they are too big, too powerful. And then they slam into me and I shatter.

* *

My reasons for staying vanish one by one as I lie awake staring at the ceiling. I try to sleep, but every time I close my eyes, I see visions of Iyla. Her fingers reaching for mine under the table as Gopal flew into one of his rages, her carefully controlled expression as she told me about her latest target, the way her eyes would flash when she was angry. And her smile—a sight so rare that glimpsing it always felt like a gift. If she were dead, wouldn't I know it? Wouldn't there be a piece of my heart that vanished along with her soul? Wouldn't I feel the space it made?

Jasu nudges at my fingers, anxious that she has caused my pain, worried that it's her fault that a dull anguish is spreading over me like frost on a windowpane.

But the fault belongs to the Nagaraja and all of the people who serve him.

I was so sure when I left the Widows' Village, when I stood in front of the Raja with my spine straight and proud, that I could do this. I was sure that I would give up anything to see the Nagaraja destroyed. But it turns out I was wrong. Balavan played his hand far better than I played mine. I came with too much to lose, and now I risk losing everything.

I can't be here. Not even for a moment more. I can't risk letting the Naga take Mani from me too.

I send Jasu to make sure that the Naga are still meeting with Balavan. My best chance of escape is when they're all preoccupied. Amoli rarely checks on me after one of their gatherings—especially ones like this that stretch late into the evening. If I leave now, it will give me a head start of several hours before she knows I'm gone.

Jasu's thoughts touch mine, and I hear the echo of Balavan's voice in Amoli's mind, feel her sleepy realization that the meeting isn't close to wrapping up. Fantasies of curling up in a cozy bed hover in Amoli's mind just beneath the drone of Balavan's words.

I pull my satchel from beneath the bed and shove several saris inside, along with my scarf and hairbrush. The snakes circle my ankles, their minds colored with panic. *Don't worry, little ones. I won't leave you.* I lift the snakes one at a time and deposit them in the bottom of my bag, where they curl up together like a pile of puppies. Their minds quiet.

I glance around my room one more time—the rumpled covers, the pillows scattered at the foot of the bed like spilled jewels, a platter of expensive, half-finished cheese on the bedside table. It's the bedchamber of a *rajakumari*. And it feels nothing like home.

The flat I shared with Mani was home. The cramped space, the tiny table, the shabby yellow curtain that concealed our bathroom. And yet when we lived there, I always longed for more. Why does it seem like fate always grants the wrong half of a wish? Both Mani and I have been living in palaces, but we're not together. And that's the only thing that ever really mattered.

I slip out and close the door softly behind me. This time, instead of passing the guards, I wait just off the path, concealed by a giant fern, and let the snakes search the men's minds. If Balavan is cunning enough to use Mani to try to control me, he'll know that threatening my brother's safety might send me over the edge. And I am right: the guards are prepared. This time they have orders to do more than report the fact that I've left.

The time passes like dripping molasses, and my legs twitch with the desire to bolt. The Naga's meeting won't last forever, and the longer I crouch here, the more likely Balavan is to catch me. But despite my sweat-slicked palms and the blood pulsing through my veins, I force myself to be patient.

Finally, more than an hour later, I find my chance. One of the guards steps off the path to relieve himself. The other man stands watch, but the thought of his comrade peeing makes the pressure in his own bladder intensify. He shifts his weight from one foot to the other. He tenses the muscles in his lower body. He curses his friend for taking far longer than seems necessary. When he can hold it no longer, he steps off the path, reasoning that it will take only a moment. And what trouble is there likely to be in the middle of the night?

I won't get a better opportunity. I dart past the checkpoint, racing along the path as silently as possible. I don't slow down until I'm sure that I'm too far away to be seen. Balavan will come after me the moment he knows I'm missing. But I hope by then I'll be long gone.

CHAPTER TWENTY

Marinda

Kadru is asleep when I burst into her tent. She lies curled on a crimson settee, her legs tucked to her chest, her breathing deep and steady. I've never seen her like this—her face smooth and expressionless, her wrists and ankles unadorned.

The sight pins me in place.

She looks so ordinary. And nothing like herself.

I clear my throat, and Kadru's eyes fly open. She presses a hand to her chest and sucks in a sharp breath. "Marinda," she says, swinging her legs to the floor. "What are you doing here?"

"I need your help."

She stares at me wide eyed for several long seconds before she finally blinks. "I didn't hear you coming."

Kadru's snakes stir at her voice. I can feel their minds reaching for hers.

"I was quiet," I tell her.

She shakes her head. "That's not what I meant."

I open my mouth to respond, but she cuts me off. "This is about Iyla again." Kadru snatches a green silk robe that's draped over the back of the settee. She pulls it over her shoulders and cinches it at the waist. "I told you, I can't help her."

"Balavan thinks she might be dead. I need you to use your snakes to find her. And to check on Mani."

"Why would you think I could . . ." Kadru's gaze drops to my hand. "Oh."

I glance down. Jasu has crept from my satchel and wrapped her small body around my wrist. I can see how it must look to Kadru, what assumptions she must be making. "No," I say, "it's not like that." *I'm not like you. I never will be.*

But she's not listening to me. Her full attention is directed to Jasu. She strokes the snake with the tip of her finger. Her expression is so tender, so sad, that it rattles something inside me.

"I need your help," I say. "Please."

"You're different, Marinda," Kadru says absently. She's still focused on Jasu instead of me.

"No," I tell her. "I'm not."

But my palms are dry. My heart isn't racing. It's the first time I've ever been in Kadru's tent without feeling like I was suffocating. With a start, I realize I can't smell the snakes.

"Kadru." I say it softly, like a plea. At the sound of her name, her gaze snaps to my face and her expression shutters. Her hand falls to her side.

She saunters to an ornately carved side table and scoops a handful of jewels from a glass dish. She slides heavy emerald bracelets onto her wrists and golden rings onto her fingers. The snakes—both mine and hers—go still, as if they sense something dangerous in the air. Kadru takes her time settling a heavy necklace over her collarbones, putting on teardrop earrings, slipping jangling bands over her slender ankles.

By the time she turns to me, her expression is distant and cold, as if she's just dressed in armor instead of emeralds.

"What were you hoping I could help you with, darling?" Kadru asks.

I swallow. "I need your snakes to search for Iyla," I tell her. "And to make sure Mani is safe."

"Not possible," she says.

The muscles in my shoulders tighten. "It's possible. I know it is."

Kadru throws back her head and laughs. "Do you?" she says. "Do you *know*?"

"Yes," I say, though a note of doubt has crept into my voice.

Kadru touches the tip of my nose. "Sweet Marinda. You train one batch of snakelets and you think you're an expert."

I take a step back. "I don't know everything," I say. "But I know the snakes can be used to gather information. And I'm guessing yours are better at it than mine."

Too late, I realize it was the wrong thing to say. That I've just admitted to spying on Balavan. I press my fingers to my mouth.

Kadru smiles. "Don't worry, darling. My lips are sealed. But it really doesn't matter—this won't be a surprise to him."

Dread curls in my stomach. So I was right. Balavan can read my thoughts just like Kadru can.

"No," Kadru says as if I've spoken out loud. "He can't. Not unless he's . . ." She presses her lips together like she's afraid she's said too much. And then after a pause she continues. "It would take a great deal of focus for him to enter your mind."

I think of the intense way Balavan looks at me, like I'm a tray of pastries. "Maybe he *has* been focusing."

"Darling, if Balavan were in your head, he wouldn't be able to do anything else. Seeing your thoughts would take his undivided attention. He wouldn't even be able to speak." She runs her palm along the length of my hair and tucks a strand behind my ear. "He's not like you and me."

Jasu's body tenses around my wrist. She tries to send me calming thoughts, but it's too late. I move out of Kadru's reach.

"Then why won't he be surprised?" I ask.

"I'd imagine your ingenuity at finding snakes to train would surprise him very much," she says. "But your disloyalty won't. He never trusted you."

I take a deep breath. None of this matters right now. My cover was compromised the moment I left—it doesn't matter if Balavan ever trusted me. I need to find out if Iyla is alive. I need to make sure Mani is safe.

If Kadru won't help me, then I'll have to do it on my own. I start toward the front of the tent.

"It's not that I *won't* help you," Kadru says. "It's that I *can't*."

I freeze and wait for an explanation.

"The snakes can only focus on one mind at a time," Kadru says. "If they leave my presence, their minds will find the Nagaraja. They will focus on him, and I'll lose control of them."

"But . . ." I think of sending the snakes to spy on Balavan's meetings. They were away from me then.

"Not very far away," Kadru says softly.

My thoughts spin in search of a solution. "Can't you control the snakes from here?"

Kadru sighs. "For a time maybe, but not long enough to do what you're asking."

"You could come with me."

"With a hundred snakes in tow?" Kadru strokes my cheek with the backs of her fingers. "I'm sorry, darling. But I think it's time you let Iyla and Mani go. There's nothing you can do to save them. You'll be happier once you've made peace with that."

I wrench away from her. "No, I won't. I shouldn't have come here. I should have known you'd do nothing."

My eyes burn, but I won't give her the satisfaction of seeing me cry.

"Why *do* you keep coming?" Kadru asks.

The question jangles inside me, and it takes me a long time to answer. "You've never lied to me." And it's true. She can be cruel, but she's always told me the truth. It was Kadru who told me I was the only *visha kanya,* Kadru who told me that I served the Nagaraja, Kadru who told me

Iyla was dying. She gives me the gift of truth even when it hurts.

Her expression softens. "Then please believe me when I tell you that there's nothing you can do. Let them go, darling."

"I can't do that," I say. "I won't."

I walk away from her and lift the flap of the tent. But before I leave, I turn and look at her one last time. She's watching me with something like pity.

"Did it ever occur to you that Balavan has no power without you? Without me?" I ask. "Don't you ever wonder what we could do if we worked with each other instead of with him?"

Kadru opens her mouth, but then she snaps it closed without speaking. And she turns her back on me.

My throat feels thick as I step into the cool night air. But I don't have time to feel sorry for myself. Balavan could be looking for me at this very moment. I need to get as far away as I can.

I pull the scarf from my satchel and examine the map. I'll have to find a different dead drop—tradecraft forbids me from using the same one twice in a row. And once I do, I'll leave a message that only Deven will understand. *As soon as you get this, find me on the path lit by the growing moon. I have a promise to keep.*

CHAPTER TWENTY-ONE

Iyla

"Iyla?"

I blink once. Twice. Light swings into my eyes and then away again. My head throbs.

"Iyla?"

Someone stands in front of me, a lantern held near his head. His face blurs in and out of focus. Fazel.

I try to sit up, but my entire body screams in protest. I ache all over. "Where am I?" The room is dark and cold. I'm lying in a bed that feels like it's made of stone, and I'm covered by a thin white sheet that looks suspiciously like a shroud.

"Crocodile Island," Fazel says. "But you already knew that. The question is, why are you here?"

I put my fingers to the back of my scalp and find a bump the size of an egg. My hair is matted with what I can only assume is dried blood. I suddenly remember falling from the tree, and the fact that I'm not dead bites into me with sharp disappointment.

"How long have I been out?" I ask. My head feels stuffed with cotton, as if I've been unconscious for days.

"You fell last night," he says, "and you slept all day. Now tell me why you're here."

Fazel is staring at me, waiting for an answer. The lantern in his hand sways from side to side, casting him in an eerie light. The irony of my situation bubbles in my throat and escapes with a harsh laugh.

I've been captured.

Only a few weeks ago, I pressed a knife to Pranesh's throat to force him to draw me a map showing the location of the Crocodile King. I lied to him that day when I told him that there were only two kinds of spies—the ones in it for the thrill and the ones who really believe in their cause. There's a third kind: the spies who only do it because they're forced, because they don't have anywhere else to go. Those spies are just as easy to turn as the first. And they don't die when captured either.

"I'm here to spy on you for the Nagaraja," I tell him.

Fazel's eyes widen. Not because of my confession—he must have already suspected that I was working for one of the Crocodile King's enemies—but because I offered the truth so freely. He was probably ready to threaten violence, and now I've saved him the trouble.

His features rearrange themselves. The surprise leaves his face and is replaced by suspicion. "You're lying."

I sigh. "I'm not."

"If you were actually working for the Nagaraja, you'd

never confess so easily," he says. "It would be a death sentence."

I press my lips into a fine line. "A death sentence? You're going to kill me?"

"I'm not, but with an admission like that, Chipkali certainly is."

"I'm assuming he's the crocodile guy? The one who eats his own followers?"

Fazel stiffens. I've hit a nerve. "Yes," he says after a long pause.

"Excellent. Bring him in and let's get this over with."

He gives an exasperated sigh. "This isn't a joke, Iyla. You have no sense of self-preservation."

I give a sharp laugh. He's more right than he knows.

"Look, we both know how this goes. Let's just skip all of the steps where you threaten and I cower, and instead go straight to me telling your leader everything he wants to know. Then we'll see if he still feels like killing me."

Fazel sits on the edge of the bed, and the movement makes me wince in pain. His face softens. "I'm trying to help you," he says. "Why do you always have to be so difficult?"

"Always? We've only spent one day together."

"And you were prickly. Except for when you were trying to woo me—to get information on Chipkali, I assume?" He sets the lantern down on the floor, and I can no longer see him clearly.

"Of course," I say. "Not that it worked."

"Yeah, well, the truth serum didn't work either, so I guess we're even."

I gasp and sit forward so hard that my ears ring. "You actually gave me truth serum?"

His laugh is low and soft. "No," he says. "I'm only kidding."

"Oh." My chest constricts. I can't tell if he's flirting with me or mocking me. I wish I could see his expression. I have the urge to reach for him in the dark, to touch his face and see if he's smiling. The impulse makes me hate myself, and I push the thought away. Fazel is threatening to turn me over to someone who he's sure is going to kill me, so how he feels about me is probably the last thing I should be concerned about. And yet every time I see him, I can't help myself. He gets under my skin in a way no one ever has before.

But I can't let him distract me. The only thing I can think about right now is finding a way to convince the Crocodile King to let me go. I have to get back to the Naga palace and warn Marinda. She's in danger every moment that she spends with Balavan, every second she thinks he's only a man.

"So when do I meet with your leader?" I ask. "I assume he wants to question me before he scarfs me down?"

Fazel grabs my leg just below my knee, and I let out a startled gasp. His fingers dig into my skin. "Stop it. You can't make comments like that to Chipkali or he won't even hear you out before he kills you."

I pry Fazel's fingers from my leg. His hands are warm, and I have to force myself to let go. "Yes, yes," I say. "I get it. Your leader is very scary. Can I see him now, please? It's important."

Fazel stands up. He snatches the lantern from the floor

and lifts it to face level. His eyes are tight. "It's the middle of the night," he says. "Chipkali is sleeping. But if you're so determined to see him, I'll make sure he visits you first thing in the morning."

"Thank you," I say.

He studies me for a moment without speaking. His brow is furrowed. His shadow pools in the space between us. "Don't thank me," he says. He turns and walks toward the door. His fingers close around the knob, but he doesn't leave. He stands motionless for several long seconds, like he's wrestling with a decision. Finally he clears his throat. "I'll see you tomorrow," he says without looking in my direction. "If you're still alive."

* *

I open my eyes to a room brightened by buttery slices of sunlight. It's the only warmth my accommodations offer— this little bit of nature that creeps between the bars on the windows and stretches across the floor and up the walls. The rest of my surroundings are grim. I'm in a square room with a dirt floor and stone walls. The mattress I'm lying on is filthy and rests on top of a crude wooden platform.

My body aches as I crawl out of bed. A wave of dizziness washes over me, and I put a palm against the cool stone wall to steady myself. I squeeze my eyes closed and take a few deep breaths. At least nothing feels broken. Once I regain my balance, I open my eyes and catch a glimpse of my damaged body. I gasp. Purple bruises bloom along my arms and legs. Blood wells in dozens of scratches.

Any thoughts of escape drain away. If it wasn't clear before, it is now. My only hope of survival is to convince the Crocodile King that I'm worth keeping alive. No small feat for someone who devours his friends. I shudder to think what he does to his enemies.

As if on cue, something behind the door rattles. I can hear the drag of heavy chains, the clink of metal, and then, finally, the handle turns and the door swings open.

Chipkali strides into the room. He's larger than he looked when I saw him from the tree in the clearing. His shoulders are broad and strong, and his face is covered in a thin layer of stubble, as if he came here straight from bed without bothering to shave first. He wears his dark hair longer than many of the other men on the peninsula; it's gathered at the base of his neck and tied with a thin leather cord.

Chipkali's gaze finds mine and cuts through me like a shard of broken glass. "Fazel tells me you requested to see me."

I swallow. "Yes."

"Are you brave or stupid?" he asks. His voice is gravelly and harsh.

"Probably both," I tell him.

He folds his arms across his chest. "Go ahead," he says. "Try to save yourself."

"Balavan sent me to spy on you," I say. I try to stand tall, to appear confident despite my injuries. "But I'm not willing to die for him. I have valuable information that I think you'll want to hear."

His eyes narrow. "Valuable information? You think I don't have my own spies?"

"Do you?" I ask. "Ones that are in the Naga's inner circle?"

His lip curls, but he doesn't answer the question. He holds my gaze for several moments, and I resist the urge to take a step back. "This is one of Balavan's oldest tricks," Chipkali says. "Sending in spies who get captured on purpose and then promise they have valuable information. Instead they learn what they can from us, and at the first opportunity they take off in the night." He crosses the room until he's looming over me. His voice goes quiet. "It's not the first time Balavan has done this."

Dread curls in my stomach and I shake my head. "That's not what happened," I say. "I didn't get captured on purpose."

"Sure you didn't," he says. "But let me ask you this: what kind of spy falls out of a tree?"

"It was an accident," I say. "My boot slipped."

His hands curl into fists at his sides. "And yet your boot didn't slip until you were close enough to the ground that the fall wouldn't be life threatening." He turns to walk away. "It was a good try," he says. "But not good enough."

"Balavan is coming to kill you," I say.

"I doubt that very much," Chipkali says over his shoulder. "But if he wants to, he's welcome to try."

"He's already killed the Tiger Queen."

At this Chipkali freezes. He turns slowly. "You lie."

"It's true," I say. "Bagharani is dead, and so are many of her followers. Balavan sent me to find the relic so that he can take you out next."

Finally the smug self-assurance slips from his face. His

jaw tenses. He flexes the muscles in his hands—fisting them so tightly that his veins bulge—over and over again. Then he steps into the hallway and speaks to the guards outside my door. I strain to hear his words.

"Send a team north to check on Bagharani," he says. "I want to know if she's dead or alive. And tell the rest of the men to get ready to move. Our location has been compromised. We need to be ready to leave by nightfall tomorrow."

He steps back into the room and fixes me with a stony gaze.

"If you're lying to me," he says, "I'll kill you in the worst possible way. I'll make sure you suffer before you die."

Until this moment I wouldn't have believed how sweet a threat could sound, how full of hope. Because no matter what his men find out about Bagharani, the information has bought me more time.

"Of course," I say. "I would expect nothing less."

And I hope that Marinda was right about Balavan killing the Tiger Queen. My life depends on it.

CHAPTER TWENTY-TWO

Marinda

Maybe the path lit by the growing moon wasn't a clear enough clue. Maybe Deven doesn't know that I meant to retrace the journey we made out of Bala City to the palace in Colapi City when we were racing against time to save Mani from the Nagaraja.

I was hoping he'd find me quickly, but I've been walking for two days now without any luck. I stop only when absolutely necessary—to use the snakes to help me steal foods I can eat on the move, *chole bhature* or *vada pao*. Or to catch a few hours of restless, shivering sleep at the base of a devil tree while the snakes stay on high alert for approaching danger. I have no idea if Balavan is searching for me, but I can almost feel his presence like a pressure at my back. It drives me forward when I barely have energy to put one foot in front of the other. I wish I'd thought to ask Deven for a key to the safe houses just in case I ever needed to flee. I'd give anything right now for a warm bed and a door with a lock.

As I trudge through valleys and over hills, I can't help but remember the last time I made this journey. How desperate I was to get to Mani, how helpless I felt. And here I am again on the same path for the same reason. The futility of the last few months gnaws a hole in my gut. I've accomplished nothing except putting Mani in danger yet again. Why did I ever think it was a good idea to leave him? Why did I think I'd be able to take down the Snake King when the Raja himself couldn't do it?

The snakes squirm in my bag and reach for my mind. Jasu reflects my exhaustion back to me. The burning sensation in my eyes. The way each step feels like dragging bags of heavy sand.

I can't stop, I tell her. But her worry falls across my mind like a shadow. I keep walking. A few minutes later my vision fractures. I stumble. Jasu's alarm clangs inside me as loudly as a dropped pot on a stone floor. Maybe the snakes are right. Maybe if I don't stop on my own, my body will stop for me.

I search for a place to rest out of sight, but the landscape before me is nothing but open field. No matter where I go, I'll be easily noticed if anyone passes by. Not that I've seen another human in hours. Finally I give up and collapse on the spot. I rest my cheek on the cool grass, pull my knees to my chest and let my eyes slide closed.

* *

I dream of Deven.

His voice is petal soft as he calls my name. His palm is warm against my cheek.

It's the same dream I've been having since I left him months ago. Some part of my mind knows it's not real, but still, I want to luxuriate in the sensation of being with him, of his skin against mine, so I don't open my eyes.

"Marinda? Marinda, please wake up."

His voice catches on the words, and it makes him sound young. Vulnerable. Desperate. This isn't how the dream usually goes. My eyes flutter open.

Deven leans over me, one hand on the side of my face and the other cradling the back of my head. His eyes are wild.

"Deven?" The word scratches my throat.

Relief floods over his face. "Oh," he says, his voice shaky. "Oh, thank the skies."

"Are you really here?" I ask. Black spots dance at the edges of my vision. "You got my message?"

"That message." He groans. "Marinda, what were you thinking? I've been searching for you for days, panicked that you were dead or captured. I've been on every moonlit path from here to Colapi City. What's the point of giving me information if I can't understand it?"

I frown. "I was trying to be cryptic."

"Well, congratulations," he says, "you succeeded."

I flinch and Deven's face softens.

"I'm sorry," he says. "That came out more harshly than I meant it. You just scared me." He puts a hand on my back and helps me to my feet. A chilly wind whips through my hair and I start to shiver. Deven pulls me close and I fit my body against his. His warmth makes me realize just how cold I am.

"How is Mani?" I ask.

Deven presses a kiss on my forehead. "He's fine. It's you I'm worried about. Let's get to a safe house and we can talk there, okay?"

I want to argue. I want to demand information about Mani now. I want to confess all of my worries, to give them to Deven one by one like stones from a bucket and let him carry them for a while. But I'm tired, and the promise of a shower and a warm place to sleep is a temptation I'm not strong enough to resist.

And I hope Mani will be safe without me for just a little while longer.

* *

I'm barely coherent when we make it to the safe house, but a few hours later—after a nap, a meal and a shower—I finally feel like myself again. It comes at a price, though. The food and warmth have crystallized my thoughts, have shaped my anxiety about Mani into a sharp blade of fear.

I emerge from the washroom, dressed in clean clothes and drying my hair with a towel, to find Deven stretched out on one of the beds, staring at the ceiling. His expression is thoughtful and faraway. I watch him until I can't bear it anymore, until the need to connect with him is stronger than the pleasure of being able to study him unnoticed. I clear my throat, and he turns onto his side and props up his head with his elbow.

"Hey," he says, giving me a faint smile. "So what happened? Why did you leave the Naga palace?"

The question makes the muscles in my stomach tight. "Balavan has someone watching Mani. Someone who's seen him recently."

Deven sits up. "No," he says. "That's not possible."

I perch on the edge of the bed. "It's true," I say. "I'm sure of it. He talked about how Mani wasn't sleeping." I swallow. "He described the hollows under his eyes."

Deven shakes his head, pulls on the back of his neck. And I can't help it, my gaze skips to the satchel propped against the wall. All five snakes are coiled at the bottom of my bag, out of sight, but alert and ready. I reach for their minds and they reach for Deven's. A series of images flash through his memory—all of the people Mani interacts with each day. The cook who prepares his meals, the servants who clean his room, the woman who tutors him in writing, reading and geography. None of them seem like spies.

"I believe you," he says. "I just can't think who it could be."

Guilt twists in my stomach. It's an invasion to search Deven's mind. And the fact that he's telling me the truth makes me feel even worse.

"We have to get Mani out of the palace," I say. "I can't take the risk."

Deven nods. "Of course. We'll leave at first light."

He puts his arm around my shoulders and I lean into him, savoring the feeling of being together again. I sigh and close my eyes. But when I open them a few seconds later,

Deven is looking at me differently—his gaze is soft and his pupils are wide. He strokes my cheek, and my heart stutters. My face heats beneath his hand. He trails his knuckles slowly down my neck, traces the contours of my collarbone with his thumb.

Our lips meet and I melt against him.

Every inch of me sparks at his touch, as if my entire body is made of fireflies. His fingers sink into my hair. All my other thoughts slip away until there's only Deven. Only this moment.

I draw him closer to me, and our kiss deepens. I trace the light stubble along his jaw, find the hollow at his throat. I wonder if being with him will always feel like this—the rush of heat, the sense of weightlessness.

Suddenly Deven freezes. He puts his hands on my shoulders and pushes me away. The rejection feels like a fist in my stomach, and my eyes fly open. But Deven's not even looking at me. His eyes are lowered, his face taut with alarm. "Don't move," he says. I follow his gaze to the floor, where Jasu is looping herself around my ankle.

"I can kill it," he says softly. "But I need you to hold still."

I gasp. "No!" I bend to scoop up the snake in my palm. Jasu wraps her body around my arm, her mind red with panic. Deven's dark thoughts have frightened her. "Don't hurt her. She's mine."

Deven's expression goes slack. "What do you mean, she's yours?"

"Well," I say, "technically, I stole them from Balavan,

but I've raised them since they were hatchlings, so it feels like they belong to me."

"Them?" he says. "They?"

My cheeks flame. "There are four more snakes in my satchel."

His expression shifts into something inscrutable, and the air between us chills.

"I can explain," I say, though I'm not sure I can. "It's a long story."

Deven stands up and rakes his fingers through his hair. "It's late," he says. "We should get some rest. We have a long day ahead of us tomorrow."

I clutch a handful of the bedspread in my fist. "They're just babies," I say.

His mouth is a thin line. He's looking at me like I'm a stranger. "Maybe," he says. "But they're still snakes."

* *

I lie awake long after Deven's eyes have fallen closed. Long after his breathing has grown deep and loud. If he's angry that I even have the snakes, what would he think if he knew I could use them to see his thoughts?

I tried all evening to resist the temptation to snoop through his mind again. The snakes kept feeding me images—flashes of anger, snippets of concern. Each time they showed me Deven's thoughts, I gently pushed them away. *No,* I told them. *Not now.*

But then one of the snakes pushed an image into my mind that sent a slow pulse of dread through me—Deven's memory of Jasu wrapped around my ankle, along with his niggling worry that maybe I deceived him. That maybe I'm on the Nagaraja's side after all.

Stop, I told the snakes. *No more.* And they tried to obey. But I've trained them too well—searching through minds is now a reflex. It's not easy for them to quit.

CHAPTER TWENTY-THREE

Iyla

Chipkali's men return the next evening just as daylight is tipping into dusk. I stand on my tiptoes and watch through the bars of the window. They must have taken an elephant once they reached the mainland to have returned so quickly. That, or Bagharani's lair is close. The men move toward the Crocodile King at a pace just short of a run. I press closer to the window. The news is urgent, then.

I'm too far away to hear the report, but Chipkali listens with his arms across his chest. As the men speak, his posture stiffens. His head dips low for just a moment before he starts barking orders. The entire camp springs into action. It must be true, then. The Tiger Queen is dead.

I sink onto the bed and pull my knees to my chest. Now all I can do is wait.

I try to discipline my thoughts, to pin them to this moment, to focus them on getting off the peninsula alive. But they keep slipping backward to the ritual I witnessed—the horror of watching Chipkali transform into the Crocodile King.

And from there my thoughts slide headlong into Marinda. My breath catches at the sudden pain in my throat. I've spent so many years resenting her, convinced that she wasn't doing enough to protect me, certain that she never thought of me at all. And yet now that it's staring me in the face, losing Marinda is the most painful thing I can imagine.

I envision Balavan transforming into the Nagaraja, and a wave of nausea rolls through me.

The chains at the door rattle. I take a deep breath and try to clear my mind. If I'm going to face Chipkali, I can't do it with the memory of Marinda pressed against my neck like a knife.

The door swings wide, but it's not Chipkali who walks through. It's Fazel.

"You're alive," he says. His eyes have dark smudges beneath them. He's wearing the same clothes he wore yesterday.

"For now," I tell him.

He sighs. "You must have told him something good."

"Something *good*? I told him that the Tiger Queen is dead. I told him that the Snake King is planning to kill him next."

Fazel's eyes go wide. "Something valuable, I meant," he says. He rubs his forehead and then scratches his face like he's not sure what to do with his hands. Finally he shoves them in his pockets. "Is all of that true?"

"You think I'd admit it to you if I gave your leader false information?"

Fazel doesn't answer right away. He just holds my gaze as if he'll be able to discover everything he needs to know just by studying my expression. And despite the uncomfortable weight of his stare—the way it makes me feel like I've swallowed a swarm of bees—I refuse to look away. "I don't think you lied," he says finally. "Even you wouldn't be that reckless." But his voice is uncertain.

"And what would you do if I had?"

"Nothing," he says.

I fold my arms across my chest. "Nothing? Now who's lying?"

He shakes his head. "It's true. This . . ." He sweeps his hand around the room, and I don't know if he means to indicate this space or this peninsula or the whole of Sundari. "All of this—taking prisoners, watching people I care about die—it's not what I signed up for."

"And yet you watched the Crocodile King eat one of your friends without a second thought."

A spasm of pain crosses Fazel's features, and I almost wish I could take it back. Almost.

"The Nagaraja doesn't require sacrifices?" he asks softly.

I think of Mani tied to the altar in the Snake Temple, his frantic cries, the naked terror in his eyes. And I stood by and did nothing to help him. The memory bathes me in shame. I have no right to judge Fazel. At least his friend knew what was happening. At least he died willingly.

"Of course he does," I say. And then, "I'm sorry. That was unfair."

He sits next to me on the bed and puts a hand on my shoulder. "I'm really glad you're not dead."

Something about the statement makes a laugh bubble up from my chest. "Are you flirting with me?" I ask.

Fazel flinches. "What? No. I'm just . . . I just . . ." He stands up and runs a palm over his short hair. "Forget it," he says, striding toward the door.

"Wait," I tell him. "Don't go. I didn't mean to offend you. It's just not the most romantic thing a guy has said to me, that's all." Except even as the words leave my mouth, I realize that I'm wrong. That it actually might be one of the sweetest things I've ever heard. Especially since Fazel is the only boy who has seen me as I really am. Not the skilled seductress that Gopal trained, but the unvarnished, irritable, real me.

Fazel stops walking, and several seconds pass before he turns toward me. "I wasn't flirting," he says.

"Understood."

A ghost of a smile quirks at the corner of his mouth. "It would be in poor taste to flirt with a prisoner."

"Extremely," I agree.

He grins and returns to sit beside me. "Okay, then. Now that we have that settled, we should figure out how to keep Chipkali from killing you."

* *

Chipkali leads his followers to the boats docked at the water's edge. The men are silent—the only noises on the peninsula are the steady fall of boots and the occasional snap of a twig or rustle of a leaf. The leaders of the group all carry flaming torches, which cast an ominous orange glow over the procession.

I'm still not sure I can trust Fazel, but when his gaze finds mine as Chipkali shoves me toward one of the boats, I feel—at least for the moment—like I've found a friend.

I settle between two of the Crocodile King's younger followers, both of whom smell like they haven't bathed in a week. I hold my breath against the stench as the boats glide toward the opposite shore.

Chipkali climbs into the boat and sits across from me but won't meet my gaze. He holds his back ramrod straight, even though everyone else is hunched against the cold.

"So where are we going?" I ask.

The boys on either side of me shrink away as if they're worried they'll be punished for my indiscretion. As if just sitting near me is enough to indict them too.

"No questions," Chipkali says without looking in my direction.

"Does that apply to both of us?" I ask. "Because I'm happy to stop answering questions."

The boy on my right stiffens. The one on my left lets out a startled gasp. Chipkali's jaw goes tight and finally his gaze meets mine. The fire from the torches dances in his eyes. "Careful, prisoner," he says. "Or I'll have you killed before we ever make it to the mountains."

I bite my lip to keep from smiling and turn away as if cowed. As I suspected, Chipkali's personality is more like Gopal's than Balavan's. He loses control when he's angry. It makes him careless and easy to manipulate; he will give away in anger what would be impossible to pry from him when he's calm. Now I just need to find out which mountains so I know how much time I have to formulate an escape plan—because there's no doubt that Chipkali will kill me eventually.

I search for Fazel among the passengers in the other boats. I finally spot him a ways off, seated in the opposite direction from me, so that we're facing each other. It's too dark to know for sure, but I feel like his gaze is already fixed on me. I told him everything earlier—how I didn't know that the Raksaka can take human form, how Marinda is in danger, how I need to get to her and warn her before something terrible happens. Fazel promised to help me escape. It's just as likely that he'll use the conversation against me and earn himself a higher place in the Crocodile King's ranks, but at this point I have nothing to lose.

I'm dying either way. I'd like to die knowing that I tried to save Marinda.

CHAPTER TWENTY-FOUR

Marinda

Deven is quieter than usual on our journey to the palace. I can feel the unease rolling off him in waves, and I'm no longer sure if it's the snakes feeding me thoughts or if it's only my own worries gnawing a hole in my gut.

"I'm sorry," I tell him when the silence has stretched on too long. "I know how it must have looked to see me with snakes after . . ." The words stick in my throat as I think of the Nagaraja attacking Mani, and it takes me a moment to find my voice again. "After all that happened. But it's not like that—"

"Don't," Deven says, and the word feels like a slap. But then his gaze finds mine, and his eyes are soft. "You don't have to justify yourself to me." He slides his hand into mine. "We do what we have to in order to survive."

Tears prickle at the corners of my eyes. Somehow his understanding hits me harder than his disapproval did.

And I wonder if my life will ever be about anything except survival. If I will ever have a chance to live for happiness instead.

By the time we make it to Colapi City, the sun is sinking beneath the horizon and I'm so tired I can barely stand up straight. But then the palace comes into view, and the promise of seeing Mani again gives me a surge of energy. Deven has to rush to keep up with me as I race past the guards and wrench open the enormous golden palace doors. And then I realize I don't know where I'm going, and I skid to a halt on the marble floor of the pavilion.

"Where is he?" I ask, turning toward Deven, who has a sheen of sweat glistening on his brow.

He gives me an amused smile. "I thought you'd forgotten I was here."

"I just . . . I need to see him. . . ."

Deven puts a hand on my arm. "I know," he says softly. "Follow me."

He leads me across the jewel-studded marble floor and around the corner to a long corridor. My heart knocks against my rib cage. The snakes stir in my satchel, reaching for my mind, their concern for me prodding at the edges of my consciousness. But my thoughts are only for Mani.

Deven opens a set of mahogany doors, and my breath lodges in my throat. Three of the walls are lined with bookshelves that soar from floor to ceiling. The fourth wall is made entirely of glass, drenching the room in golden sunlight.

Mani is curled on a red sofa in the center of the room. His eyes are closed, and he's clutching a book to his chest as if he's worried it will disappear while he sleeps. It reminds me forcefully of our days in Japa's bookshop. Of the many times I went searching for Mani only to find him snoozing on the purple cushion in the corner of the shop, an open book splayed across his nose.

My throat is thick with emotion. I cross the room and kneel at his side, stroking his cheek with the backs of my fingers.

"Mani," I say. "Mani, I'm here."

His eyes flutter open, but he doesn't speak, doesn't move. Fear seizes my heart.

"Mani?"

He blinks once. Twice. "I know you're not there," he says. The statement robs my breath.

I take his face in my palms. "I am, monkey. I'm right here."

He squints at me then, his expression wary. He's looking at me like I'm a mirage—like he's been tricked before, and my return is too much to hope for.

My heart splits in half.

Mani lifts a hand to my cheek. "Really? It's really you?" The hope in his voice chips at my self-control, and soon the tears are streaming down my face. I gather him in my arms.

"I'm here," I tell him. "Really, really."

His face crumples and he throws his arms around my neck. "I thought you'd never come back for me," he says. His tears soak through my shirt as I hold him tight and rock him back and forth.

Deven comes to my side and lays a hand on my shoulder. "You can kiss him now," he says. "He's immune."

My chest gets tight. It seems too much to hope for. "Are you sure?"

Mani pulls away and wipes at his eyes. "It's true," he says. "I've had more venom in my body than anyone in the whole palace. Everybody says so." He puffs out his chest and holds up his left arm like it's a source of pride.

"Are you sure you want your sister kissing you?" I ask. Mani shrugs and tries to act nonchalant, but I know him too well. I cast one more glance Deven's way and he nods.

"I promise," he mouths.

I lean in and kiss Mani on his cheek.

He wrinkles his nose. "That tickles," he says, and my heart pinches. No one has ever kissed him on his face before. I always had to be so careful, planting kisses on the top of his messy mop of hair, avoiding his skin.

"Hmm," I say. "Maybe I did it wrong." I kiss his other cheek and he giggles.

"That tickles too."

"Yeah?" I kiss his forehead and his chin and the crook of his neck, and soon he's laughing so hard that he can scarcely breathe. I tickle him as I rain kisses down on his entire face, and soon Deven joins in, laughing and tickling too. For a shimmering moment I'm filled with a joy so big my body can't contain it. And then I remember Kadru's warning—that I'll grow more and more deadly as time passes. That someday even my touch will be enough to kill. My happiness vanishes as quickly as it came. I let him go and lean back on my elbows.

Mani catches his breath and then lets out a contented sigh. A few moments later he climbs into my lap, his face suddenly serious. "Don't leave me, Marinda," he says. "Please."

"Never again," I tell him. "I promise."

* *

Deven, Mani and I are on the path to the Widows' Village a few hours later. Deven wanted to wait until dawn, but Balavan's description of Mani—the hollows under his eyes, how haunted he looked—echoed in my mind. It was so accurate that it rubbed my soul raw, and I didn't want to stay in the palace another moment, let alone an entire night. I can't protect Mani from a threat I can't see.

"Will we stay in the Blue House?" Mani asks as we walk. His hand is firmly clasped in mine, and for the first time in months I feel whole again.

"Yes," I say. "I imagine we will."

He turns toward Deven. "Will we get to meet your grandmother?"

Deven stiffens. His eyes go unfocused for just a moment, as if he's lost in a memory, and then he tousles Mani's hair. "No, I'm afraid we won't."

Mani stops walking. "Why not?"

"She died a few months ago," Deven says softly, his gaze fixed on the ground.

I touch his shoulder. "You didn't tell me." I think of all the time I spent studying the faces of the widows in the village, desperate to find Deven's grandmother among them. And she wasn't there.

He meets my gaze and his eyes are tight, his mouth a

thin line. "I didn't know," he says. "She died shortly after I met you, but my father decided not to tell me." His voice is strained, as if it cost him something to say it out loud.

I pull in a sharp breath and curl my fingers around his. "Why?"

"I was doing well working with Japa," he says. "My father didn't want me to get distracted and lose focus."

What kind of man doesn't tell his son that he's lost someone close to him, doesn't give him the chance to say goodbye or to grieve? But then I remember the Raja's soldiers—their callous disregard for Bagharani's followers, how they cut them down without hesitation. And I know exactly what kind of man does something like that. "I'm sorry," I tell him.

He gives me a small nod and squeezes my hand.

"I hate when people die," Mani says suddenly, and something in his tone chills my blood. Japa is the only person he's ever known who died. Except for Gopal, which could hardly be considered a loss. But I get the sense he's not talking about Japa.

I kneel next to him and look into his eyes. "What do you mean, monkey? When who dies?"

His gaze roams over my face. He bites his lip. "Nothing," he says finally. "Never mind."

"Mani, what is it?"

But he won't meet my gaze. So I reach for Jasu's mind and ask her to reach for Mani's. And when she does, I cover my mouth in horror. Mani's mind is full of images of me dying. Vivid nightmares of me being murdered in a variety of grisly ways—the Nagaraja tearing out my throat, the Nagaraja ripping me apart limb from limb, the Nagaraja slashing through my chest with a sharp fang and then feasting on my organs while Mani watches.

Tears well in my eyes and I pull Mani close to me. No wonder he can't sleep. He's been torturing himself for months, and I've been too far away to help him. "I'm right here, monkey. And I'm not going anywhere."

Mani buries his face in my neck and holds me tight. But he doesn't say that he believes me.

CHAPTER TWENTY-FIVE

Iyla

I thought navigating Crocodile Island was hard, but that was nothing compared with navigating the rocky hills of the mainland with my hands tied behind my back. The terrain is uneven, and without my arms to lend me balance, I keep stumbling. The knees of my pants are soaked through with blood from my last fall, and my body still aches from my earlier injuries, but Chipkali refuses to untie me.

The moment the boat pulled ashore, he called for rope and then wrenched my arms behind my back as he tied my wrists together. I sucked in my bottom lip to keep from crying out, but he must have seen my expression, because he gave a dark laugh.

"What is it, prisoner?" he said, his voice full of grim satisfaction. "No sharp comment this time?"

Maybe I pushed him too far. It's going to be a lot harder to escape without the use of my hands. I want to look for

Fazel, but he's somewhere behind me, and I don't dare crane my neck to get a better view. If I'm being watched, I don't want to draw attention to him.

We hike for hours before Chipkali finally calls for the men to make camp. Moonlight filters through the trees and casts the leaves in silvery light. It looks eerily like the night I watched Chipkali transform into the Crocodile King and eat one of his own followers. A shiver goes through me at the thought. Maybe this time it will be me.

But the men don't set up an altar. They start pitching tents.

"Would you like me to start a cook fire, master?" one of the men asks.

"We can't risk the smoke giving away our location," Chipkali says. "Distribute dry rations." He glances at me and frowns. "The prisoner only eats once the others are satisfied."

My stomach grumbles in protest, but I won't give him the pleasure of seeing me look disappointed. I study the trees as if I find them fascinating. From the corner of my eye I see the sharp look he gives me, but then he walks away and I'm left standing in the clearing alone.

I make my way to a fallen log and sit. The men work around me—setting up lavishly decorated tents, unfurling sleeping carpets, passing out dried meat and loaves of flatbread. But no one dares glance in my direction. They act as if I'm invisible.

Maybe it makes sense not to look your master's meal in the eye.

My shoulders ache from being confined so long in such an unnatural position. I try to turn my wrists to loosen the bindings, but they're too tight—the rope digs into the soft flesh at my wrists.

I study my surroundings, but it's too dark to plan an escape route—all I can see in the distance are trees. I soon realize it's hopeless and give up.

I spot Fazel across the clearing. A younger boy holds a flaming torch nearby, angling it so that Fazel can see to work. It's just enough light to make out the muscles rippling beneath his shirt as he sets down the wooden chest he's been carrying. He pries open the lid and pulls out a tent decorated with bold blue peacocks and bright red blossoms against a creamy background—it's too opulent to belong to anyone but Chipkali.

My heart sinks. The Crocodile King trusts Fazel, and everything I've learned about tradecraft tells me I shouldn't. We hardly know each other, and no one understands better than I how affections can be faked in order to manipulate. But then Fazel darts a glance in my direction. The firelight falls on his face, and I notice a smudge of dirt on his cheek that sends a wave of tenderness rippling through me. I have the urge to rub it away with the pad of my thumb. If only I were closer. Or untied.

Fazel returns to his task, but he smiles as he works, and somehow I know that smile is meant for me.

It takes some effort, but I pull my gaze away from him and study the other men in the camp. I can't risk letting Chipkali see me staring at one person for too long. The men work with quick, efficient movements, but there's a palpable sense of unease among them. They don't speak to one another. Their brows are pulled together in concern.

Whatever news came from the scouts Chipkali sent out this morning has the men on edge.

A few minutes later one of the men approaches me and sets a bowl of dried figs in my lap before turning to walk away.

"Are you going to untie me so I can eat?" I ask.

He turns to face me. "Chipkali said your hands are to remain tied."

"How am I supposed to eat without my hands?"

The man stares at the ground near my feet. He won't meet my gaze. "Sorry," he says under his breath, and then returns to his post.

I find Chipkali a ways off, watching me with his arms folded across his chest. He wants to see what I'll do. He wants to watch me eat directly from my bowl like a dog. I turn away. I'd rather go hungry than give him the satisfaction.

* *

It's not until hours later that the activity in the camp finally starts to wind down. The low buzz of small talk dwindles, the trunks of food and supplies are closed and locked, men drift, yawning, into the tents.

At first I think the Crocodile King plans to leave me exactly as I am, sitting here on this log, my hands tied behind my back. I've been twisting my arms for hours, trying to loosen the knots at my wrists, but I'm no closer to escaping. And the thought of having to stay here all night, of not being able to lie down and sleep for a few hours, fills me with grim dread.

But then Chipkali glances in my direction and barks orders at one of his men, who jogs over to me and roughly grabs my elbow. "Bedtime," he says as he hauls me to my feet.

My shoulder screams in pain, and I have to bite the inside of my cheek to keep from crying out.

"I need a personal moment," I say through gritted teeth.

"What are you talking about?"

I cock my head to one side and give him a pointed look.

"Oh," he says. "I don't know if . . ."

"You're seriously not going to let me pee?"

He hesitates before he lets out a long sigh and pulls me toward the edge of the camp. "Go over there," he says, pointing to a copse of trees. "No more than ten paces. You have two minutes."

"I'll need you to untie me," I tell him.

He gives a dark laugh. "I'm not that stupid, sweetheart. Sorry."

"How do you expect me to . . ."

He shrugs. "Not my problem."

I'm tempted to kick him in the shin, but I settle for a dirty look before stomping off.

But I don't even make it to the tree line before the camp breaks into chaos.

The heavy pounding of a dozen pairs of boots, the shouts of men as they're pulled half-asleep from tents. And cutting through it all a silky voice that makes my blood run cold. Balavan. "Gather them all in the clearing," he says. "But bring Chipkali to me."

My guard glances over his shoulder and jabs a finger in my direction. "Don't you move." Then he runs toward the center of the camp like a fool. But I have no intention of obeying his orders, of standing here and waiting to die. I spin on my heel and run. I make it only a short distance before I trip and fall flat on my face.

Balavan's voice booms through the camp, "Either I get what I want or all of you are going to die."

I wriggle, snakelike, and conceal myself behind a giant banyan. It's not nearly good enough, but it's the best I can do.

Chipkali's gruff laugh ricochets off the trees. "I wouldn't be so sure *you're* not going to be the one to die, old friend." His voice betrays none of the worry I saw in his eyes earlier.

"You should know that Bagharani is dead," Balavan says. "She spilled her own blood to protect her followers. But I'm guessing I'll need to use a different approach with you. You've never struck me as the selfless type."

A long silence stretches over the forest and I creep farther forward, straining to hear. Sticky leaves adhere to my cheeks like glue.

"You're not surprised that the Tiger Queen is dead," Balavan says. It's too dark to see him, but I can picture him pacing in front of the Crocodile King, his fingers steepled in front of him. "Interesting. So you questioned Iyla before you killed her? Or is she still alive?"

Chipkali doesn't reply, and Balavan gives a dramatic sigh. "No matter. She'll be dead in a matter of months either way. But *you,* my friend, will be dead by morning."

My breath sticks in my throat. What does he mean? That he'll capture me? Or that I don't have as much life left as he promised?

And why doesn't Chipkali simply transform into the Crocodile King? How can Balavan possibly expect to kill him when he knows what Chipkali can become?

"I'm going to torture you slowly," Balavan says. "Until you beg to spill your own blood."

In one swift motion I'm yanked to my feet. I try to scream, but the sound is swallowed by the rough flesh of a palm pressed against my lips. I arch my back and try to land a kick, but without being able to use my arms, without being able even to see my assailant to know where to aim, I'm helpless.

He drags me away from the tree and pulls me deeper into the forest. I'm filled with sudden dread. I thought I had prepared myself to die, but the fear that claws at my throat is a stark realization that I'm not ready.

My attacker adjusts his hold, and the hand covering my lips shifts just a little. I open my mouth to scream.

"Stop." A hiss against my ear.

I go still. Fazel.

I don't know if it's a betrayal or an escape.

We move farther away from camp. Fazel keeps his hand over my mouth. I try to shake him off, to reassure him that I won't cry out, but he still trudges forward, half carrying, half dragging me. My shoulders scream in pain—they feel like they're being wrenched from their sockets.

Finally, after what seems like an hour, Fazel stops. He pulls a knife from his belt and steps behind me. I squeeze my eyes closed and wait for the cool metal to bite against my throat, but I feel it against my wrists instead. Fazel slices through the rope in one fluid motion, and my arms are suddenly free.

Relief stings my eyes.

"Is that better?" Fazel asks, his breath stirring against my neck.

I roll my shoulders. Every inch of me aches. "Yes," I tell him. "Though you could have done that a long time ago. I would have come willingly."

"Sorry," he says. "I had only a small window of opportunity to get away. I couldn't risk you screaming."

"For an hour?"

I can barely see him in the darkness, but his voice is apologetic when he answers. "If we got caught on the way out, I thought we'd both be safer if you looked like a prisoner."

"*You'd* be safer, you mean." I can still feel the pressure of his hand against my mouth, the sharp panic of not being able to breathe.

"Are you angry? Because I just risked my life to get you out of there."

"Would you be angry if you'd been tied up all night and then dragged through the forest like a dead animal?"

"I was trying to help," he says.

"Well, if that's what you consider help, then I think I'll go it alone. Thanks anyway." I spin on my heel and stomp off.

"You're headed back toward camp," Fazel calls out.

I stop walking and blink up at the black velvet sky. A storm of confusion rages in my chest—I don't know if I want to punch Fazel or fall into his arms and thank him. I ache all over and I'm so tired. I slide to my knees.

A hand falls on my shoulder. "Iyla, let me help you. I thought you needed to get to your friend."

I shake him off. "Why are you doing this?" I ask.

He sighs. "Why am I doing what? Helping you? Maybe because I don't want you to die."

I look up and try to study Fazel's expression, but he's nothing more than a shadow.

"I don't believe you."

"You think I want you dead?"

"I think people don't risk their lives for someone they just met. I think you took me so that if you got caught on the way out, you could turn me over to Balavan in exchange for your own life. That or I'm just a pawn in whatever game you're playing with the Crocodile King, a stepping-stone to getting more power."

Fazel sucks in a sharp breath. "The man Chipkali sacrificed was my best friend's father." The low, strained tone of his voice slides under my skin like a sharp sliver. "The two of them were like family to me—at least until . . ." Fazel's voice breaks, and something inside me cracks open. I want to comfort him, but the words stick in my throat.

"Kalan lost his mother a year ago to a sudden illness, and her death changed him. He withdrew from everyone— even me—and he hasn't been the same since. Chipkali knew that he was struggling, that the grief was overwhelming. He knew it better than anyone. But still he turned Kalan into an orphan." Fazel scrubs a hand over his face, and when he speaks again, his voice is weary. "So, no, Iyla. I'm not using you as a stepping-stone to get more power. I'm just tired of watching people die."

A trembling silence stretches between us, and I wish I could take my earlier words back. But it's too late. It's always too late.

"I'm sorry," I tell him.

He doesn't answer. He just stands up and starts walking. I scramble to follow him and wonder if I'm so broken that I can't tell the difference between the people who care about me and the people who want to kill me. Because right now everyone feels like an enemy.

CHAPTER TWENTY-SIX

Marinda

There are no safe houses on the path between Colapi City and the Widows' Village, and none of us are up for walking all night, so we sleep under the stars. I curl my body around Mani's and bury my face in his hair until he's snoring softly. Each time he stirs in the night, I hold him tighter and tell him that he's safe. And each time Deven hears me whispering, he puts a palm on my shoulder to tell me the same thing.

When morning comes, Deven and I have barely slept at all, but Mani looks better rested than he did yesterday, so my bleary eyes and the headache pulsing at my temples are worth it. At least for one night I could chase the bad dreams away.

"How much farther?" Mani asks as we roll our blankets and stuff them into our packs.

Deven pats him on the shoulder. "We'll be there before dark."

And for the first time since we left the Raja's palace, I see Mani smile.

* *

We arrive in the Widows' Village just as the sun is starting to set. The houses spilling across the landscape in a shock of blue always fill me with a raw kind of wonder.

The path widens as it dips into the valley, and I reach for Deven's hand. Our eyes meet and he must see the worry in my expression, because he stops and cups my face in his hands.

"It's going to be okay," he says. "We're safe here."

I don't remember the last time I truly felt safe, but I give him a thin smile. "I hope so."

The small blue cottage Iyla and I stayed in a few months ago is just around the bend, nestled alongside dozens of other houses painted the same bright hue. The muscles in my shoulders start to unwind.

Then we turn the corner and I freeze. My hand flies to my mouth. A man stands on the porch, his back to us.

Balavan.

"What is it?" Deven asks. His hand tightens around mine.

"How did he find me?" The snakes stir in my satchel, tasting my panic. My heart slams against my rib cage.

"Talk to me." Deven's voice is low and urgent. "What is it?"

"It's Balavan." I take a step backward. "He's the leader of the Naga."

"Marinda," Mani says, his voice trembling. "What's wrong?"

I squeeze Mani's fingers. "Don't let go of me," I tell him. "Do you understand?"

But it's too late to run. Balavan has already turned, has already seen the three of us standing hand in hand. A smile stretches across his face.

"Rajakumari," he says, moving in our direction with the grace and speed of a mountain lion. "You disappoint me." His eyes gleam like puddles of spilled ink.

I gently push Mani behind me without letting go of his hand. Deven stands next to me so that Mani is completely blocked from view.

"I'm not coming back with you," I tell him.

Balavan gives a cold laugh that sounds like shattering glass. "You're brave," he says, taking a step toward us. "I'll give you that. But you always speak too soon."

"Just go." My voice is tight. I can barely get the words out. "You don't need me."

"I underestimated you." Balavan circles us like a predator. Deven and I move along with him so that Mani stays behind us. "I thought mentioning the boy would make you more compliant. But now look what you've done. You've made it so much easier to kill him."

Behind us, a sharp intake of breath. A whimper. Mani presses his face into my back.

"You aren't killing anyone," Deven says. He moves closer to me.

"There would be no point in killing him," I say. "It would gain you nothing."

"Oh, but that's where you're wrong, *rajakumari*. I think killing him is the only way to get everything I want."

"What is it you want?" I ask.

Deven stiffens beside me. "This isn't a negotiation," he says in a low voice. But it is. I'll do whatever it takes to protect Mani.

One of the cottage doors opens, and a widow steps out onto the porch. "Marinda? Is that you? Are you all right, love?"

I don't take my eyes off Balavan. "Yes," I call. "I'm fine." I repeat my question, softly this time so the woman won't overhear. "What do you want?"

"What I've always wanted," he says. "Absolute power."

"You don't need to kill Mani to get that."

More doors have opened, and the widows of the village are spilling into the lane. They surround us like a small army, but I wish they were younger, stronger. I wish they had weapons.

"Oh, but I do," Balavan says. "Letting the boy live didn't work so well the last time."

My palm slicks against Deven's. My mouth goes dry. "What do you mean, the last time?"

Balavan takes a step toward us. "You will serve me," he says. "Or you will be compelled to serve me."

Deven starts to move between me and Balavan, his hands curling into fists. But then he recoils as if he's been struck. My vision fractures and bends. The air around Balavan seems to fuzz at the edges, and my nose is filled with a smell I would recognize anywhere. Musky. Reptilian. The odor of the Nagaraja.

I spin, expecting to find the Snake King at my back, but

I only find dozens of widows with their hands pressed to their mouths.

I turn back to Balavan. His skin is rippling, turning from deep bronze to pale white. His neck and body stretch and elongate. Huge scales emerge along his body. Before my eyes, Balavan transforms into the Nagaraja. Cold horror rolls over me.

Mani screams.

Deven yanks on my arm. His eyes are wild. "Come on," he says. "We need to run."

A dark cloak falls over my mind, warm and comforting. Like the moment just before falling asleep. I touch my wrist, expecting to find Jasu, but she's not there.

Daughter.

The word slices through my mind, and I stumble backward. This isn't one of my snakelets.

"Marinda," says a voice at my side. "Listen to me." Deven. I turn my head and see his panicked expression, hear the chaos erupting around us, see the widows streaming from their houses. If I could . . .

Stop fighting me.

My gaze goes back to the Nagaraja. I want to stop fighting.

Good, he says. *Yes.*

He dips his head low until I can see my reflection in his pitch-black eyes. And Mani is standing beside me. Mani. I have to protect him.

I turn toward my brother, and his expression goes vacant. I think of what Kadru said about snakes, how they can focus on only one mind at a time. If I can make the

Nagaraja concentrate on me, maybe he won't be able to control Mani.

"Someone bring me a weapon!" Deven shouts. I resist the urge to turn to him. I have to distract the Snake King. Mani's face is slack. He takes a step forward.

I burrow my voice into the Nagaraja's mind. *Leave him alone.*

Deven grabs me around the waist and tries to force me to move, but I push him away. I have to help Mani.

You will serve me.

I know I need to hold on to my own thoughts. But they're like water—slippery and impossible to control.

Pledge your loyalty to me, Marinda. It's the only option.

The Nagaraja's gaze falls on my face like a flame. His eyes swallow me.

Yes, I tell him. I take a step forward.

My mind floods with the Nagaraja's approval. He stretches toward the sky. Large yellow drops of venom fall from his fangs as his mouth opens wide.

But his thoughts waver and he swivels, looking at something behind me. Our connection breaks. Awareness rushes over me like a cold gust of wind. Deven is scooping Mani into his arms. He starts to run and the Nagaraja roars in frustration.

The ground trembles.

Panic chokes the breath from my lungs. "Deven!" I shout, sprinting toward him. He looks over his shoulder, one moment of hesitation that's just long enough to lose his footing. The Nagaraja crashes into him from behind. Mani flies from his arms as Deven slams to the ground.

Watching them is like drowning just under the surface of the water. Like being able to see the shimmering light just above me, but knowing I might run out of air before I can get there. Something inside me fractures. I'm going to lose them both. Deven clambers to his feet, but he's too late. The Nagaraja is already going for Mani.

My blood spikes with fire. I race toward my brother, flinging myself on top of him and curling my body around his. Above us, the Snake King unhinges his jaw. He's going to devour us.

"That's enough."

I turn to see who spoke. Vara—the widow who took care of me and Iyla when we first arrived in the Widows' Village—stands with her hands on her hips. The snake turns toward her, mouth agape. He rears back as if surprised. I want to shout at her, to tell her to save herself while she can, but Mani's trembling body, his small, soft sobs, make the words stick in my throat. I can't risk drawing the Snake King's attention back to us.

Deven runs toward me and Mani and pulls us into his arms. We sit together in a huddle.

"Stop," Vara says. "Be gone from this place."

The Nagaraja lets out a hiss that chills my blood. He whips his head toward the three of us, his tongue flicking from his mouth to taste the air. Mani squeezes his eyes closed and clings to me.

My mind scrambles for a way to keep the Nagaraja out of my head. *Jasu. Help me.* She reaches for me without hesitation. She shows me Deven's thoughts, colored red with panic. She shows me Mani's terror. The other snakes join in, and my mind is filled with the thoughts of the people I love. The agony pulsing through my chest feels like it might break me in half, but at least I know I'm me.

And then a voice, powerful and razor sharp, silences every thought but one.

Come to me, Marinda. There is no pain here. No suffering.

My thoughts are washed clean of worry and fear. I stand. A yank on my arm nearly pulls me back down, but I resist.

No pain. No suffering.

A vision of Vara crowds into my mind, and I shake my head, confused. The Nagaraja's grip on me has slipped. Jasu. She's still trying earnestly to help me. Now she must be grasping for any mind within her reach. But the real Vara never looked like this, fierce and ready for battle. Jasu's thoughts are getting muddled.

Marinda. My worries vanish again, and the relief is like a drug.

Distantly I remember that I'm supposed to be resisting something. But it's like trying to wake from a dream—hovering on the cusp of two realities, but not fully present in either. I push through the gauzy film around my thoughts, and the Nagaraja's grip on me falters.

Jasu's mind is frantic. She gives me one vision after another to try to keep me tethered to reality, but they've stopped making sense. Vara stands behind the Snake King. The air around her vibrates, and then in one fluid movement her body is gone in a burst of blue and green and feathers.

Garuda.

I suck in a sharp breath.

I can't tell if the bird is real or not until the Snake King swivels to face her. He strikes, but she's too fast for him. She soars above his head. She's so big she blots out the setting sun.

Deven grabs both my hand and Mani's and drags us to our feet. "Run," he says. And we do. We race toward the path that leads out of the Widows' Village, but Mani's legs are too short to keep pace. Deven gathers him up midstride and presses forward. Behind us I can hear the rustle of giant feathers. The hiss of the Snake King. The shriek of Garuda either attacking the Nagaraja or distracting him, I can't tell which.

I throw a glance over my shoulder.

"Don't," Deven says. "Keep going."

"We'll never escape," I tell him. "There's nowhere to go." But I don't slow down.

Deven's breathing is ragged. Mani's arms and legs are wrapped so tightly around his neck that they cut off his air supply. But Deven doesn't slow down either. We're nearly to the trail that leads out of the valley when my desire to run is abruptly snuffed out like a candle in a stiff breeze. I turn.

"No," Deven says. "Marinda, please, no."

The Nagaraja's eyes meet mine. *Aren't you tired of feeling powerless?*

Yes.

I take a step toward him. Two steps. Three.

Another mind—a tiny, trembling one—pokes at the edge of my thoughts. It's a pinprick of light that breaks through the darkness. I stop walking. Jasu pulls my attention upward. Garuda hovers above us, her wings flapping against an orange sky.

The Nagaraja roars in frustration. *You will serve me.*

"Do something!" Deven shouts, and I'm not sure if he's talking to me or the bird. His fingers circle my wrist and he pulls me toward him. He shifts Mani with his other arm. "We need to move, Marinda, please."

I can feel myself being drawn toward the Nagaraja like a shell caught in the tide. I try to resist, but the weight of his mind is too much.

Your loyalty or your death. Choose.

I can't hold on much longer. I manage to pull my gaze away long enough to see Garuda tuck her wings to her sides and dive toward the earth. My heart gives a leap of hope. If she attacks the Nagaraja, we might have a chance to escape.

But when I glance at the giant bird again, she's not diving toward the Snake King.

She's aiming for us.

CHAPTER TWENTY-SEVEN

Marinda

One moment I'm pledging my loyalty to the Nagaraja, and the next I'm soaring through the sky in a cage made of bone.

I used to have dreams like this as a little girl—gliding through the air, the world blurring and tilting beneath me, until I woke with a sharp sting of disappointment. But this doesn't feel the same. My stomach lurches and my eyes burn. It's all wrong for dreaming. Something feathers across my hand, drawing my gaze sideways. Deven caught in a cage of his own. He holds Mani with one arm and reaches across the space between us with the other, his fingers barely grazing mine.

"Is this real?" I ask, but the wind snatches my words away.

I try to make sense of what happened back in the Widows' Village, but my mind is still swathed in a confused fog. I remember Balavan circling me, threats shooting from his lips like arrows. I remember trying to remain calm. Trying to find any exposed weakness, any way to kill him before he killed Mani.

And then it seemed . . . for just a moment it seemed like Balavan *transformed* into the Nagaraja. But that can't be right. Maybe he summoned the Snake King. And once the Nagaraja was there, I lost all sense of reality. Because there are other things that don't make sense. Like my vision of Garuda.

My mind has finally splintered. Maybe the Nagaraja has killed me after all, and these are the last delusions of the dying. Yet . . . the cage does look suspiciously like the foot of a bird. And the sharp edge digging into the small of my back could be a talon. I squeeze my eyes closed.

If we really are in the clutches of Garuda, does that mean she saved us from the Snake King? Or did she win us in the battle only to kill us herself?

We slow down, and my stomach flips as the ground rises to meet us. Just before we touch down, the cages spring open, and the three of us tumble onto the grass and roll to a stop.

Mani scrambles for me and flings himself into my arms. His eyes are streaming, and I'm not sure if his tears are from the wind or if he's crying. I pick him up and he buries his face in my shoulder. Deven laces his hand through mine, and together we turn.

A bird the size of a house stands just a few steps away. Her body is sapphire blue with emerald-tipped wings. Her head tilts to one side as she studies us. I've barely taken her in when her body starts to shimmer and shrink. And before

I know what's happened, she's transformed into a woman. My chest gets tight.

"Vara?"

It really is her. Jasu's thoughts weren't as jumbled as I suspected. But Vara? She brought me and Iyla warm loaves of naan and taught us how to plant brinjal seeds. And if she's Garuda . . . my mouth goes dry. Balavan is the Nagaraja. My mind wasn't playing tricks on me. A wave of nausea rolls over me. It was one thing to work with the Naga to try to bring the Snake King down, but to think that I've been sharing a home with the Nagaraja himself. That I've broken bread with the creature that tried to kill my brother. I press a hand to my stomach.

"I'm sorry I frightened you," Vara says, smoothing her palms over her brown sari as if she's worried the flight has left her clothing wrinkled. "But I was rather out of options."

My mouth can't work fast enough to form all of the questions that pool on my tongue. "What . . . how . . ."

"Come inside," she says, "and we'll talk."

I take in my surroundings. We're on the top of a mountain, and just behind Vara is a small house, oddly shaped and roughly hewn from individual pieces of wood. It looks very much like a bird's nest. Deven and I exchange a glance, but there's really no choice but to follow her.

The interior of the cottage is bigger than I expected, though still smaller than all of the homes in the village. A rustic wooden table is nestled in a tiny kitchen off to the left. On the other side of the room is a seating area with a sofa and several soft chairs. Brightly colored rugs are scattered over the uneven floor.

Vara opens a cupboard and pulls out a copper kettle. "Would anyone care for some tea?" she asks, as if we've just dropped in for a visit. As if she didn't just transform into a giant bird and carry us here.

Mani is the first to answer. "Yes, please," he says, squirming out of my arms. A flash of surprise goes through me. Maybe he feels like the offer of a warm beverage is the only normal thing that's happened in hours. Maybe it makes him feel as if the world is starting to make sense again. I wish I could say the same.

The three of us take a seat in the kitchen and wait while Vara fills the kettle with water and puts it over the heat. She hums as she works, and the sound is out of place alongside my frantic pulse. Deven reaches for my hand under the table, and the pressure of his fingers curled around mine makes me feel like I can breathe again. It's then that I realize I'm feeling not only my own fear but Mani's and Deven's too. Miraculously, my satchel is still slung across my body. Relief washes over me as I slip my fingers inside and count five small heads.

I reach out with my mind to comfort them, and I find their thoughts as frightened and hectic as my own. Poor babies. *It's okay,* I tell them. *You're safe now.*

"I imagine you have questions," Vara says a few minutes later as she settles in the chair directly across from me and slides a tray filled with cups of steaming ginger tea between us.

Deven is the first to speak. "The Raksaka are human?" Once he says it out loud—the question that's been haunting me for the past several minutes, the question that seemed too unreal even to consider—a chill crawls down my neck.

"Yes," Vara says. "We are."

Mani's eyes go wide and he sucks in a sharp breath.

"Oh, monkey—"

"I'm thirsty," Mani interrupts, taking a cup from the tray. He's trembling so much that tea sloshes onto the table, but he doesn't seem to notice. He plunks a handful of sugar cubes into the hot liquid and stirs as if watching the crystals melt is the most fascinating thing he's ever seen.

I put a hand on his shoulder and he glances up at me. His expression is exactly the same one I've seen on his face a dozen times—fear masked by a grim determination to be brave. It's the look he used to get every time Gopal turned up with a breathing treatment, every time I had to leave him in Gita's care to do a job. My heart aches for all the ways I've failed to protect him.

I turn back toward Vara. "How is that possible?" I ask. "For the Raksaka to be human?"

"It should never have been possible for us to be anything other than human," she says. "But I suppose you wouldn't have any way of knowing that. The histories have been lost." She flinches at her own words. "No, that's not true. We destroyed them. We didn't want future generations to know the horrible things we'd done."

Deven lets go of my hand. His palms fall flat against the table. "I think you'd better start at the beginning," he says.

Vara sighs and her gaze gets far away. "Thousands of years ago the four of us were Sundari's most skilled warriors—

gifted, yes, but nothing more. We helped stop an invasion from a neighboring kingdom, and as a way of honoring us, the Raja who was in power at the time named us the Raksaka—the four protectors of Sundari."

She takes a cup of tea and stirs it absently, as if she's forgotten we're here. I don't dare say anything to break the spell.

"It felt good," she says finally. "We had the love and adulation of the people. They trusted us to protect them and we did." She sets her spoon on the edge of her saucer. "It was partially the Raja's fault too. He turned us into living legends. He exaggerated the stories of our skill—if the people believed that the four of us were an unbeatable weapon, it would keep them in line. And it would dissuade other kingdoms from attacking Sundari.

"And then we started to age. Our followers could see that we wouldn't be around forever, that the kingdom would one day be vulnerable again. A handful stepped forward and offered up one of their ten lives so that we could live for another generation."

My breath catches in my throat. "Did you accept the offer?"

Vara meets my gaze, and the lines in her forehead seem to deepen. "It seemed like the right thing to do at the time."

"But . . . that's terrible." To use people's fear to take from them their most precious asset—one of their lives—it's unconscionable.

"It gets worse." Vara's gaze drops to her tea, and several seconds pass before she starts speaking again. "Our followers suggested that we'd be doing a service to our kingdom if we took all the remaining lives of truly evil people—those who had committed unforgivable crimes. After all, we'd use the lives more nobly than they would. We'd use them to protect Sundari, while the criminals would likely make the same choices in a new life that they'd made in their current one."

Deven's hands curl into fists. "But if you took every life, they would be denied a second chance. Their souls would cease to exist." The silence grows heavy in the room. "Please tell me you didn't do it."

Vara presses her lips together. "We did. That and so much worse. Eventually the dungeons were empty. There were no more truly evil people in Sundari—none that got caught, anyway. Losing all ten lives was a forceful deterrent. But, sadly, we had grown power hungry. We started taking any lives we could get, evil or not."

The information curdles in my stomach. All this time I thought that finding Garuda was the answer. I took the tattoo on Deven's shoulder, and the fact that the Naga wanted the Pakshi dead, as an endorsement. But just because she's the Snake King's enemy doesn't mean she isn't as evil as he is.

"But how did you get to be a *bird*?" Mani asks.

The question breaks the tension and we all laugh. I put my arm around Mani's waist and pull him close. He leans his head on my shoulder.

Vara smiles and directs her answer toward Mani. "Humans have ten lives, but did you know that higher animals, like birds and crocodiles and tigers, have unlimited lives?"

He shakes his head. "I didn't know that. So Smudge will be able to come back?" My throat aches at the hope in Mani's voice.

"Smudge was our cat," I tell Vara softly. The one Gopal killed to teach me a lesson.

Vara lays a hand on Mani's wrist. "She probably already has. Perhaps she'll find you again."

He gives her a tremulous smile. "Really?"

"Animals often try to replicate the life that made them the happiest. Your Smudge may find you yet."

Mani sighs happily, his original question forgotten.

"You know, monkey, maybe it's time for you to get some rest," I say. He's probably heard enough disturbing information for one evening. I turn toward Vara. "Is there a place he could lie down?"

"I have a bedroom just down the hall," she says, but Mani is already shaking his head.

"I don't want to be alone."

I bite my lip. I also don't want him hearing the rest of our conversation. "How about if you lie on the sofa right over there? You'll still be in the same room, but you can rest."

He shrugs. "I guess."

As I settle Mani on the sofa and pull a blanket up to his chin, a knot lodges in my chest. I wish I could curl up beside him, close my eyes and forget all my troubles. But I can't. I press a kiss on the top of his head and join the others in the kitchen. It's going to be a long night.

* *

My tea has grown cold.

But I curl my fingers around the cup anyway and I keep sipping, just to give my hands something to do. Darkness has enveloped the cottage. Outside the window, stars scatter across the inky sky.

"Let me make more," Vara says, reaching for my cup, and I wonder if her hands need a job too. She refills the kettle, puts it over the heat and then joins us at the table again.

"So what is the answer to Mani's question?" Deven asks softly. "How did you become a bird?"

Vara takes a deep breath before she begins talking. "Because animals can live forever, we found a way to"—her gaze darts to Mani for just an instant, and her voice gets even softer—"to take on enough of their lives that we could become them at will." She phrases the sentence carefully so that she doesn't upset Mani in case he's still listening, but I understand the meaning. More bloodshed, more sacrifice in the Raksaka's quest for power. My stomach turns at the thought of the four of them killing animals over and over again in order to live forever. I suddenly remember when Deven first told me about the Raksaka. He said that the animals physically grew bigger as their followers increased. Goose bumps race across my arms at the thought that maybe they gained size not because more people were willing to live for them but because more were willing to die for them.

"Why are you telling us all this?" Deven asks. The question lights a spark of hope inside me. Because if Vara were truly as evil as the Nagaraja, she wouldn't have saved us in the Widows' Village. She wouldn't be explaining herself now. And her expression wouldn't be so full of regret.

Vara traces a finger around the rim of her teacup. She doesn't answer for a long time, but when she finally looks up, her eyes are shiny with tears. "Redemption," she says. "Hope. Trust that you can make a better future than we did. Our followers wanted to turn us into gods." A single tear tumbles from her lashes and crawls down her cheek. "And when we agreed to let them, we turned ourselves into monsters."

I have the urge to cover her hand with my own, to offer her some kind of comfort, but I can't bring myself to do it. I'm not sure she deserves forgiveness. "Where have you been all this time?" I ask. "Why have you been hiding instead of helping?"

Vara dabs the moisture from her face with the back of her hand. "I had been growing uneasy with our . . . arrangement for decades. I started spending more and more time in my human form. I stopped killing. And because I wasn't taking more lives, I started to age. I tried to persuade the others that the era of the Raksaka was over and that it was time to let ourselves die. I made a little headway with Bagharani and even with Chipkali, but Balavan wanted no part of it. Ultimately, he was more persuasive than I was, and it created a rift between me and the others. But Balavan was furious I'd even tried to suggest that we were wrong. He declared war against me. I fought hard for a long time, but then something happened that made me realize I couldn't win against him, that I couldn't stand to lose anything else, that I was so tired of fighting."

I open my mouth to ask what it was, but Vara waves a hand in the air. "It doesn't matter," she says. "Suffice it to say I was heartbroken. So I hid myself away in the Widows' Village, where I could live in peace. They've been the happiest years of my life."

I swallow. "Until we brought the Nagaraja to your doorstep."

She squeezes my hand. "It was going to happen sooner or later," she says. "I couldn't hide forever."

The teakettle whistles and I jump in my seat. Vara gives me a small smile. She pours the tea into fresh cups, and the smell of ginger fills the air.

"So what do we do now?" Deven asks. "How do we destroy him?"

Vara sighs. "That's the tricky part. We have to convince him to destroy himself."

"What do you mean?" I ask. "Why?"

"If we kill him, he'll simply be reborn. His supply of lives is nearly endless—when the Raksaka learned how to take on animal form, we could only hold so many extra lives at once. So we got around the problem by creating relics."

All the air leaves my lungs. "He's been hunting for relics," I say. "I've heard him talk about them. But I haven't been able to figure out what they are or what they mean."

Vara presses her lips together. "The relics were created from parts of the giant animals we became—mine is a large blue feather, Bagharani's is a claw, Chipkali's is a tooth and Balavan's is a snake scale. They serve as reservoirs for the lives we've taken—they can hold a nearly limitless number of years, and when we need more, we can simply draw from the relic. The only way to truly kill any one of us is to destroy our relic. And the only way to destroy the relic is by our own blood. But there's a catch. The blood has to be willingly shed."

"Why?"

Her voice is soft when she answers. "Sacrifice has enormous power, but sacrifice given instead of taken is the most powerful thing of all. When our followers started giving up their lives as tokens of their devotion, as gifts—it made us nearly unstoppable. Such great strength can't be stolen. It must be set aside. The only thing strong enough to destroy a power so immense is the blood of the power itself."

"But then how did the Nagaraja kill the Tiger Queen?"

Vara sucks in a sharp breath. "Is that true?" she asks. "Bagharani is really dead?" The raw look of pain on her face slices through me. It makes me think of Iyla—of the way I felt when I heard Balavan claim she was likely dead—and this time I can't resist taking Vara's hand. My own grief rises in my throat, and it takes me a full minute before I can speak. The snakes stir in the satchel at my feet. Vara's hand trembles in mine.

"I'm so sorry," I say softly. "But it's true. I heard Balavan telling the members of the Naga about how he'd killed her. And then I saw her followers rioting in the city."

"He must have convinced her to spill her own blood," Vara says. "It's the only explanation."

"But how would he have done that?"

Vara shakes her head. "I don't know."

"The Nagaraja will never willingly die," I tell her. "There must be another way."

Something flits across Vara's expression. Deven must have noticed too, because he sits forward.

"You have an idea," he says. "What is it?"

She shakes her head. "It's probably nothing. It's just . . . years ago I heard—now, it was just a rumor, mind you—but I heard that Balavan had fathered a daughter. If that's true, then her blood could destroy the relic also. Provided she could be found, of course. And then turned against her father." Vara pinches the bridge of her nose. "Which is unlikely on both counts."

My stomach plunges. My mind chills. *Daughter.* It's what the Nagaraja has called me both times I've faced him.

Bile rises in my throat. Balavan is my father. And my blood is the key to destroying him.

CHAPTER TWENTY-EIGHT

Iyla

Fazel and I hike until dawn. I'm so exhausted I can barely stay upright, but the threat of being caught by either Balavan or the Crocodile King is like a wind at my back pushing me forward. No matter which of them survived, they'll want me dead.

"We should find a place to rest," Fazel says. The pink light from the sky makes his eyes luminous.

"No," I tell him. "We need to get farther away."

He pulls on the back of his neck, leaving angry red handprints. "We can't keep walking forever."

I give him a sidelong glance. "Maybe you can't."

He comes to an abrupt stop. "Did your parents slap you every time you showed kindness or something? Is that why you can't seem to serve up a single comment without a side of vinegar?"

His words are laced with acid, and they spill over the

raw wounds that fester in my chest. I try to keep the pain from showing on my face. "I don't have parents," I tell him. "I was kidnapped as a baby to serve the Nagaraja. So maybe keep your commentary to yourself."

Fazel's shoulders slump and he lets out a long breath. "I'm such a jerk. I'm tired and I'm hungry and . . . I'm so sorry." The tenderness in his expression makes it hard to look at him.

I shrug. "It's not your fault," I say. "You're not the one who kidnapped me."

"Iyla." His hand catches mine and he spins me toward him. "I'm trying here."

I press my lips together and study the ground. Finally I meet his gaze. "Trying what, exactly?"

He throws his other hand in the air. "Trying to apologize. Trying to connect with you." His jaw tightens. "Trying not to kill you."

"Well," I say, "you're doing it all very nicely."

His lips twitch like he's struggling to hold back a smile. "Give me a little bit of a break?"

I give him a small nod instead of an answer.

We start walking again, but Fazel doesn't let go of my hand. I could pull away, but I don't. I tell myself it's because I need the extra support to remain on my feet. I tell myself that I need to stay on Fazel's good side so that he'll keep helping me. I tell myself a thousand lies so I don't have to let go.

"So what about you? Did you have some kind of horrible childhood that led you straight to the Crocodile King?"

"No," Fazel says. "I had a great childhood and parents

who told me I could be and do anything. Unfortunately, what I wanted to do was have adventures, and what I wanted to be was a hero."

"And now you've thrown all that away to traipse through the kingdom with me."

"Oh, I don't know about that. Saving a pretty girl from certain death—it has a nice heroic ring to it, don't you think?"

He smiles like he's teasing, but something flutters in my stomach. It makes me feel off-balance and out of control. I can't decide if it's a pleasant sensation or a horrible one.

"Maybe I rescued *you* from certain death," I tell him. "You might have been Chipkali's next meal. Or Balavan's."

Fazel laughs and my stomach spins and swoops. Definitely an unpleasant sensation. "Yeah," he says. "Maybe you're right." He squeezes my fingers. "Or maybe we saved each other."

My heart clenches. I search for a caustic retort, something that will push him so far away that I won't have to risk his choosing to leave on his own. But my mouth feels glued shut. And then the moment slips away and it's too late to argue with him.

Maybe he's right. Maybe we did save each other.

* *

Morning slides into afternoon, and the forest gives way to a small village—the trees have been thinning for hours now, and in the distance we can see a herd of cattle and a collection of small huts with thatched roofs and walls made of clay.

"I smell food," I say. My stomach grumbles, and a wave of dizziness washes over me.

"Let's hope they take pity on us," Fazel says. We hurry forward. A cluster of children play in the sand in front of one of the huts, and their laughter floats to us on the breeze. Not far away a group of women cook over a fire pit—one woman stirs a huge pot of curry with a large stick. Another woman flips chapati in a hot pan. My mouth waters. I'm ready to run toward the village and beg the women for a bite.

But then Fazel's sharp intake of breath makes my heart stutter. He puts a hand out to stop me from moving and presses a finger to his lips. I follow his gaze, and my stomach clenches.

Several of Balavan's men—members of the Naga who are vaguely familiar—approach from the opposite direction and begin to circulate among the children. We crouch behind an oxcart piled high with hay. My pulse thunders in my ears. How did they beat us here? But then I remember how quickly they were able to find Chipkali and his people even after they'd packed up and left the peninsula.

We're too far away to hear what the men are saying, but they seem to be describing us. One of the men holds a hand, palm down, just above his head—probably to show them that Fazel is a bit taller than he is—and then he does the same gesture near his shoulder to indicate my height.

At first the children give the men little notice. They shrug and continue scooping sand into piles at their feet. And then one of the men reaches into his pocket and pulls out a handful of coins. They glint in his palm like jewels.

The children stand—he has their full attention now. They bob their heads up and down. They grab for the money with eager fingers.

If the children spot us, they will sell us out without a second thought. And I wouldn't blame them. Their homes are tiny with crooked walls. Their knobby arms and legs protrude from their clothing like twigs. And the money they're gazing at is enough to feed every man, woman and child in their village for a month. The Naga man shakes the coins one more time before he pulls them out of reach and slips them back into his pocket.

There's a price on our heads.

The children groan in protest, and one of the women leaves the cook fire to investigate. As the men talk, her gaze sweeps across the horizon. I flinch and duck out of sight. Several long seconds pass before I dare move enough to see what's happening, and by that time the men are gone.

"What are we going to do?" I ask Fazel.

His expression is tense. "I don't know. I had planned on going back to my flat or maybe even to my parents' cottage just to be safe." He shakes his head. "But if the Naga are already searching for us, neither of those places is an option."

I glance around for any sign of a landmark. "Where are we, exactly? Do you know?"

"In a tight spot, I'd say."

Fazel and I both spin toward the voice. The woman who was talking to Balavan's men a few minutes ago now stands behind us with her hands on her hips.

The little hope I still harbored drains away. I start to

stand—better to face my fate with dignity than to cower in fear—but the woman gives a sharp shake of her head.

"Stay where you are," she says. "I have no intention of turning you over, but if any of the children see you . . ." She looks back toward the village and her eyes go soft. "Well, their grumbling bellies are likely to win out over their kindness."

"How did you know we were here?" I ask.

She purses her lips. "I could see your feet peeking beneath the wheels," she says. "Next time you might want to find a more solid hiding place."

"We didn't exactly have a lot of options," I say sharply. "Why are you even helping us? You're probably going to turn us over the next chance you get." Fazel pinches the skin above my elbow. He means it to be a warning, but it makes anger flare in my chest. I slap his hand away.

The woman narrows her eyes. "I don't sell people," she says. "No matter the price." She swipes a strand of silver hair from her forehead. "I'll bring you something to eat in a bit. In the meantime, stay out of sight."

Fazel and I don't speak for several minutes after the woman leaves. And then he clears his throat softly. "I'm sorry I pinched you," he says finally.

"No, you're not."

He sighs and drops his head into his hands. And I feel it again, that inextricable pull toward him. The desire to say more than I should. The urge to move closer to him when it would be smarter to move away.

"I just meant that I understand why you did it," I say. "I

know you were trying to keep me from saying something that would make her decide to turn us over to Balavan's men."

"You assume the worst of people," he says.

"I wasn't assuming the worst of you," I tell him. "I was—"

"No," Fazel says. "You assumed the worst of *her*. She was trying to help us, and you—"

"Served up my comments with a side of vinegar?" The words have been echoing in my mind since Fazel said them earlier today. They still sting.

"Yes," he says.

"I have trouble trusting kindness."

Fazel turns toward me, and his gaze falls on my face like sunshine.

"Why?" he asks.

A lump forms in my throat. "Because . . ." I fumble for an explanation that will make sense to him. "Because my whole life it's never been given for free." A beautiful flat, a new sari, an expensive bottle of perfume, all came with price tags—finding the Naga targets to kill, letting Kadru drain away my life, keeping Marinda in the dark about who we were really working for. Even kindness from Marinda came with strings attached—the price of her friendship was that she expected mine in return. And that may have been the steepest price of all.

Fazel circles my wrist with his fingers, his thumb stroking my skin and leaving a trail of heat behind. Then he turns my hand over and gently traces the lines on my palm like he's a fortune-teller and touching me will reveal all my secrets. Sparks dance down my spine.

He leans toward me, and my pulse goes erratic. His breath moves across my cheeks like a warm breeze. His eyes are two bright coins.

A throat clears behind us and we spring apart. "Sorry to interrupt," the woman says. She hands each of us a thin metal platter laden with thick, fragrant curry, chapati and a mug of water. My stomach growls.

"Thank you," I say. "I can't tell you how much we appreciate this."

The woman tilts her head to one side as if she can't puzzle out whether I'm being sarcastic or sincere, and I feel a little pang in my chest.

"Leave the dishes here when you're finished," she says. "I'll collect them later. And then once the children go inside, it's time for you to move along."

"Thank you," Fazel says. The woman gives him a small nod—there seems to be no question that his gratitude is heartfelt.

"You're about a two days' walk south of the capital," the woman says. "Stay safe." She turns on her heel and walks back toward the village.

Fazel and I eat in silence. We scoop up curry with bits of chapati and stuff it into our mouths. We lick our fingers and sip our water without saying a word.

Finally, when our platters are empty, Fazel speaks. "I think we should start heading east. We can make it back to my flat in Bala City in a few days."

I set my tray on the ground. "But the longer we're out in the open, the more likely Chipkali is to find us. I think we should go west, toward the Raja's palace."

Fazel laughs. "And then what? Knock on the door and ask if we can hide out for a while?"

"Yes," I tell him. "I know someone there who might be able to help us."

"Who?"

I bite my lip. "The *rajakumar*."

His eyes widen. "The *rajakumar*? You know the prince of Sundari?"

I shrug. "A little."

"You are full of surprises," Fazel says, and I can't help feeling a tug of satisfaction at the expression of wonder on his face. Now I just have to hope that Deven is at the palace. And that he'll be willing to help us.

CHAPTER TWENTY-NINE

Marinda

My mind is like a floor covered in broken glass. No matter which way my thoughts turn, they run into sharp edges that pierce and slice and make me bleed.

If Balavan is my father, what does that say about me? That the raw materials used to make me are flawed? That I was broken before I was ever born? I've always mourned the fact that the snakes poisoned my blood. But if Balavan is my father, maybe it already came that way.

Mani's gentle snores rumble through the room. He's been out for hours. Deven is lying next to me on the floor, his breathing deep and even, one hand buried in my hair. It seems I'm the only one who heard the crack as the world split in two. I'm the only one who can't imagine relaxing enough to rest ever again.

And yet . . . my eyes grow heavy and I lurch into a fit-ful sleep. I toss and turn and wake suddenly in a cold sweat, only to stumble into nightmares again. When I finally open my eyes to a room filled with soft light from the gray dawn, a headache pulses in my temples. I touch Deven's shoulder. He stretches and scoots into a sitting position. His hair sticks up in all directions, and despite the pain in my head, the sight of him pulls a smile from me.

"Good morning," he says through a yawn.

But I don't answer. Because the sofa Mani slept on last night is empty, except for a tangled pile of blankets.

"Mani?" I jump to my feet and hurry to the back of the cottage. "Mani?"

Deven follows close behind me. "Mani?" he calls, his voice tinged with as much panic as my own. "Where are you?"

Vara hurries from the back bedroom in a pumpkin-colored silk robe. Her dark hair falls in a long braid at her back. "What's wrong?"

"Mani is missing." My breath comes in small gasps.

Her eyes go soft with concern, and she touches me gently on the elbow. "He can't have gone far, love. We'll find him."

But something is wrong—it seeps into my bones like an icy wind. The three of us search through the cottage, opening every cabinet, peeking under every piece of furniture, calling Mani's name in increasingly alarmed voices. But it's no use. He's not here.

I run to the front door and yank it open. The chill mountain air slaps me in the face and steals the breath from my lungs. "Mani?"

Deven follows me outside and pulls me into his arms. I bury my face in his chest, and he rests his chin on the top of my head.

Vara joins us outside. She shivers and pulls her robe tightly around her body. "He's probably just exploring," she says. "He wouldn't have just wandered off in the middle of the night."

Deven's arms tense around me before they fall away. "Actually, he might have."

Vara tilts her head. "What do you mean?"

"He has nightmares," Deven says. "And sometimes he wanders."

I make a strangled sound at the back of my throat. "He wanders?" At the waterfall Deven told me that Mani had started walking in his sleep, and I pictured him stumbling around his bedroom, bumping into furniture. But this— disappearing from the top of a mountain—it's more than sleepwalking.

I go to the edge of the cliff and peer at the sheer path that leads downward. My stomach pitches at the sight. "He could be dead."

"He's not dead," Deven says, but I'm not sure if he's trying to convince me or himself.

Vara pinches the bridge of her nose. "I can't imagine he would have tried to make his way down," she says. "What could he have been thinking?"

Her comment lights a spark in my mind. I turn toward Deven. "Search for bugs," I tell him.

A crease appears between his brows. "Bugs?"

"Or small rodents—mice, gophers, moles—anything will work."

"Marinda." He says my name carefully, like he's trying to get me to back away from a cliff. "How will that—"

"Just do it," I say, spinning around and running into the cottage.

I find my satchel on the floor near the sofa and coax the snakes onto my lap. All five of them are hungry, and their minds pulse with worry and dread. I don't know if the emotions are their own or if they're only reflecting my own thoughts back to me.

I need your help, I tell them.

The snakes' minds bend toward mine, eager. Just then Deven walks into the cottage and freezes. I know how it must look to him—five small white bodies wrapped around my arms, when only a few months ago even the thought of being in the same room with a snake made me break out in hives. But this is different. My snakes are only babies, and they're loyal to me, not Kadru.

"Where do you want these?" He doesn't quite meet my eyes as he holds out his cupped palms. Dirt clings to his knuckles and fingernails, and a handful of beetles wriggle against his skin.

I dip my head toward the rug. "Come sit with me."

Deven lowers himself to the floor. He's grown a hint of stubble overnight, and I have the sudden urge to run my thumb along his jaw. Instead I clear my throat and hold up one of the snakes. "This is Jasu," I say. "And I hope she can help us find Mani."

His expression shutters, and for a moment I worry that he's going to ignore me. Or worse, storm out of the cottage. But then, in a soft voice, he says, "How?"

Vara comes inside and sits in a chair across the room. If she's shocked by the scene before her, she doesn't show it.

I absently run my fingers down the length of Jasu's body while I try to find the words. "Ever since the Nagaraja entered my mind in the cave . . ." I swallow. This is harder than I thought. "I've been able to command snakes."

Deven's sharp intake of breath sends a stab of pain through me. "I'm not turning into Kadru," I tell him. His eyes narrow just a fraction. "I'm not. It's just, when I realized that I could see inside their minds and that they could see inside the minds of other people . . ."

"You knew you could use them to help you spy on the Naga," Vara says.

I turn toward her. "Yes," I say, talking only to Vara now, but hoping Deven will hear, will listen. "I stole several snake eggs. I waited for them to hatch and then I trained them. It's how I found out about Bagharani." My gaze flicks to Deven. "And how I found out that Iyla is missing."

Deven stands and chews on his bottom lip. He shifts his weight. "So how will the snakes help us find Mani?"

"They're hungry right now," I say. "But I'm hoping once they've eaten—once they can focus—they'll be able to remember Mani's thoughts last night. And, with any luck, that will give us a hint about where he's gone."

"Clever girl," Vara says. "Let's hope it works."

I pluck the insects from Deven's palm one by one, and as I feed the snakes, I nudge their minds toward Mani. At first I can't get them to focus on anything except the sensation of food—the crunching of tiny bodies, the gulping and swallowing. But then, eventually, their stomachs fill and their thoughts are more easily guided.

Focus on Mani, I tell them. *What was he thinking about last night?* When Jasu finally finds a thread of thought that I recognize as my brother's, a pulse of horror seizes my heart. Her impression of Mani's mind has a familiar quality to it—the hypnotic pull toward the will of another, the sense of being swallowed up and consumed. It's exactly the way I felt both times the Nagaraja took control of my mind. What if the Snake King formed a connection with Mani when he bit him? What if Mani's nightmares are more than just dreams? What if Balavan can control Mani like I can control the snakes? The room starts slowly spinning. I've forgotten how to breathe. Jasu's panic presses her thoughts even more firmly into my mind, like stepping on a rock in wet sand. And there are only two clear words she can remember from Mani's sleep-fogged mind—*palace* and *Nagaraja.*

I spin toward Deven and Vara. "I think . . . I think he went to the Naga palace." The words feel strangled as they leave my throat.

The snakes scurry back into the satchel as if they already know we're leaving. And we are. We're leaving now.

But I'll never get there in time. Deven must see the stricken look on my face, because he takes my hand. "Maybe Mani didn't leave that long ago," he says. "Maybe we can still catch him."

"Maybe," I say. But I don't believe it. If I'm right about Balavan being able to control Mani, then he already has my brother. And he likely provided a faster way for Mani to get down the mountain. It's already too late.

Suddenly my ability to communicate with the snakes seems more like a curse than a gift—one more thing that connects me to Balavan. One more thing that proves we're alike. The thought curdles in my stomach.

I climb to my feet and turn in a slow circle around the cottage, as if I might find answers scrawled on the walls or dangling from the rafters. But there's only emptiness. And silence. And a hopelessness so thick that it makes the air hard to breathe.

Vara touches my elbow and I yank away from her. I'm too broken to be touched.

"I can help," she says.

My cheeks are wet and my legs feel spongy, like they might give out at any moment. "I don't see how."

She cups my face in her hands and looks at me with the kind of tenderness usually reserved for children. "Tell me where we're going, love, and I'll fly you there."

CHAPTER THIRTY

Marinda

We fly over the mountains so fast that it feels like pieces of me are falling away. Or maybe it's just the sensation of my heart breaking.

I wish I could wind back time like a ribbon on a spool. I wish I could start over and make different choices—to leave Sundari forever instead of trying to take down the Naga, to go so far that they would never be able to find me.

Mani would be safe then. I wouldn't know I was Balavan's daughter. I wouldn't feel so powerless.

The landscape blurs beneath me and I squeeze my eyes closed.

A few minutes later, at the edge of the rain forest, Garuda unclenches her feet and releases me and Deven from her grip. This time I'm prepared and I land softly on the ground. I turn to see the giant bird shrinking, her form growing fuzzy at the edges as she changes. It's not until she's fully human again that I see there's something wrong. Vara's skin is ashen, and her hair is pasted to her damp forehead. She's trembling.

I rush to her side. "What's wrong?"

She tries to take a step, but she falters and nearly falls. "It's been too long," she says, clutching my arm. "Becoming Garuda twice in such a short time . . ." She trails off, and it takes a moment for her to catch her breath. "It's too much."

A weight settles on my heart. We can't just leave her here. But I'm desperate to get to Mani—the feeling burns in my lungs like I'm underwater.

Vara gives me a weary smile. "Go," she says. "I'll be fine."

But she won't. She's struggling to remain upright. Her eyes are glassy.

My gaze flicks to Deven. "Will you stay with her?"

His expression goes tight around the eyes. He shakes his head. "No. I'm not letting you go alone. Balavan could kill you."

"If he decides to kill me, there won't be anything you can do about it." The truth of the statement trembles between us for a long moment before Deven sighs and runs a hand over his face.

"I don't like it," he says. It's as close as I'll get to a concession.

Deven takes Vara's arm and helps her sit. Her back rests against a thick tree trunk, and her head is tipped toward the sky, eyes closed, as if she's already asleep and dreaming of flying.

"Take care of her," I say, squeezing Deven's fingers before I turn and walk away.

"Marinda, wait." Deven jogs toward me and wraps an arm around my waist, pulling me tightly against him. His lips meet mine, at first soft and then urgent—like the kiss is a message in a language only we understand. Like it's a goodbye. I pull away while I still have the strength.

"Be careful." Deven says the words against my mouth, so that I swallow them. So that they become part of me.

I run my knuckles across his scruffy jaw without making any promises. I can't afford to be careful. Not when I need to be brave.

"Marinda." Deven's voice frays at the edges. I can tell what he wants to say. *Don't go.* But he knows me well enough not to say it. I take his hand in mine and press a kiss to his palm. His skin is warm, and it takes all the restraint I have not to wrap myself up in him.

But when I start up the path to the Naga palace, I don't look back.

* *

The guards are missing. The abandoned trail curves in front of me like a beckoning finger. Panic flutters in my chest. It's a trap. And my only choice is to walk into it with my eyes wide open.

As I climb the steep staircase that leads to the front door, the only sound is my sandals slapping against the stone. The rain forest is as silent as a held breath.

I enter the palace without knocking. Amoli isn't in the foyer to greet me or to ask me where I've been.

I reach for Jasu's mind to see if she can find Mani, and

then, with a sharp stab of regret, I realize that in all the commotion and worry about Vara, I left my satchel behind. My mouth goes dry. The snakes can't access Balavan's mind anyway, but I still feel defenseless without them. The thought sparks a memory, and I rush to my bedchamber.

The room looks more or less as I left it, though the bed has been made—the silky coverlet is pulled taut and covered with artfully placed pillows. The platters of food have been cleared away. But there's still a sari draped over one of the chairs, as if Amoli thought I might return at any moment and need something clean to wear. I hope that means she wasn't too thorough when she tidied up.

I kneel beside the mahogany wardrobe and reach into the far corner. It takes a moment of fumbling in the dark before my hand closes around the jewel-encrusted dagger I took on the day we questioned Pranesh.

I thought Iyla was being ridiculous when she insisted I choose a weapon—I thought I was the last person in the world who needed another way to kill—and until a few moments ago I'd almost forgotten I had it at all. But now I make a mental note to tell her she was right. Fresh pain seizes me. If I ever see her again. The wound of losing Iyla is still too raw to acknowledge for more than a moment at a time.

I pull in a deep breath and try to empty my mind of every thought except confronting Balavan and getting Mani back.

The dagger probably won't help me with either of those things, but I like the weight of it in my hand. It gives me something to hold on to. Some promise that I'm not as powerless as I feel.

The corridor is as tomb silent as the rest of the palace. I take off my sandals and sling them over one finger so that I can slip quietly toward Balavan's rooms. My heart flutters like hummingbird wings against my rib cage. What if the snakes were wrong? What if Mani isn't here at all?

I ease the door open and my breath catches. Balavan sits on the floor with his legs crossed and his hands resting softly on his knees. His eyes are closed, and his head is tipped upward as if in prayer.

The pose is so relaxed, so unconcerned, that it makes me want to shake him until his eyes rattle from their sockets. I clear my throat, and his eyes fly open.

"Where is Mani?"

Balavan blinks. He shakes his head, disoriented, like he's been startled from sleep.

"Where is my brother?" A range of emotions flit over his face until finally he seems to register my presence.

And then he laughs.

Rage explodes in my chest. I stride forward and slap him hard across the face. My fist tightens around the dagger in my other hand, and I swing it toward his neck. But I'm too slow. Balavan catches my wrist and twists it sharply. I gasp at the sudden jolt of pain. The weapon falls from my fingers and clatters to the floor.

He clucks his tongue like I'm a misbehaving child. His hold on my wrist softens, and he absently runs his thumb over the scars there. "Poor *rajakumari*," he says. "How you've suffered."

I yank away from him, and my gaze darts around the room. "Where is Mani?"

Balavan rises to his feet. "You can't possibly think he's here."

My certainty wobbles, but I try to keep my expression blank. It's only a game, and Balavan is trying to keep the upper hand. "I know he's here," I say.

"Do you?" Balavan's eyes glitter. He's taking too much satisfaction in this. Which means I'm wrong about something.

My heart gives a slow pulse of dread.

"He's just a little boy," I say, and my voice sounds small and far away. "He's done nothing to you. If you want to hurt someone, hurt me."

"Oh, Marinda, my love." Balavan steps close to me and tucks a stray lock of hair behind my ear. "Mani has actually done a great deal for me. I don't want to hurt him. I want to use him." He laughs. "And unlike you, he's more than happy to oblige."

My stomach lurches. "What are you talking about?" I ask. "Use him for what?"

His fingertips move along the curve of my cheek. "For whatever I want."

I was right. Balavan can control Mani. A whirlpool of emotion rages inside me. "Where is he?" I ask softly. "What did you do?"

"I didn't do anything. But your brother . . . he's in Colapi City delivering what I hope will be a crushing blow to our enemies."

The words fall like knives.

I chose the wrong palace.

When the snakes showed me the words *Nagaraja* and

palace, I just assumed that Mani would be here. Not at the Raja's palace. I press a palm to my chest to try to keep my heart from escaping.

Balavan sighs. "Don't you see, Marinda? You keep trying to play a game that I've already won."

He's right. I can't meet his eyes, can't bear to let him see the resignation in my expression. Instead I glance around the room—at the glazed-tile walls and the rich furniture swathed in silk. The endless bowls of fruit and the gleaming hardwood floors. It's the room of a man who gets everything he desires.

And now he'll get whatever he wants from me too. As long as Mani is safe, I will give him the entire world in my open palms.

My gaze lands on the diamond-shaped pearl mirror on the wall. Something catches in my mind, and my pulse speeds up. I remember seeing it the first time I visited this room. *Even the mirrors are made of gems,* I thought. But on closer inspection, it doesn't particularly look like a mirror. I only assumed it was one because Balavan examined his reflection on its surface.

It actually looks more like a giant snake scale.

Understanding seeps into me. It's the relic—the reservoir that holds all of Balavan's extra lives. Only Balavan would have the arrogance to keep it on display. To gaze into it like a mirror and let it reflect invincibility back at him. But then again, who would ever think to look for it here? Maybe hidden in plain sight is the most secret place of all. I take a step back toward where the dagger lies on the floor.

I need to keep talking to distract Balavan, or he'll never let me get close enough.

"What do you want from me?" I ask.

"I want you to stop fighting," he says. "I want you to take your place by my side, where you were always meant to be."

"Why would I do that?" Another step. And then another. The dagger is within reach now, but I don't dare look at it.

"Because I control Mani," he says. "And that means I control you."

I let my face go slack. I sink to my knees and drop my head in my hands. My hair is loose, and it falls around me like a dark curtain, shielding my hands from Balavan's view. In one fluid motion I snatch the dagger from the floor and spring to my feet.

Balavan's gaze drops to the weapon. His eyes widen and then he laughs. The sound hits my ears like breaking glass.

"Oh, Marinda," he says. "That would be a very bad idea."

He takes a step toward me and I back away, inching closer to where the scale hangs on the wall.

"Maybe," I say. "Or maybe it's the best idea I've ever had."

He moves forward again and I twist away, like he's my partner in a carefully orchestrated dance. I try to remember exactly what Vara said about destroying the relics. *Blood . . . willingly shed. The blood of the power itself.* And then, *I heard that Balavan had fathered a daughter.* If I'm his daughter—if we share blood—then I should be able to destroy the relic.

"You really think such a small blade can defeat me?"

My fingers inch along the handle of the dagger until I'm holding the blade in my palm. I squeeze as hard as I can. Sharp pain bites into my flesh, and bright blood wells at the wound. I run toward the wall and press my hand to the giant scale.

And nothing happens.

CHAPTER THIRTY-ONE

Iyla

Fazel and I slept under the stars last night, curled on a patch of unyielding ground, and now I can't quite roll the stiffness from my neck. I arch my back and stretch my arms above my head. From the corner of my eye I catch Fazel studying me with an expression on his face that I can't quite name.

When he sees me looking, he drops his gaze and suddenly finds a thread on his sleeve that seems to need his urgent attention.

"Is everything okay?" I ask.

There's a hint of red at the tips of his ears. "Sure," he says without looking up. "Of course."

I want to press him—I know there's something wrong—but he seems so uncomfortable that I decide to let it drop. Ever since he nearly kissed me, something has shifted between us, like the pressure in the air right before a storm.

"We should get moving," I say. The Raja's palace is only a handful of hours from here, and the less time we're out in the open, the better.

Fazel's shoulders relax at the change of subject. "Lead the way."

He aggressively avoids touching me as we walk. Before, he didn't hesitate to lay a hand on my forearm to emphasize a point, or squeeze my shoulder to get my attention. But now he walks with his hands clenched at his sides. The space between us is conspicuously large.

It shouldn't bother me. And yet . . . in that moment when Fazel's breath danced across my cheeks, I thought I might actually have the first kiss that wasn't ordered by someone else. That wasn't part of a job. That wasn't initiated by me. The possibility of having that choice—to be offered affection and have the option to accept or reject it—made me feel desired and powerful and important.

Until Fazel pulled away. And now he seems awash in regret.

The cold weight of being someone's mistake presses on my chest.

As we get closer to the palace, a fragrance drifts to us on the wind—at first it's delicate, and then, with every step we take, it grows more oppressive, more cloying. It reminds me of when Gita used to make chutney, and the smell of the boiling fruit would burn the inside of my nostrils like I was being suffocated with the scent of sugar.

When we finally crest the hill, the palace stretches across the valley floor like a giant, glittering dragon. Fazel lets out an appreciative sigh, but we barely have time to take it all in before I see smoke in the distance. It curls above the tree-tops in a massive brown column. Fazel and I break into a run. And we aren't the only ones. The palace doors emit servants in a frantic stream. They carry water in buckets and barrels and even bare hands as they rush toward the fire.

Time seems to slow as I take in the scene before me. The air is filled with the crackle of breaking branches, the shouts of people racing toward the fire, the thud of damaged trees hitting the ground. The wind changes direction and clears the smoke directly in front of me.

Orange flames lick up trees that hang heavy with pale fruit. In the center of it all is a small form. I squint. A boy.

And one of his arms is missing below the elbow.

Slick dread goes through me as I race forward. Why isn't anyone doing anything? Why isn't anyone trying to help him?

"Mani!" I shout. "Run." But my voice is swallowed up in the chaos.

"What's wrong?" Fazel asks as he pulls alongside me.

I point toward Mani. "I know him," I say. "He's my . . ." I choke back a sob. "We have to get to him."

Fazel gasps as he spots Mani. He grabs my hand—the first time he's touched me all day—and we hurry forward.

"Mani!" I call again. "Run." But he isn't moving. He stands motionless in the midst of the smoke and flames, as if he's oblivious to the danger around him. As if he's the eye in a storm of his own making. A gust of wind changes the direction of the smoke and obscures Mani from my sight.

I try to speed up, but I can't make my legs move fast enough.

My throat starts to close from the dirty air. "There's a little boy in the fire!" I shout to the men entering the orchard from the opposite side. "You have to help him." But no one is listening to me. No one cares. The wind shifts again and the smoke clears.

And Mani slumps to the ground.

CHAPTER THIRTY-TWO

Marinda

Blood drips from my palm and trickles toward my elbow. I cut myself too deeply, and the sight of the wound makes me light-headed. The giant snake scale is painted with my crimson handprint, the fingers smeared and unnaturally long. My blood has ruined the beauty of the luminescent surface but otherwise seems useless.

My hand throbs. Maybe I'm expecting too much of a change. Maybe Balavan will quietly die without anything happening to the scale. I turn to face him, my injured palm cradled in the opposite hand. The jeweled dagger lies at my feet.

Balavan holds perfectly still. His gaze jumps from the scale on the wall to the blood running down my arm. His head is cocked to one side, his lips pursed, and then, like clouds parting, understanding dawns on his face.

"Garuda told you about the relics." He says it so softly

I barely hear. His voice has lost the mocking arrogance it had earlier. Now his tone is full of something quieter and far more dangerous. Seething rage. He gives a harsh laugh. "You thought you were my *daughter*? You thought you could destroy me?"

The hair on the back of my neck prickles. My mouth goes dry.

Balavan takes a step toward me. "Was it the title that confused you?" he asks. "The fact that we made you our *rajakumari*? It's true that the title of princess is usually reserved for the daughter of a king. But not in this case."

A tremble builds in my legs. I'm not sure if it's from the blood loss or the raw fear of being in the same room with a man I just tried—and failed—to kill. But once I start shaking, I can't stop.

Balavan strides to his wardrobe, yanks open a drawer and pulls out a white dhoti. He rips off a section and holds it out to me. I blink in confusion.

"For your hand," he says. "You'll ruin my rugs."

I take the cloth and wrap it tightly around my palm. Blood blooms against the white fabric.

"You're not a beloved child, Marinda," Balavan says. "You're a spoil of war."

My voice is trapped in my throat. What does he mean? Which war? The war between him and the Raja? Between him and the other members of the Raksaka?

"I don't understand," I say. The room seems to tilt, and I have to lean against a chair to keep from toppling over.

Balavan steps close to me and runs his cold knuckles along my cheek. His liquid eyes stay fixed on my face like he's drinking me in. I can't look away. His eyes in human form are nearly as mesmerizing as they are when he becomes the Nagaraja. I should have known who he was from the moment I met him.

"Darling Marinda," he says. "I value you so dearly because you represent my greatest victory over my enemy."

I swallow. "What victory?" I ask. "Creating a *visha kanya*?"

He smiles. "Not just creating a *visha kanya*," he says. "Creating a *visha kanya* out of *you*."

"Stop speaking in riddles." I mean for it to sound forceful, but it comes out faint and strained. My hand throbs.

"Let me see," Balavan says. He takes my palm in his and wraps it with a fresh piece of cloth, putting pressure on the wound until the bleeding finally slows. I'm desperate to ask about Mani. Where he is. If he's safe. But now that I know Balavan can control my brother, I don't dare draw his attention away from me.

"So much blood," he says. And then, as if it's an afterthought, "Your blood *could* destroy a relic, you know. Just not mine."

All the air leaves my lungs in a rush of understanding. A spoil of war. The Nagaraja is not my father. Garuda is my mother. Her words come back to me. *He declared war against me. . . . But then something happened that made me realize I couldn't win against him, that I couldn't stand to lose anything else, that I was so tired of fighting.*

What if that something was losing me?

Balavan must see the dawning realization on my face, because he laughs. "What better revenge than stealing Vara's

· 265 ·

daughter and turning her into a weapon who would kill her own mother's followers?"

Horror wells in my chest. Not just at Balavan's actions, but that Vara gave up on fighting him. That she gave up on *me*.

"You're a monster," I say.

He gives me a rueful smile. "That's true," he says. "But aren't we all?"

I back away slowly. Inch by inch I move toward the door.

"Go ahead," he says. "Run back to her." I freeze. It must be a trick—he's baiting me. I spin on my heel and dash out of the room, but Balavan doesn't even bother to chase me. It's like he knows he can get to me whenever he wants.

But still I run.

When I finally stumble from the rain forest, Deven gasps. His gaze travels from my blood-splattered sari to the cloth wrapped around my hand that's soaked and dripping red. He rushes to my side and I fall against him.

"What happened?" he asks, and then before I can answer, "I never should have let you go in there alone."

I lift my eyes to his. "Mani is in Colapi City. At the palace."

He smooths the hair away from my face. His hands are trembling. "But that's good, right? He went home."

I shake my head. "No. I don't think so."

"Why not? Marinda, talk to me. What happened in there?" Deven's voice is jagged.

"We have to get to him," I say. "Balavan can control him."

"What do you mean, control him?"

"Mani wasn't having nightmares. Balavan was taking over his mind."

Deven sucks in a sharp breath. I can see him putting it together—the sleepwalking, the destroying things, the haunted look in Mani's eyes. "I'm so sorry," he says. "I . . . Is he in danger? Has Balavan hurt him?"

"I don't know. He said something about using Mani to defeat his enemies. I'm not going to feel better until I have Mani in my arms."

Vara lifts herself from the ground. "Balavan doesn't have the boy, but he let you go?"

I bite my lip. "He wanted you to see me," I say. "He wanted you to know what he'd done."

Vara sways on her feet. She shakes her head, confused. "What he'd done?"

"To your daughter."

"To my . . ."

The air around us stills. A spasm of disbelief crosses Vara's face, and then a dozen other emotions flit across her features—pain, sorrow, regret, acceptance—before her expression melts into tenderness. She cups my chin in her palms. "Is it true?" Her voice breaks. "I thought he killed you."

I flinch. "No," I say. "He thought it would be better revenge to use me to kill the people who believe in you."

Vara's hands tremble. "He was wrong."

Her expression is so raw, so gentle, that it stirs something inside me, but I don't know if it's love or hate. Pain or joy.

"I can't . . . I can't do this right now. I have to get to Mani."

Vara catches one of my tears with her thumb before she drops her hands to her sides. "Of course," she says. "Let's focus on your brother. We can talk later."

I turn to Deven. "How will we ever get to him in time?"

He pulls me against his chest and presses his lips to the top of my head. "We will," he says. "We'll get an elephant."

"It won't be fast enough."

"I'll take you," Vara says softly. "We can be there in a few minutes."

I spin to face her. "You're not strong enough," I say. "You're still shaking from bringing us here."

"I can manage. It will be all right."

"But what if the journey kills you?"

"If I die making sure you are able to hold someone you love in your arms again, it will be a worthy sacrifice." Vara smiles sadly. "I've given you so little," she says. "Let me give you this."

CHAPTER THIRTY-THREE

Marinda

Garuda shudders as she flies. Her body tips and bobs, careening through the sky like she can barely maintain control. When we finally touch down, air surges back into my lungs. I didn't realize I was holding my breath.

But my relief lasts only a moment. Something is wrong.

The palace grounds are swarming with people, and the smell of something sickly sweet hangs in the air. Behind me, Vara groans. She's struggling to climb to her feet. Her face is pale, and her breath is coming in shallow gasps.

I grab Deven's elbow, but I don't even need to ask before he's already springing into action. He scoops Vara into his arms. "I'll take her to my father's physician," he says. "Go find Mani."

"Thank you." I press a kiss against his cheek and hurry away.

I'm running toward the palace when I spot Iyla in the

distance. A weight lifts from my chest. So much has gone wrong today that the sight of her is like a jug of sunlight spilling over me.

She's alive.

Hope nudges aside my worry for just a moment. Iyla is alive.

She's sitting on the ground in the middle of a clearing. Her back is to me, and she's bent over like she's searching for something. For a moment I waver between rushing toward her and running toward Mani's room in the palace. But maybe Iyla has seen Mani. Maybe she can help me find him.

A young man kneels next to her, his hand on her shoulder. He's tall, with hair cropped close to his scalp. He whispers something to her as he strokes her hair. Her shoulders start to tremble.

My heart strains against my rib cage, understanding before my mind does. The trees surrounding Iyla are charred and black. Smoke hangs heavy in the air, along with the scent of burning fruit, and I suddenly realize where I am. This isn't just a clearing in a copse of trees.

It's the Raja's maraka orchard.

A series of scenes flash through my mind. Balavan asking me how so many of the Raja's men were able to survive my kiss. The answer falling from my lips like liquid poison as I told him about the antidote and the orchards. And then, just a few hours ago, Balavan in his rooms, his face tipped to the sky, trance-like, as if whatever task he was engaged in required his full concentration. I interrupted him. I pulled his attention away.

And now Iyla is curled toward the earth. Her shoulders shake, her body racked with sobs. I don't want to know why she's crying. I don't want to know what she holds in her arms. But my feet don't seem to care what I want. They take me toward her anyway.

"Iyla." The word is ragged as it leaves my throat.

She turns. Her face is smudged with soot, dirty except for where tears have cleared a crooked path.

Mani lies limp in her arms. His eyes are wide and still, as if his own death has caught him by surprise.

I fall to my knees. My throat closes as I push Iyla aside and gather Mani in my arms.

I thought I had known pain before, but I was wrong. Nothing I've felt before compares with this sudden, brutal slash of despair that leaves me breathless and bleeding. Bleeding out hope. Bleeding out regret for the last few months that I've spent far away from Mani, missing him every second but not holding him in my arms. Bleeding out every misguided, horrible decision that has brought me to this moment where my tiny brother is dead and I'm not.

A strange keening sound fills the air, as if the very sky grieves along with me.

It takes a long time before I realize that the sound is coming from me.

* *

Dark clouds roll across the sky, and thick raindrops soak through my sari, splatter on my bare arms, plaster Mani's hair to his small forehead. And still I don't move.

"Marinda." Iyla's hand is gentle on my shoulder. "Let's take him inside."

I don't answer, and so she sits beside me and rests her forehead on her knees.

"This is my fault," she says finally.

"No," I tell her woodenly. "It's not."

"Balavan asked me what you cared about," she says. "I told him the only thing that was really important to you was Mani." Her voice breaks. "I'm so sorry, Marinda. I didn't think . . . I never thought . . ."

My chest is hollow where my heart and lungs used to be. "Balavan didn't need you to tell him what was important to me. Not when I'd stabbed him to protect Mani. You didn't do this. I did. *I* told him about the orchard. *I* told him about the antidote." I stare off into the distance, but I don't see anything except my own regret. "And then I interrupted him while he was controlling Mani, so he never gave Mani the order to leave the orchard. So Mani never woke up from his nightmare."

"Oh, Marinda." She leans her head on my shoulder. "Don't do that to yourself." She wraps one arm tightly around my waist and rests the other on my knee, as if by sheer force of will she can hold me together.

But no one can. Not anymore.

I brush the hair from Mani's forehead. I'd give anything to have him back. I'd sacrifice every life I have left if I could just . . . I spin toward Iyla. "Go get Vara."

She gives me a blank stare like I've spoken a different language.

"I'm sorry." She touches my arm gently. "Vara's not here. She's back in the Widows' Village."

I shake my head. "No. She flew us here. Deven took her to the palace physician."

Iyla bites her lip. "Marinda . . ."

"Vara is Garuda," I say.

Iyla's eyes widen, but she doesn't look nearly as shocked as I would have expected.

"Vara can fly Mani to Kadru. And Kadru will know how to give him life back."

Understanding washes over Iyla's expression, and without another word, she clambers to her feet and sprints toward the palace.

Kadru has refused to help me twice now, but this time I won't take no for an answer.

CHAPTER THIRTY-FOUR

Iyla

Fazel is waiting for me at the edge of the orchard. When Marinda found us, he left, mumbling something about privacy, about not belonging. I thought he'd use the opportunity to slip away. I was sure I'd never see him again.

But he stayed.

Everyone is always leaving me, but Fazel stayed.

"How can I help?" he asks. The question pricks my heart.

"We need to find Deven," I tell him.

He doesn't ask why, doesn't ask what Deven looks like or where he might be. He just catches my hand in his and we run together.

* *

The palace halls are choked with smoke. At first Fazel and I nearly turn back, but then I notice that people aren't streaming for the entrance. They're holding their noses and throwing open windows. The fire must already be contained. But the gossip isn't.

Dozens of frenzied conversations blend into a low buzz, and it takes three tries before someone finally tells us how to find the physician.

"He's not working from his regular quarters," says a tiny woman with a shock of long silver hair. She extends a bony finger toward a passageway directly opposite from where we're standing. "But last I saw, he was down that way, and around the bend." She looks both Fazel and me up and down. "Which one of you is hurt?"

I don't bother to answer her as we hurry away.

We're about to turn the corner when I hear arguing. I pull on Fazel's arm and we both stop, just out of sight.

"Why would you bring her here? She's a stranger. She means nothing to me, and now my valuable resources have been squandered helping her."

I unlace my fingers from Fazel's and move so that I can see around the corner. Deven and a man I assume is his father face each other. The Raja's arms are folded over his chest.

"It's a long story," Deven says. "But believe me, I wouldn't have if it wasn't important."

The Raja's jaw tightens. "The physician is rather busy at the moment, seeing as the boy set fire to his rooms."

Deven reels back as if the Raja struck him. "Mani did this?"

"The physician's rooms and the orchards both. It's all gone—the venom, the antidote. Every maraka tree. Every piece of fruit. Every tool we have to protect us from the *vish kanya*."

"Is he all right?"

"The physician?"

"No," Deven says. "Mani."

Sickening dread pulses through me. Deven doesn't know.

The Raja's arms drop to his sides. His hands curl into fists. "I have no idea. Nor do I care."

"But . . ."

"But nothing. The Nagaraja used the boy to destroy us, and I refuse to worry about whether we'll return his weapon to him unharmed."

"You *knew*?" Deven says.

"That the Snake King has been giving him orders from afar?" The Raja waves a hand in front of his face, as if swatting away a troublesome fly. "Of course I knew. Following the boy during his spells was providing some useful intelligence—at least it gave us some idea what the Nagaraja was interested in. But now . . ." He rubs a hand over his chin. "I never expected this."

"How could you? We could have tried to break the connection. We could have helped him."

"And lose a valuable source of information? Don't be sentimental, Deven. They have spies. We have spies. This is war, not a childhood game."

"If anything happens to Mani," Deven says, "I will never forgive you."

"I don't need your forgiveness. I need you to learn how to lead." The Raja storms away but calls back over his shoulder, "Before I see you again, I expect you to pull your-self together."

Deven closes his eyes and massages his forehead. I try to call to him, but it comes out as a small, strangled noise at the back of my throat. Deven freezes. Turns.

"Iyla? What are you doing here?" And then he must see the look on my face, because his expression goes tight. "Have you seen Mani?"

I nod. Bite my lip.

"Is he . . ."

I shake my head, and Deven sinks to his knees. He shoves his fist into his mouth. Fazel puts an arm around me, as if I were the one falling apart. Maybe he knows I am.

Finally Deven scrubs at his face. "I need to get to Marinda," he says.

"She's asking for you," I tell him. "She said to bring Vara."

CHAPTER THIRTY-FIVE

Marinda

It takes Vara several tries to transform into Garuda. Her face paled when I asked. "The Raksaka . . . We don't usually change so often. Even when I was still"—she swallowed hard—"accepting sacrifices, I was weak if I spent too long out of human form."

The physician was able to give Vara something to ease her pain, and she had a short time to rest, but it wasn't nearly enough. In any other circumstance it would have been too much to ask. But my tiny, dead brother was heavy in my arms.

"Please," I said.

Now, for the fourth time in less than two days, we fly over Sundari clutched in the grasp of a giant bird. But this time Garuda's grip is not as firm. Her feet quiver violently. Giant blue feathers break loose from her wings and flutter to the ground. I wrap a fist tightly around her ankle, terrified that at any moment her body will give out and she will send us plummeting to the earth.

In my other arm Mani is clutched tightly to my chest. And though Deven must be as terrified as I am, he holds on to only me.

Iyla and Fazel are curled in Garuda's other foot. Their eyes are squeezed shut, and I think they might be screaming—the wind makes it impossible to tell.

Garuda descends over a small park not far from the marketplace. I asked her to take us directly to the front of Kadru's tent, but she must have decided it was too conspicuous to have a giant bird gliding above the crowded streets.

We land hard. Garuda loses her grip before her feet touch down, and the five of us tumble to the ground in a heap. I curl my body around Mani to cushion his fall before I remember that he's gone. That he can't feel anything anymore. My legs are like lead as I climb to my feet.

I'm adjusting my hold on Mani when Vara crumples to the ground. I can't tell if she's breathing.

Fresh pain snatches the air from my lungs. *What have I done?*

"She'll be okay," Deven says, but his worried expression doesn't match his words. "Go. We'll catch up with you." He bends over Vara to check her breathing, to feel for a pulse in her neck.

My gaze skips from Mani to Vara—both of them are still and lifeless. My heart breaks in two, but I do what I've always done.

I choose Mani.

Kadru is pacing outside her tent, lips pressed together in a thin line, arms folded across her chest. When she sees me, a spasm of relief crosses her face.

"Your thoughts are so muddy." She says it like an accusation. Then her eyes drop to Mani. "What happened?"

"You're going to help me," I tell her. "Whether you want to or not."

Her expression goes stony. "Bring him inside." She lifts the flap of the tent and I duck under her arm.

I lay Mani down on a ruby-colored sofa. His neck has already stiffened. His jaw is tight. His body is pale and cold.

Kadru kneels near the sofa and bends her face toward Mani. She's careful not to touch him as she turns her cheek so that it rests near his nose and mouth.

Her eyes are wide when she meets my gaze. "He's already dead."

The words pierce through me. I swallow. "I know."

She rises to her feet. "Marinda . . . what were you hoping I could do?"

"Give him life," I tell her. She opens her mouth to speak and I hold up a hand. "I'm not asking you to sacrifice any of *your* lives. Give him mine. Take everything I have left and pour it into him."

She shakes her head. "I'm sorry, darling . . . I can't—"

"No! Don't tell me you can't. Just do it."

Her gaze falls on me like a shadow. Sad. Dark. Hopeless.

"Do it," I say, softly this time. "Please."

"I would if I could," she says. "But I'm an executioner, not a resurrectionist."

Doubt catches in my heart like a fishhook. "You're lying."

"My abilities don't include reanimating the dead. I could pour lives into him, but they wouldn't bring him back. They would just be stored in his dead body until they were removed again. Lives are for the living."

Tears blur my vision. I refuse to believe her.

She trails a hand from my shoulder to my fingers. And then she opens her mind to mine. I'm so startled I take a step back. But then I stop and let myself be swallowed up in her thoughts.

I can find no lies in Kadru's mind. But it's the compassion I find there—the raw pain that mirrors my own—that finally convinces me she's telling the truth.

Mani is really gone.

Grief swells in my throat and I slide to the floor, boneless. Losing all hope a second time is worse, like being sliced open and then—when you've finally stemmed the bleeding—having the dagger plunged into the wound again. I bury my face against Mani's neck and sob. I smooth the hair from his forehead. I murmur apologies for leaving, for failing him, for choosing revenge instead of safety. I cry until my soul is vacant, until I'm numb.

When Kadru finally speaks, it's like being snatched from sleep and thrust into icy water. "You're bleeding."

I glance down at my cloth-wrapped hand. Fresh blood seeps through the fabric. "I tried to kill Balavan," I say, "but it didn't work."

Her eyes widen in alarm. "What do you mean, you tried to kill him? How?"

The world seems to blur at the edges. Nothing feels quite real. "I don't have the right blood." My voice is wooden. It sounds like it belongs to a stranger. "I thought I was his daughter, but I'm not."

I tip my head back against the sofa and close my eyes. I want to let sleep overtake me, to slip away to a place where there's no pain.

"What are you talking about?" Kadru says. But I don't have the energy to answer her.

"Marinda," she says sharply. I blink. Usually Kadru's gaze is lazy, unconcerned. Like a cat's. But right now she's studying me with an intensity that sets her eyes ablaze.

I lift my head.

"Why would it matter if you were Balavan's daughter?" Her voice has an urgency that I don't understand.

And then I realize I've signed my death warrant by coming here. It didn't matter where her loyalties were when I thought I could force her to help Mani—I didn't think I'd walk out of this tent alive. But now . . . Last time I was here, Kadru proved that she would choose Balavan over me. And Balavan will hunt me like an animal.

"He's going to kill me," I say, as much to myself as to her.

Kadru sighs. "Your thoughts are jumping all over the place. I'm not following you."

I almost laugh. As if her lack of access to my mind is my biggest concern right now. Kadru purses her lips and then grabs the strap of my satchel and lifts it over my head. I've grown so used to the feel of the bag slung across my body that I forgot it was there. She tips it upside down, and all five of my little snakes tumble onto my lap. Jasu scrambles to wrap herself around my wrist, and my thoughts are infused with both her worry and her comfort.

"Is that better?" Kadru asks.

I don't want to admit to her that it is. My brother is dead. Nothing should make me feel better.

"Why did you think you could kill Balavan?" she asks again.

"Did you know I'm Garuda's daughter?" I ask. "Did you know he stole me as a baby to punish her?"

Kadru doesn't answer.

"Did you know that Balavan is the Nagaraja? That he was controlling my brother?"

She sits quietly and doesn't take her gaze from my face. Maybe my thoughts are coming more clearly to her now. I give her an image of the burning orchard, of the physician's quarters reduced to ashes. She flinches and I feel a sharp stab of satisfaction.

"The maraka fruit is gone," I say. "Along with every single dose of venom. There's no limit to Balavan's power now."

"Why did you think you could kill him?" It's the third time she's asked me some version of the same question. I suddenly feel like I'm on trial. Like she'll use the answer to convict me, to find a suitable punishment.

She lays a hand on my arm. "Marinda, this is important."

"Only his own blood can destroy his relic. And since he

always called me daughter . . ." I think of my conversation with Vara and let the snakes show Kadru my thoughts and fill in the rest. I can't speak the words. I'm too hollowed out.

As she looks through my mind, Kadru's expression slowly changes to something I've never seen on her face before: astonishment.

She starts pacing around the tent, her ankle bracelets clinking together as she walks, as if she's moving to music. "Can this really be true?"

I narrow my eyes. Balavan tells Kadru everything. Why wouldn't she know about the relic? Unless . . .

"You're his daughter." The words tumble from my mouth before I can stop them. "He didn't tell you because you're the one person who can destroy him."

Kadru stiffens. A huge white snake slithers from a bamboo pole and settles around her neck. Her expression is inscrutable. "Yes."

I swallow. *Balavan's daughter.* I've just confessed to his own child that I tried to kill him. In one swift motion I scoop Mani into my arms. It's time to get out of here.

"Put him down, Marinda." Kadru's voice is a freshly sharpened blade. I hesitate. *"Now,"* she says.

I slide Mani back to the sofa and turn to face her. My heart feels like lead. "Let me give him a proper burial before you report to Balavan. I won't resist you after that. Please."

Kadru throws her head back and laughs. "Oh, my darling." She leans close to me and strokes my cheek with the back of her hand. "You were right before. Maybe it's time you and I start being loyal to each other."

I go still. "What do you mean?"

"Where is the relic, Marinda? Tell me and I'll use *my* blood to destroy it."

It's a trap. It has to be. The image of the relic nearly surfaces in my mind, but I replace it with thoughts of blue skies and bright sunlight, waterfalls and flowering trees. It takes more focus to think of happy things when I'm filled with despair. I hope it makes the information Kadru's searching for harder to reach.

"You said it yourself—I've never lied to you. And I'm not lying now. Tell me where the relic is, Marinda."

I chew my lower lip. I don't know if I can trust Kadru, but I don't have much left to lose. If I don't tell her, she'll report me to Balavan and he'll kill me. She *still* might betray me if I do help her, but maybe I can get something from her first. Maybe I can save someone today.

"Are the five hundred years you took from Iyla stored in the relic?" I ask. It's almost impossible to talk about the giant snake scale without thinking of it, but I take a deep breath and fill my mind with memories of our old cat, Smudge, and how she used to love to chase Mani around the flat. I sing a familiar lullaby in my mind. I count to ten.

Kadru hesitates. "Yes."

"I'll tell you where it is if you promise to give Iyla's lives back before you destroy it."

"Marinda . . ."

"That's the deal," I say. "Take it or leave it."

"Do you really think Balavan is going to trust me if I show up with *Iyla*?"

"Find a way," I tell her. "She's going to be gone forever

if we don't do something." I glance at Mani's still form, and my throat aches. "I can't lose anyone else."

"Balavan will never believe I care about helping Iyla," Kadru says. "It won't work. Not unless we can give him something in return."

The flap of the tent rustles open. "Give him me." Both Kadru and I spin toward the voice.

Vara.

She's alive.

CHAPTER THIRTY-SIX

Iyla

My heartbeat roars in my ears as I struggle to take in the scene in front of me. Vara holding back the flap of the tent. Mani's tiny body resting on a red sofa, just as lifeless as he was an hour ago. Snakes everywhere—curled in baskets, lounging on furniture, dangling from poles and wrapped around not just Kadru's neck but Marinda's wrist. I can't tell if the snake is an accessory or a shackle.

But it's the conversation I overheard as the four of us approached that's still reverberating in my mind like the clash of cymbals. My missing years—not fifty, but *five hundred* of them. If that's true . . .

Bile rises in the back of my throat.

My thoughts feel slow, like I'm seeing everything from underwater. Marinda was supposed to be forcing Kadru to save Mani, but she's not. It sounded like she was pleading to save me. I press a hand to my neck, but even though the sound of my pulse is loud inside my head, I can't feel it against my skin.

Marinda's palm flies to her chest. "Vara," she says, "you're okay."

I can't breathe. I need to get out of here. I take a step backward, and Fazel laces his fingers through mine. I know he'll come with me if I run. But then Marinda turns toward me, and the naked expression of grief on her face pins me in place. "You heard," she says. "Oh, Iyla. You weren't supposed to find out that way."

I can't manage more than a nod. Marinda's already-bloodshot eyes fill with tears. Her despair is a mirror I can't bear to look at.

I turn toward Kadru. "Is it true?" I ask. "Did you really take five hundred years from me?" But she's not paying attention. Her gaze is fixed on Vara.

"Who are you?" Kadru asks, her voice laced with venom. "And what makes you think Balavan will care?"

Vara is still unsteady on her feet. Her face is ashen, and she holds on to Deven's arm for support. But when she speaks, her voice is strong. "My name is Vara," she says. "But you probably know me as the great bird Garuda."

Kadru laughs, and the sound chills my blood. "I don't believe you."

"She flew us here," Fazel says. "Believe her."

Kadru's eyes narrow. She opens her mouth to say something more, but I won't let her get away with not answering my question.

"Did you take *five hundred* years from me?" I ask again. This time my voice is sharp and loud.

Kadru's eyes flick to me. "Yes."

My stomach goes cold. "How many years do I have left? Do you even know?"

"None. Your time is probably measured in months, not years." She says it flippantly, as if she were relaying the weather.

It's like being pushed from a cliff. The icy shock of falling, arms spinning in search of something to hold on to— some miracle in the form of a branch or rock—but finding only air. Kadru didn't just steal years from my current life. To take that many years, she had to have robbed me of my future too, of every life that could have redeemed me from this one. She stole my hope and left me grasping at air. But air can't catch a falling body.

"We're going to fix it," Marinda says. "Your lives are stored in Balavan's relic. Kadru is going to give them back to you."

Kadru shakes her head, and Marinda gives her a withering stare.

"Unless she really is Garuda," Kadru says, motioning toward Vara. "*And* she's willing to die for you. I suppose Balavan might be persuaded with that on the table."

Vara barely knows me. She'll never . . .

"Yes," Vara says. "I'll do it."

My heart leaps into my throat. Marinda looks from Vara to me and back again. "There has to be another way," she says. Her voice sounds small and bled of hope.

Vara squeezes her fingers. "I won't have to die, love. Balavan just has to think I'm willing."

But a heavy silence settles over all of us. Because that's a promise Vara is in no position to keep.

* *

We don't leave for the Naga palace right away. Kadru insists that Marinda needs time to process Mani's death, to have his body cremated, that Vara needs time to rest, that we need to formulate a plan. But the longer we wait, the more my anxiety grows.

We have no reason to trust Kadru. And she has so many motivations to betray us. I can't stop thinking of everything that happened on Crocodile Island. Vara's eyes grew misty when Fazel and I told her our story, especially when she heard Balavan's tale of killing the Tiger Queen. But then the corner of her mouth ticked up. A small, sad smile. "Bagharani died to save her people," she said. "That sounds like the old friend I knew."

"How would dying save them?" Fazel asked.

Vara explained about blood willingly shed. And suddenly the exchange between Chipkali and Balavan made perfect sense. Balavan was going to torture him until he *chose* to die. Until he spilled his own blood to stop the pain. And now something deep in my gut tells me it worked. The Crocodile King is dead. Which leaves only Balavan and Vara.

Kadru will be a hero to the Naga if she shows up at their palace with the ultimate prize. The great bird Garuda, delivered right through the front door like a beautifully wrapped gift.

And yet . . . I want my lives back. The desire aches at the back of my throat like thirst. If I were a better person, I might try to convince the others not to go. But I can't force myself to say the words. Because in the back of my mind is this selfish thought: maybe Kadru will give my lives back *before* she betrays us. Maybe even if Vara dies, I won't have to. I hate myself for thinking it, but not enough that it loosens my tongue.

We stay in Kadru's tent while we plan. The snakes keep their distance—they congregate near the back of the tent as if they've been commanded to give us a wide berth. I'd rather wait almost anywhere else, but there is no safe place for us.

Returning to the palace isn't an option—Deven says the Raja can't be trusted to protect Marinda. Not after what happened to the orchard. Balavan knows about the Widows' Village now, so we can't return to the Blue House. And if by some chance the Crocodile King is still alive, he'll be looking for us too.

We will be hunted from all sides.

There's no safe place for our grief either. It hangs so heavy that it nearly suffocates us. Mani is everywhere. He's in Marinda's haunted gaze as she moves through the tent like an apparition. He's in the tight set of Deven's jaw. And his memory wraps around my heart like a noose, squeezing so tight I can scarcely breathe. Even Fazel, who never even knew Mani, is subdued, as if our collective sorrow has snuffed the light from his eyes.

Such a little boy, and yet loving him has slain us all.

My guilt is almost as heavy as my grief. I should have been kinder to Mani, should have protected him more. But for years I treated him as an interloper—the person who stole Marinda's attention, who had first dibs on her love. It was only when he was lying lifeless in my arms that I realized somewhere along the way he'd become family, that I couldn't bear to lose him. That I loved him. But by then it was too late.

Fazel held me for hours on the night Mani died—he pulled me close to him and let me weep against his chest like he'd known me my whole life. Like he could absorb some of my sadness into his own body to relieve the burden.

But since then he's kept his distance.

Our fingers brushed this morning as we both reached for the same basket of naan, and he snatched his hand away as if he'd been burned. My heart shriveled in my chest.

Maybe he's seen enough to know the truth about me—I want all my lives back, but I'm not sure I deserve them.

CHAPTER THIRTY-SEVEN

Marinda

Kadru knows the relic is at the Naga palace—I've told her that much—but I won't give her an exact location. Not until we get there. I want to believe she'll keep her word, but we have too much history for me to trust her completely. And she doesn't care about Iyla like I do. I can't be sure she'll fight for her.

The six of us make the journey in relative silence. Kadru leads the way, and she glides through the streets of Sundari like an elegant cyclone—the crowd parts as she approaches, as if all can sense how deadly she is.

The snakes in my satchel are a constant tug at my thoughts as we travel. They offer a strange kind of comfort with their innocent worry. And each time grief threatens to overtake me, Jasu feeds me the feelings of the others—Iyla's worry that she's putting us in danger by trying to get her lives back, the way Deven's heart aches for me, Fazel's growing devotion to Iyla. Their thoughts make my heart swell even as it's breaking.

We trudge through the rain forest in single file like a funeral procession. When we finally make it to the Naga palace, the guards can't seem to get out of the way fast enough. They don't ask for a password; they just nod at Kadru without making eye contact and then practically dive off the path.

The sun disappears behind a cloud and plunges us into shadow. We ascend the steep steps that lead to the entrance, and Kadru opens the door without knocking.

The palace is silent as a tomb.

"Something is wrong," I say. Not a single member of the Naga is anywhere in sight. Not even Amoli greets us at the door.

"Relax, darling," Kadru says. "Everything is fine." But she's wrong. It feels as if the walls are holding their breath.

Kadru touches my elbow gently. "When the other members of the Naga see me coming, they generally make themselves scarce."

I remember the night of Balavan's party—the way everyone looked at her with fear in their eyes, how lonely she seemed—and a lump forms in my throat. So much pain with her power.

"Marinda will come with me," Kadru says. "Iyla will take the rest of you to one of the bedchambers to wait until you're needed."

I feel Deven stiffen beside me. "No," he says, folding his arms across his chest, "that's unacceptable."

Kadru's mouth quirks in amusement, as if she's watching a child having a tantrum.

"And what would you suggest, young prince?" she asks. "Would you like for us all to march into Balavan's bedchamber and announce we're there to destroy him? Because I'm sure that would work out splendidly."

Deven's jaw goes tight and he turns to me. "The last time I saw you with Balavan, he was trying to kill you. The last time you saw him on your own, he left you bleeding and delirious." He takes both of my hands in his. He dips his head toward Kadru. "And she works for him. She's his daughter. She's done unspeakable things to you. Marinda"—his voice catches on my name, and his eyes go soft—"I don't like this."

I stand on my tiptoes and kiss him gently on the lips. I would be lying if I told him that I didn't have misgivings about Kadru. I do. But Mani's death shifted something inside me, and I don't feel like running anymore. My brother died because I was trying to take down the Nagaraja. Right now it seems like it was all for nothing, but if I can get Iyla's lives back, maybe it will help close the yawning chasm that has opened in my chest. Maybe it won't feel like I was created to destroy everything I touch.

"I have to do this," I tell Deven. "Please trust me."

But then a horrible thought occurs to me. I spin toward Kadru.

"What if Balavan transforms?" I don't know why it didn't occur to me until just now. Maybe because Balavan and the Snake King still seem like separate entities to me. But they're not. And we'll never be able to stop him if he becomes the Nagaraja.

"He won't," Kadru says.

"But how do you know?"

Kadru touches my cheek with the back of her hand. "Because he can't keep any secrets from me in snake form, darling. He hasn't changed in my presence for many, many years."

I swallow. I've spent months wondering why Kadru wasn't in the Snake Temple the night I first saw the Naga-raja. It's one of the reasons I trusted her—I thought it might be a sign she wasn't as loyal as some of the other members of the Naga. But it must have been Balavan's choice not to have her there. He's afraid of her power. And if my destiny is to become like Kadru, then someday he will be afraid of mine too. The thought gives me a jolt of courage.

"Balavan keeps the relic in his bedchamber," I say. "It's hanging on the wall like a mirror."

Kadru's eyes flash. She smiles. "I'm ready when you are."

* *

Balavan opens the door right away. I can't see his expression—Kadru is blocking my view—but his voice is full of warmth. "Darling," he says, leaning to kiss both of her cheeks, "to what do I owe the pleasure?"

"I brought you a gift." She steps aside so he can see me, and his eyes widen in delight.

"You found her."

Kadru laughs. "Of course I did." She puts a hand on the small of my back and pushes me into the room. "I told you

Marinda would come to me." Her eyes flick in my direction, and they are as cold as if she were dead. "She always does."

Dread settles over me like an iron shawl. They've spoken since I was last here. I walked into Kadru's trap. And I brought everyone I care about with me.

"I never should have doubted you," Balavan says. Fresh pain blooms in my chest at the sight of his easy smile. At his lack of suffering for Mani's death. My fingers long to curl around his neck. They twitch at my sides.

Kadru sinks onto a turquoise sofa and curls her feet beneath her. "It's even better," she says. "I brought you Garuda."

His face is alight. "You didn't."

Kadru presses her palms together. Her face is triumphant. "Yes," she says. "I did."

Balavan's hungry expression sends a wave of nausea through me. "Where is she?" he says. "Bring her to me."

"She's agreed to hand herself over if you give Iyla her lives back," Kadru says. "I'm not sure why all of them are so obsessed with that trifling girl, but there you have it."

My eyes slide to where Iyla's lives are stored. To the giant snake scale hanging on the wall like a mirror. Except it's not there. An actual glass mirror hangs in its place, as if the whole thing were a figment of my imagination. My pulse thrums in my ears.

"If Vara is already here, we don't have to agree to anything."

Kadru stretches her legs out and crosses one foot over

the other. "True," she says. "But she didn't bring her relic with her. And isn't that what you're really after?"

"I can get her to tell me where her relic is. . . ." He gives a wolfish smile. "Eventually."

"Torturing her could take days," Kadru says, waving a hand in front of her face like she's shooing away a fly. "This will be so much faster. And once you have the relic . . ." She raises her eyebrows meaningfully. "It's not like Iyla's going anywhere."

Balavan throws his head back and laughs. "You always were clever," he says. "Of course. Once I've destroyed Garuda's feather, I can just take the lives back and kill the girl."

"No," I say. "Kadru . . ." But she won't look at me. My throat aches. "Kadru, please."

Finally she meets my gaze. The spark of connection between us is gone. Maybe it was never there in the first place. A series of images flash through my mind. Kadru's large, kind eyes the first time I met her. The way she pulled me gently onto her lap. Her breath soft against my cheek. And then her satisfied smile as her snakes sank their fangs into me, the searing pain followed by the cold shock at having misjudged her cunning for kindness. It's like suddenly hearing the notes of a tune I forgot I knew.

Kadru lifts a small silver bell from the mahogany table at her elbow and shakes it gently. A few seconds later Amoli appears. She gulps when she sees Kadru, but tries to cover it with a trembling smile. "What can I do for you?" she asks.

"I brought a few guests with me," Kadru says. "They're

waiting in the *rajakumari*'s bedchamber. Invite them to join us."

"Of course," Amoli says before she scurries away.

My heart slams against my rib cage. I have to find a way to warn them.

Kadru turns to me and smiles sweetly. "Don't even try, darling," she says. "I'd hate to have to kill your boyfriend."

CHAPTER THIRTY-EIGHT

Marinda

I sit numbly as my friends are led into the room. Listen wordlessly as Balavan tells Vara she must bring her relic to the palace to save Iyla. Bite back a scream as she agrees. Both she and Iyla are going to die for nothing.

Deven tries to catch my gaze, but I can't look at him. I'm afraid of what he'll see in my eyes.

My mind scrambles for a solution, but it's like groping in the dark for something I'm not convinced is there. And each time I open my mouth to blurt out a warning, Kadru's gaze cuts sharply to me. A single word inside my head. *No.*

The snakes in my satchel mirror my panic. They stir, restless. Eager for an assignment. But the only minds that could help me are closed to them.

Morning melts into afternoon. And still we wait.

Iyla paces in front of the window. Her fingers drum out

a restless beat against her thigh. Her expression teeters between hope and fear.

Finally Vara returns. She stumbles into the room balancing a giant sapphire-blue feather across her forearms. Her face is drawn and a fine sheen of sweat beads on her forehead. Why is she giving in to Balavan so easily? She must know he's going to kill her.

"Set it down there," Balavan says, motioning toward a tall table in the center of the room. Vara heaves the feather onto the surface like it's made of glass or bone. "You don't look well, my friend. Your lofty principles haven't been kind to your appearance."

Vara fixes him with a steely gaze. "Your lack of scruples hasn't been kind to your disposition. And we haven't been friends in a long time."

He laughs and circles her like he might pounce at any moment. "Did you *fly* here? You must have, to have returned so quickly." His eyes rake over her disheveled hair, her shaking knees, but Vara just stares blankly ahead. "I'm amazed you can still transform at all. Perhaps I've been too conservative in how often I allow myself to become the Nagaraja." Balavan taps his bottom lip as if lost in thought. "I could change before I kill you. It would be so satisfying to devour my final prize, and you look far too weak to stop me."

My breath catches in my throat, but then I notice Balavan's eyes flick to Kadru as if he forgot she was there.

"Then again," he says, "there will be something oddly satisfying about watching this through my human eyes."

"Give Iyla her lives back," Vara says. "And then I'll do whatever you ask."

I can see the calculation in Balavan's expression. With both Vara and the relic in the same place, he doesn't have to hold to his agreement. Vara must see it too. "You'll keep your end of the bargain," she says softly, "or this will get very messy." Her gaze slides pointedly to Kadru and back again. It's a subtle threat—Vara will tell Kadru how to destroy the relic if he doesn't cooperate—and Balavan seems to understand perfectly.

"Very well," he says. "Kadru, darling, you can take five hundred years from me and give them to Iyla. I've recently replenished."

The last of my hope dissipates like the air from a popped balloon. Now that I've seen the relic, he has no intention of letting me lay eyes on it again. I've lost. We all have.

CHAPTER THIRTY-NINE

Iyla

The idea of getting lives directly from Balavan makes me feel ill, like I've just been offered a bit of half-chewed bread from grimy fingers. But I'm not exactly in a position to be picky.

Balavan and I sit side by side in matching chairs. Marinda watches from across the room with two fingers pressed to her mouth.

Kadru saunters around the back of my seat. When she reaches for me, I flinch.

"You need to hold still," she says. "If my skin touches yours, you'll be dead within the hour. Which would rather defeat the purpose, don't you think?" Her laughter ripples across my cheek.

"Wait," Fazel says, "if you touch her, she *dies*?"

"Would you like her to demonstrate on you?" Balavan asks sharply.

Fazel's fingers flex at his sides, and I feel Kadru stiffen behind me. I can't see her expression, but whatever it is, it makes Fazel shrink a little. I give him a small smile that I hope is reassuring. He drops his eyes and blows a stream of air through pursed lips.

Kadru cups Balavan's neck in her palm, and then slides her other hand under my hair and presses the tips of her fingernails against my skin. My muscles tremble as I try not to move. The sensation of Kadru's fingernails on my neck is like walking into a familiar nightmare. It's always followed by pain.

I squeeze my eyes closed, but instead of the sharp, wrenching agony of losing lives, this feels like the years are being firmly pressed inside me until I own them, like being kneaded with practiced fingers, until my whole body is as soft and malleable as bread dough. When Kadru finally pulls away, I'm pleasantly drowsy. My chest expands, and for a moment I wonder if it's possible to feel the extra life teeming inside my body. And then I realize this is what people mean when they say their heart is full. This is what hope feels like.

Beside me Balavan looks stunned. A sheen of sweat glimmers on his brow. He blinks.

"Amoli," he calls, "bring me the dagger."

CHAPTER FORTY

Marinda

Amoli brings the dagger on a silver tray. The handle is enameled and inlaid with rubies and turquoise. My blood has dried on the blade.

"Recognize this, *rajakumari*?" Balavan asks. His voice is like liquid silver. "Go ahead. Take it."

Fear slides under my skin. I keep my hands at my sides.

Amoli's gaze darts from Balavan to me and back again. The tray in her hand trembles.

"If you want Iyla to keep all the years I just gave her, you'll *take the dagger*."

But we both know he won't let her keep them no matter what I do. And if he thought I had any power to save her, he wouldn't be offering me a weapon.

A lump forms in my throat. Even though Iyla's expression is worried, her face is radiant. She looks lit from within. And Balavan is going to snuff the light from her eyes. But I can buy her more time if I obey him.

I wrap my fingers around the hilt of the dagger. Amoli doesn't hesitate; she just snatches the tray from beneath my hand and hurries away.

Balavan's smile is slow and wicked. "Destroy your mother's relic."

Even though I knew exactly what he would say, the command makes me feel as if I've swallowed a stone.

Vara clears her throat. "This isn't necessary," she says. "I'll do it myself."

"No," Balavan says. "I want your daughter to do it. I want you to look into your child's eyes while she unmakes you."

Vara stands up and cups my chin in her hands. Her palms are cool against my face. "Everything will be fine," she says, her voice barely above a whisper. "I wasn't ever going to use the lives again anyway." Vara's brown eyes are glassy with tears, but still she smiles. Why did she put me in this position? Why did she bring the relic here knowing it would cost us the only advantage we had?

"I'm waiting, *rajakumari*," Balavan says sharply. Vara flinches at the possessive nickname. She drops her arms and gives my hand a final squeeze.

The feather glistens like a jewel. I run my fingers along the surface, expecting it to feel like glass, but the velvety tufts tickle my palm. I think of all the lives hidden inside the relic. All the people who will never get another chance. I lift my head. Every gaze is fixed on me. They all watch with a mixture of fascination and horror. I wince as I slice into the fleshy part of my hand. Blood wells at the cut, trickles down my arm and drips on the feather. A mist begins to rise from the relic, growing thicker with each crimson drop. The beautiful blue dims to the dull gray of day-old fish.

Balavan laughs darkly. I look up just in time to see him lunge for Deven and press a dagger to his throat. My legs go weak.

"I did what you asked," I say. "Let him go."

Iyla, Vara and Fazel look on helplessly. Kadru stands between them and Balavan. One touch from her will kill any one of them.

Deven winces as Balavan digs the metal into his skin. A single drop of blood beads against the blade.

"It's time to make a choice," Balavan says. "Deven or Vara."

I stagger backward. "What?"

"Either you kill her, or I slit his throat."

My stomach clenches. "You'll kill them both," I say. "It doesn't matter what I do."

"Maybe," he says. "But is that a chance you're willing to take?"

Balavan knows he's already won, but still he's going to play this game all the way to the end. Until he's the only one left standing.

The blade at Deven's throat trembles. "Choose," Balavan says. I swallow. Something about that blade . . .

When Kadru took five years from me in exchange for a vial of venom, I was unconscious for hours. And weak for hours after that. She just took five hundred from Balavan.

My satchel still hangs across my chest. Jasu catches the

thread of my thoughts. She bends her mind toward mine, and the other snakes follow suit. I lift the satchel from my neck and set it on the floor. I kneel in front of Deven and brush my thumb against his cheek.

"I'm sorry," I tell him. His eyes meet mine and I hope he understands. "I love you. I always will."

Balavan leans forward, eager. He doesn't notice the snakes creeping from my satchel. The dagger at Deven's neck twitches.

Now. On my command all five snakes sink their fangs into Balavan's ankles. His eyes fly open, and his dagger slips from his fingers. He dives forward to snatch it from the air, but he's too late. I'm already on my feet; my dagger is still firmly in my grasp. Before he can regain his balance, I stab him between the shoulder blades.

Balavan makes a strangled sound at the back of his throat. He reaches behind him and swipes at his shirt. His hand comes away red, and he stares at his fingers as if he doesn't understand what's happening. He has thousands of lives and a room full of prisoners, and yet the blood is seeping from his body. He staggers backward and falls to his knees.

Kadru watches him impassively until he calls out her name.

"Please." He nearly chokes on the word. "The relic."

She follows his gaze to a large, intricately carved wooden box against the wall. "There?"

Relief sweeps across his expression, but he can only manage a nod.

I watch in horror as she slides the giant snake scale from its hiding place behind the trunk.

Balavan crawls forward, his breath rattling in his chest. His fingers curl toward the scale, but Kadru steps in front of him, blocking his path.

"You need someone to help you," Kadru says, her voice dripping with sweetness, "but I'm afraid I can't do that." She draws a sharp fingernail across her wrist. Blood beads at the wound. "My father taught me that mercy is weakness." She flips her hand over and holds it above the scale. Balavan's eyes widen in panic. A single crimson drop clings to Kadru's skin, dangling from her wrist for several agonizing seconds before it breaks free. Balavan makes a gurgling noise that sounds like a plea, but mist is already rising from the relic as it slowly turns gray. Balavan gasps one last time before he slumps to the ground.

Tears of relief sting my eyes. It's finally over. Kadru was on my side after all.

But then she snaps her fingers, and a half-dozen giant snakes slither into the room. Their minds are fixated on only one thought: getting to me.

CHAPTER FORTY-ONE

Marinda

It happens so fast I don't have time to react. The largest snake wraps himself around my legs and torso, pinning me firmly in place. Two smaller snakes bind my hands in front of me.

"What are you doing!" Deven shouts. "Let her go."

Please. My thoughts are for the snakes, for Kadru, for any gods who will listen. *Please don't do this.*

Kadru stands in front of me. She takes my face in her hands. "You killed him," she says softly, and I don't know if it's accusation or approval. "You were right, darling. We were more powerful when we worked together. But it's time I let you go."

I think of the many times Kadru pleaded with me to let Iyla go. To let Mani go. "You were never supposed to have human connections," she said. I wasn't wrong that she'd grown to care about me. I was just wrong to hope it might change her.

I can hear the others begging for Kadru to release me, but their voices are far away and distorted. My head swims. *Why won't they do something?* But then I remember that it's hard to fight someone you can't touch. Jasu's tiny mind is colored with panic. She tries to get to me, but she's too small. Kadru's snakes are no match for her or any of my other baby snakes.

Tears leak from my eyes and trickle down my cheeks, and Kadru wipes them away with the pads of her thumbs. "You deserved better," she says tenderly. "I'm sorry I couldn't give it to you."

She leans forward and plants a kiss on my forehead.

My skin prickles and then blazes. I feel a tug deep inside, like Kadru has found the string that holds me together and is slowly unraveling me. I'm being unmade. I try to pull away, but the snakes squeeze even tighter. Kadru strokes my hair softly, but her lips stay firmly planted, and the sensation of being drained overwhelms me. Black spots rush into my vision. The irony strikes me then as I feel my life ebbing away. I'm getting exactly what I deserve.

I'm going to die by a poisoned kiss.

CHAPTER FORTY-TWO

Marinda

The snakes abruptly release me, and I gasp as air rushes into my lungs. Kadru sucks in a sharp breath and staggers backward, falling heavily into a chair.

Deven rushes to my side. "What was that?" he yells in Kadru's general direction. "What did you do to her?"

I fall into his arms. I don't know why Kadru stopped just shy of killing me. She looks dazed as she massages her temples. Maybe she didn't intend to. Maybe she didn't have the strength to take all my lives at once.

Deven's fingers roam over my face as if searching for damage. "Are you okay?" he asks.

I shake my head. "I don't know."

He whirls on Kadru. "I'd kill you if I could," he says. A vein in his temple bulges. His hands are curled into fists at his sides. "Did you take her lives?"

"No," Kadru says quietly. "I set her free."

I lift my head from Deven's chest and turn toward her.

"I didn't drain you of life, Marinda. I drained you of poison."

My heart gives a single slow beat. "What do you mean?"

"You're no longer a *visha kanya*." She gives me a trembling smile. "You're free."

What she's saying can't be possible. I look at her more closely. Fine lines have feathered at the corners of her eyes. Her skin is dull.

"What did you do?"

"I used the poison in your body to eliminate my excess years," she says.

"You took lives from *yourself*?" I ask. Shock seeps into me like cold. "And poisoned them?"

"I did," she says. "Though, to be fair, *you* poisoned them. It took hundreds of my years to use up all of your poison, but I did. And now you're free."

A lump forms in my throat. "What about you?"

"Balavan is dead," she says. "I'm free too."

But it's not what I'm asking, and we both know it. She wouldn't have used the snakes to restrain me unless she thought she needed to, unless she thought I wouldn't agree on my own. She used them so she wouldn't have to lie.

"Are you . . ." I swallow hard. "Are you going to die?"

"Yes," she says evenly. "But it's about time."

A small sob escapes me. Kadru reaches out like she's going to tuck a stray hair behind my ear, but then pulls her hand back at the last moment. "I'm sorry," she says. "You've been the only person I've been able to touch for years. But you have no protection from me now."

I'm no longer poisoned and no longer immune. Her touch is just as deadly to me as to anyone else.

I think of how Kadru never saw me without stroking my cheek, or grabbing my hand, or running her fingers through my hair. I always thought it was about power. It never occurred to me that she was starved for affection. My chest aches. I think of all the venomous thoughts I've pushed in her direction over the last few hours.

"Why didn't you just tell me what you were planning?" I ask. "You could have let me see your thoughts. Balavan never would have known."

"Oh, but he would have. You've never been as good at deception as you think you are. If you hadn't actually believed I'd betrayed you, he never would have believed it either." She sighs. "When I saw that the relic was gone, I knew we'd have to trick Balavan into telling us where it was. And he was never going to do that unless he needed it urgently."

Unless he was about to die.

"But how did you know I would stab him?"

"You risked your life multiple times for them," she says, motioning toward Iyla and Deven. "I had no doubt if I weakened Balavan enough by taking lives from him, you'd kill him to protect your friends."

But I couldn't protect Mani.

The grief is like a living thing inside me—a beast with giant wings—quiet for a stretch before waking again, and digging into my heart with sharp claws.

Instinctively I reach for Jasu's mind, craving her uncomplicated comfort. But she's not there. I spin in a slow circle, my gaze raking across the floor. And then I spot her near the other snakes. They're curled in a pile in the far corner of the room. Jasu lifts her head and stares at me. She tilts her head inquisitively, like she's waiting for me to answer a question that I haven't heard.

Our connection is broken.

My throat burns. "I'm sorry," Kadru says. "Your freedom comes with a price. But I promise I'll take good care of her while I still can."

Jasu makes her way to Kadru as if she's been summoned—which no doubt she has—and Kadru lifts the snake onto her shoulder. The pressure in my chest grows.

"Goodbye, little one," I say, stroking Jasu's head with the tip of my finger. And then to Kadru, "Thank you."

Kadru's gaze meets mine, and something tender and raw passes between us. Her eyes glimmer in the fading light. She blinks once and then clears her throat. "Goodbye, darling," she says. "It's time for you to go home."

Tears well in my eyes. I feel like a rag doll, incapable of moving.

"What is it?" Kadru asks softly. "What are you thinking?" It's the first time she's ever asked me that question. The first time she's needed to.

"I don't *have* a home," I tell her.

"Your life is your own now," she says. "You'll find one."

CHAPTER FORTY-THREE

Iyla

Marinda and I settle into a cottage in a quiet neighborhood in Bala City. It's a compromise. I wanted to go back to the Blue House, but the Widows' Village is too fraught with pain for Marinda. She says it's a sliver in her heart—a reminder of everything she's lost.

But I couldn't bear the idea of living in a flat in the middle of the city—it's a reminder of everything I used to be. Of the lives that I ruined and the lives I almost lost.

We agreed that maybe it was time to leave our memories behind—both the good and the bad ones—and start somewhere new. The cottage is painted in bright colors—squares of purple, yellow, green and red—as if the previous owners couldn't decide on one hue and so chose them all.

I'm sweeping the floor when I hear a knock on the door. My pulse spikes and I have to remind myself that I'm safe now. That it won't be Gopal or Gita to give me a new assignment. I lean the broom against the wall and swing open the door.

Fazel stands at the entrance. He's rocking back and forth on his heels, a box clutched in his hands. My stomach flutters at the sight of him.

He grins. "I brought you something." He shoves the box of sweets toward me. "I mean, not just you, both you and Marinda—and Deven too if he likes sweets. Does he? Like sweets, I mean?" He licks his lips.

I smile. "I'm sure he does, yes. Do you want to come in?" I push the door wider and Fazel steps over the threshold.

We sit together on the sofa and my knee brushes against his. Silence stretches between us. Fazel clears his throat and turns slightly so we're not touching anymore. "Is Marinda . . . ? Are the others here?"

My stomach sinks. I had hoped . . . but no, I was wrong. Fazel has gotten close to Deven. And Marinda too. We're his friends and nothing more.

"They're not," I tell him. "They went for a walk."

"Oh. Do you think they'll be back soon?" He glances toward the window. "It's getting dark."

The sun has set, and the sky is painted in shades of indigo.

"You don't have to stay," I tell him. "I can tell Deven and Marinda you stopped by when they get back."

Fazel scrubs a hand over his jaw. "Are you kicking me out?"

"Of course not. It's just clear you'd rather not be here."

"What makes you say that?"

I give a harsh laugh. "Oh, I don't know. Maybe because

you're treating me like I have some kind of disease? Like if you touch me, you might break out in huge, pus-filled boils."

A hint of a smile tugs at his mouth. "Pus-filled boils?"

"It's not funny."

His smiles fades. "What's not funny is that you think I don't want to be here."

"So, what, then? It's that you don't want to be here with *me*?"

"Iyla . . ." He says my name softly, but I don't stop talking.

"I'm sorry that you're so ashamed to have almost kissed me when we were trying to escape from Chipkali."

"Iyla . . ."

"And I'm sorry that I lost it when Mani died, and I forced you to deal with me, but I really loved him and . . ."

"Iyla . . ."

"But I'm fine now and so you can just go back to . . . wherever . . . and pretend that you never met me."

"Iyla!" This time his voice is insistent enough that I stop talking. He leans forward and slides a hand behind my neck, burying his fingers in my hair. He pulls me so close that his breath skims across my mouth. "I didn't want to take advantage of you when you're stressed and scared and grieving. But believe me, it's taken every ounce of self-control I have not to."

Fazel's gaze roams over my face, and I forget how to breathe.

"What?" he asks. "You don't have a snappish retort for me?"

I swallow. "No."

I'm not sure my mouth could form words if my life depended on it. I'm still waiting for Fazel to confess that he's teasing me, that his words before were a cruel joke and that he's leaving after all. My vision feels fractured and fuzzy, like I'm dreaming instead of actually sitting here with Fazel, our knees touching, his fingers warm on the back of my neck.

He grins as his thumb moves idly over my cheek. And then our eyes lock and his smile melts away. He pulls me closer and his lips meet mine. He kisses me slowly, tenderly. And I kiss him back. I pour my soul into him—my grief, my heartache, my worries, my fears and my passion. I give him all the pent-up emotions that have chased me these past few months.

My whole body feels like it's in bloom.

And when we finally pull apart, breathless, it's as if something has shifted inside me. As if there's finally room for an emotion besides despair.

I lean my head on Fazel's chest and he pulls me tightly against him, so that I'm nestled in the curve of his body.

"I miss Mani," I say. The words have been burning inside me for weeks, but I haven't been able to say them to Marinda. Not when her grief is so much bigger than mine.

He lays a cheek on the top of my head. "I know."

"I should have treated him better."

Fazel doesn't respond, and the only sound is the chirping of the crickets outside. I worry that I've said too much, that I've given myself away for the heartless person I often was when it came to Mani.

But then Fazel clears his throat. "When I was twelve, my sister died." His voice is tight and strained. I sit up and turn toward him so I can see his face. "It was an accident—unexpected. The day before, we'd gotten in a huge fight. I told her I hated her." He closes his eyes, as if the memory still pains him. "For years I lived with that regret. But I was just a child. And so was she. And if she had lived, I think she would have forgiven me. So eventually, I had to learn to forgive myself."

My throat is thick with emotion. He is so quick to assume the best of me, to offer redemption with no strings attached. I lace my fingers through his.

I think of Mani the last time I spent any real time with him. He had just returned to the Widows' Village, and despite everything I'd done, he wrapped his arm around my waist. I told him I was sorry and he squeezed me tight. "I know," he said. And he did.

A warmth expands in my chest, and I know what Fazel said is true. Mani would have forgiven me. He already had.

"I'm sorry about your sister," I say.

He presses a kiss to my forehead. "I'm sorry about your friend."

I lean my head on his shoulder and tuck my body against his. And for the first time in many years, I feel safe.

CHAPTER FORTY-FOUR

Marinda

Mani's ashes rest in a clay jar on my bedside table.

It shouldn't be possible for a boy who filled my heart so completely to be reduced to so little. And yet this is all that's left of him—a pile of dust that could fit in the palms of my cupped hands.

I run my fingers along the container's red-hued stone and wish that my gift had been to bestow life instead of take it away.

"Have you decided where to release him?" Iyla's voice in the doorway startles me, and I drop my hands to my lap. It's a question I've been thinking about for weeks—I want to scatter Mani's ashes in the perfect spot, somewhere he felt only love, but so many of our special places have been tainted with one horror or another. He loved the bookshop, until the Naga killed Japa and kidnapped him. Our flat was the only home Mani ever remembered clearly, but the last time we were there, we found Smudge dead and our things ransacked. Every other possibility is the same. The Raja's palace. The Widows' Village. All the places Mani was loved, he was also tormented.

But then early this morning the answer came, warm and comforting, like sunlight on my face. "Yes," I tell Iyla. "I'd like to release him at the waterfall."

She smiles. "That's perfect."

* *

All five of us—me, Deven, Iyla, Fazel and Vara—sit at the edge of the waterfall, the spray gently misting our faces. Last time I was here, the branches were barren, but now they're bright with new growth. Delicate leaves quiver in a gentle breeze. It's as if the mountainside has taken a deep breath and started over.

I hold the clay jar in my lap. I know it's time to let Mani go, but I don't know if I can find the strength.

Deven's fingers trace circles on the small of my back. "My favorite memory of Mani," he says, "is how easily he got excited. Simple things made him happy—pastries, books, discovering a stray coin in his pocket—he found joy everywhere."

My heart stretches and squeezes at once. An exquisite blend of joy and pain.

"He was so smart," Iyla says. "He never let me get away with anything. But he was forgiving too. And I loved him even if I didn't show it very well."

"He was the best thing that ever happened to me," I say. "Loving him made me a better person."

"He sounds like a great kid," Fazel says.

"He was," I say. "He was perfect."

Vara sighs. "I wish I'd gotten to know him better before . . ." And then she breaks off, not wanting to skirt too close to Mani's death.

"It's all right," I tell her. "We can't tiptoe around it forever." But I have a feeling I always will, that Mani will be with me at every turn. That his memory will cut short every laugh and darken every sunrise.

"It will get easier," Vara says. She takes my hand in hers. "It won't ever go away, but eventually Mani won't be the very first thought when you wake up. And someday you'll be able to feel something besides emptiness."

Mani not being my first thought every morning doesn't sound like a good thing. I pull my hand away and toy with the bracelets on my wrists. "How long did it take for you?" I ask. "To get over losing me?"

Vara presses her lips together and closes her eyes. "I gave up too soon," she says. "I should have kept fighting."

"You didn't answer my question."

"Never," she says softly. "I never got over it." She touches my elbow. "But don't make the same mistake I did. I let my grief be a victory for Balavan. And that's no way to honor Mani's memory."

The emptiness inside me aches. I turn toward Vara. "Do you remember what you told Mani about Smudge?" I ask. Her words have been tumbling through my mind for weeks. "That animals often try to replicate the life that made them the happiest?"

Her eyes are soft. "Yes," she says. "I remember."

"Do you think . . ." A lump forms in my throat that makes it hard to speak. Deven squeezes my fingers, and it gives me the courage to keep going. "Do you think people are the same?"

"You mean, do I think there's a chance that Mani will—in some form or another—return to you?"

My heart trembles, afraid of her answer. I bite my lip and nod.

"As deeply as that little boy loved you," she says, "I would be very surprised if he didn't."

A tiny seed of hope sprouts in my chest. I want a better life for Mani than the one I gave him—a life without want, or fear, or pain. But maybe, someday, our paths will cross again. Maybe I'll have the privilege of catching a glimpse of him, even if it's from afar, even if I don't recognize him. The thought makes me smile.

I stand at the water's edge and tip the jar upside down. The ashes drift in the wind, land softly on the water and disappear.

＊ ＊

One spring passes and then another. Deven and I walk along a grassy riverbank, our shoes dangling from our fingertips, our feet sinking into the cool grass.

He stops and circles his arms around my waist. I lift my chin so I can look into his eyes. "I love you," he says. "I'm really glad you decided not to kill me."

I laugh. "It's not too late, you know. You could forget

my birthday. Or force me to sit through another of your father's awful state banquets."

His fingers press into my back and he pulls me close to him. "That day in the Naga palace when Balavan told you to choose between me and Vara, I thought you might."

"You're teasing me," I tell him. "You're trying to guilt me into kissing you."

He widens his eyes, feigning offense. "I'm far too handsome to have to resort to dirty tricks."

"And yet . . ."

"To be fair, you did have a dagger in your hand," he says. "You can understand why I might have thought you'd take me out."

"You're insufferable," I tell him.

He shrugs and gives me a smile that makes my knees go weak. "I wouldn't have blamed you," he says. "You were in a tough spot."

I stand on my tiptoes and run my thumb along the stubble at his jaw. "With all I went through to save you?" I say. "I could never."

And then I kiss him.

CHAPTER FORTY-FIVE

Ten Years Later

Deven holds my hand as another sharp pain seizes me. "I can't take any more," I tell him. Sweat beads on my forehead, pools at the small of my back.

"Hold on," Deven says. "It's almost over."

I squeeze my eyes closed and release a stream of air through pursed lips. My hair sticks to the back of my neck.

Iyla comes into the room with a bowl of ice chips and a wet sponge. "How are you holding up?"

I'm in too much pain to speak, so Deven answers for me. "She's doing great," he says. But it's a lie and we both know it.

Iyla spoons ice into my mouth and dabs at my forehead with the sponge. "The whole palace is already awake and pacing," she says. "Feel free to scream."

I press my lips together and shake my head. "What would people think?"

"Hmm," Iyla says, "you're right. You wouldn't want them to realize you're human."

The pain subsides for a moment, and I let my head fall back on the pillow. I close my eyes. "Why is everyone pacing?" I ask. "Why can't they just go about their business?" I spent so many years trying to be invisible that it feels unsettling to have my life subject to such scrutiny.

Deven smooths the damp hair from my forehead. "They're just excited to meet the new heir."

My middle tightens again, and I grab Deven's forearm, my fingers digging into his skin. He gives me a smile through clenched teeth.

Each moment feels like a day, but finally the midwife announces that it's time. I sigh in relief, but it's still more than an hour before she finally places a swaddled baby in my arms.

"Congratulations, Your Majesty. It's a boy."

I gaze into his small face, and my pain feels like a distant memory. His skin is velvet soft, and his head is covered with a cap of dark, downy hair. I stroke his wrinkled palm, and he closes his tiny fist around my finger. My heart feels too big for my chest.

He's perfect.

He blinks, his long lashes fluttering against his cheek, and looks up at me with dark, solemn eyes.

My breath catches. I'd recognize those eyes anywhere.

"Hi there, monkey," I say softly. "Welcome home."

A NOTE FROM THE AUTHOR

Writing the second book in a duology is a unique challenge. On the one hand, I wanted to give readers more of the elements they enjoyed in the first book—more of Marinda's grappling with what it means to be a *visha kanya,* more of her relationships with Deven and Mani. But on the other hand, I wanted to offer a different, fresh experience. A bigger, more complex world to discover.

While *Poison's Kiss* was an examination of what would happen to a girl who'd been turned into an assassin against her will, in *Poison's Cage* I was excited to expand on and deepen the mythology I'd introduced in the first book, especially as it related to the Naga, the Nagaraja, and Garuda.

These figures are found in both Hindu and Buddhist mythology. In the Mahabharata—one of two ancient Hindu epics—the Naga make frequent appearances. Often they are portrayed as having a mixture of human and serpentine traits. In the Buddhist tradition, the Naga are generally described as large cobra-like snakes, sometimes with only one head and sometimes with many. And at least some of the Naga are portrayed as having the ability to transform into humans.

Garuda also appears in both mythologies, though in slightly different form. The Mahabharata casts Garuda as a singular being—a giant half-man, half-bird (though in *Poison's Kiss* and *Poison's Cage,* I've taken creative license and made my Garuda female). In Buddhism, the Garuda are a mythical species of huge, highly intelligent predatory birds. In both traditions, Garuda is an enemy of the Naga and hunts snakes at every opportunity.

The hints of humanity for both Garuda and the Naga in these legends fascinate me. Though I find large, powerful creatures frightening, they're not nearly as terrifying as a monster who looks like a man or a woman. After all, the enemy who can hide in plain sight, who can conceal his or her malevolence behind a human face, is so much more dangerous than an enemy who has the good manners to look like one.

I couldn't wait to explore this idea in *Poison's Cage*—how the Raksaka went from humanity to monstrosity, and how these qualities can overlap even in regular people. I wanted to put Marinda at the intersection of the two and see what she would choose. I hope you enjoyed taking the journey along with her.

For readers who are interested in exploring more of the mythology that inspired both *Poison's Kiss* and *Poison's Cage,* I recommend seeking out the Mahabharata or the Ramayana (the second of the two great Hindu epics). The original texts are in Sanskrit, but English translations are widely available in bookstores and libraries. Another wonderful resource for further reading is *Folktales from India: A Selection of Oral Tales from Twenty-Two Languages,* collected and edited by A. K. Ramanujan. It's filled with captivating stories from across the Indian subcontinent that have been translated into English.

Poison's Cage has been a joy to write. Thank you so much for reading it!

ACKNOWLEDGMENTS

Here I am again at the end of another book and with a heart so full of gratitude, I'm sure I won't find words to adequately express it. But I'm not a quitter, so I'll give it a shot.

First, to my talented editor, Caroline Abbey, thank you for pushing me in all the best ways. This book is so much better than it would have been without you. I treasure every note in the margins—both the hearts and the question marks.

To my wonderful agent, Kathleen Rushall, who has been with me through the highs and the lows of both publishing and life over the last few years. Thanks for always being willing to either celebrate or comfort and advise, as the occasion requires. I'm so happy to have you in my corner.

Thank you to all the wonderful people at Random House who worked on this book—everyone from copyediting to design to marketing and publicity. I haven't met all of you, but I know each one of you exists, and I'm grateful for your wonderful work on this book. And special thanks to Ray Shappell for the beautiful cover design.

To all my fellow writer friends—both those I've met in the flesh and those I haven't (yet!)—thank you for sharing this journey with me. For the exclamation points in happy times and the commiseration when the going gets tough. I treasure you all. And thank you to Holly Black for being such a wonderful mentor and patiently answering all my newbie questions. You are as generous as you are talented.

A huge, huge, Garuda-sized thank-you to my readers! Thank you for your enthusiasm, for your reviews, and for loving these characters enough to read the second book. I wish I could hug each one of you individually.

As always, thanks to my parents, siblings, and in-laws for all your support. I *can* hug each one of you individually, and I plan to the next time we're together. Love to each of you.

To my three terrific kids, who are wise, and kind, and better than me in almost every way. Someday you'll come to appreciate both my off-key singing and my helpful lectures. I promise.

And to Justin, my first reader and best friend, I'm so glad we're on the same half of the globe for this one.

ABOUT THE AUTHOR

BREEANA SHIELDS has a BA in English from Brigham Young University and is an active member of SCBWI. When she's not writing, Breeana loves reading, traveling, and spending time with her husband, her three children, and an extremely spoiled miniature poodle. Visit her online at breeanashields.com or follow her on Twitter at @BreeanaShields.